Sarek nodded at McCoy. McCoy stared straight ahead.

'Bones – ' Kirk said urgently under his breath.

McCoy finally replied. 'I am,' he said hesitantly, 'McCoy . . . Leonard H.' He took a long breath of the rarefied air of Vulcan and shivered.

The Vulcan priestess spoke. 'Since thou art human, we cannot expect thee to understand fully what Sarek has requested. Spock's body lives. With your aproval, we will use all our powers to return to his body that which you possess: his essence. But, McCoy . . .'

Kirk could see the faint sheen of sweat on McCoy's forehead.

'You must now be warned,' the priestess said. 'The danger to thee is as grave as the danger to Spock.'

Paramount Pictures Presents
a Harve Bennett Production
STAR TREK® III:
THE SEARCH FOR SPOCK
Starring
WILLIAM SHATNER   DeFOREST KELLEY
Co-Starring
JAMES DOOHAN   GEORGE TAKEI
WALTER KOENIG   NICHELLE NICHOLS
MERRITT BUTRICK   CHRISTOPHER LLOYD
Executive Consultant GENE RODDENBERRY
Music by JAMES HORNER
Executive Producer GARY NARDINO
Visual Effects by INDUSTRIAL LIGHT and MAGIC
Based on STAR TREK
Created by GENE RODDENBERRY
Written and Produced by HARVE BENNETT
Directed by LEONARD NIMOY
DOLBY
MPAA
PANAVISION®

VONDA N. McINTYRE

Star Trek III

The Search for Spock

A Star Trek® Novel

PANTHER
Granada Publishing

Panther Books
Granada Publishing Ltd
8 Grafton Street, London W1X 3LA

Published by Panther Books 1984

First published in the USA by
Pocket Books 1984

ISBN 0-586-06442-7

Printed and bound in Great Britain by
Collins, Glasgow

Set in Times

This novel is a work of fiction. Names, characters,
places and incidents are either the product of the
author's imagination or are used fictitiously. Any
resemblance to actual events or locales or persons,
living or dead, is entirely coincidental.

1

Spock was dead.

The company of the *Enterprise* gathered together on the recreation deck to remember their friend.

Dr Leonard McCoy, ship's surgeon, moved half a pace into the circle. As he raised his glass in a final toast, he glanced at each of his compatriots in turn.

Admiral James Kirk and Dr Carol Marcus stood on either side of Carol's grown son, David Marcus. David was Jim's son, as well, unknown until now, but now acknowledged.

Commander Uhura, Chief Engineer Montgomery Scott, Commander Pavel Chekov, and Hikaru Sulu, recently promoted to captain, had clustered together along one arc of the circle. Every member of the ship's company showed the strain of the harrowing past few days, except Lieutenant Saavik. Her Vulcan training required her to be imperturbable, and so she appeared. If her Romulan upbringing gave her the capacity to feel grief or loss or anger at the death of Spock, her teacher, McCoy could see no shadow of the emotions.

McCoy had known the rest of the ship's company, the trainees, only a short time, not even long enough to learn their names. He knew for sure only that they were terribly young.

'To Spock,' McCoy said. 'He gave his life for ours.'

'To Spock,' they replied in unison, except for Jim, who brought his attention back to the ship from some other time, some other place, a thousand light-years distant.

A moment after the others had spoken, he said, 'To Spock.'

Everyone else drank. McCoy put his glass to his lips. The pungent odor of Kentucky bourbon rose around his face. He grimaced. The liquor was raw and new, straight out of the ship's synthesizer. He had nothing better. The *Enterprise*'s mission had been an emergency, an unexpected voyage into tragedy, and Leonard McCoy had come most poorly prepared.

He lowered the drink without tasting it.

'To Peter,' Montgomery Scott said. His young nephew, Cadet Peter Preston, had also died in the battle that took Spock's life. Scott made as if to say more, could not get out the words, and instead drained his glass in one gulp. Again, McCoy could not bring himself to choke down any liquor.

When all the glasses had been refilled, David Marcus stepped forward.

'To our friends on Spacelab,' he said.

McCoy pretended to drink. He felt as if the alcohol fumes alone were making him drunk.

When no one else came forward to propose a toast, the quiet circle dissolved into small groups. Almost everyone had begun to feel the effects of the liquor, but the drinking was a futile effort to numb their grief.

Whose stupid idea was it to have a wake, anyway? McCoy wondered. Who thought this would help? And then he remembered, Oh, right, it was me and Scott.

He orbited the serving table. It gleamed with an array of bottles. He picked one up, paying little attention to what it was, and filled another glass. McCoy and Scott had spent all day preparing for the wake. The synthesizer had tried to keep up with their programming, but it was badly overloaded. Ethyl alcohol was a simple enough chemical, but the congeners any decent liquor required were foreign

6

to the ship's data banks. Everything smelled the same: strong and rough.

Montgomery Scott beetled toward McCoy, stopped, and gazed blankly at the table full of half-emptied bottles. McCoy picked one at random and handed it to the ship's chief engineer.

'That's scotch,' he said. 'Or anyway, close enough.'

Scott's eyes were glazed with exhaustion and grief.

'I recall a time, when the lad was nobbut a bairn, that he . . .' Scott stopped, unable to continue the story. 'I recall a time when Mr Spock . . .' He stopped again and drank straight from the bottle, choking on the first gulp, but swallowing and swallowing again. Obsession and compulsion drove him. He and McCoy had planned the wake and insisted on holding it, though it was foreign to the traditions of most of the people on board and quite alien to the traditions of one of its subjects.

'This isna helping, doctor,' Scotty said. 'I canna bear it any longer.'

McCoy climbed onto a chair. Looking down, he hesitated. The deck lay ridiculously far away and at a strange angle, as if the artificial gravity had gone on the blink. McCoy steadied himself and stepped up on the table, placing his feet carefully between bottles bright with amber. Then he remembered an alien liquor called 'amber' by Earth people. He had not ordered it from the synthesizer because it required the inclusion of an alien insect to bring out its fullest flavor, like wormwood in absinthe. McCoy felt vaguely sick.

His foot brushed one of the bottles – quite gently, he thought – and the bottle crashed onto its side. It spun around and its contents gurgled out, spilling across the table, splashing on the floor. McCoy ignored it.

'This is a wake, not a funeral!' he said, then stopped, confused. Somehow that sounded wrong. He started

again. 'We're here to celebrate the lives of our friends –
not to mourn their deaths!' Everyone was looking at him.
That bothered him until he thought, Why did you get up
on the table, if you didn't want everyone to look at you?

'Grief,' McCoy said slowly, 'is not logical.'

'Bones,' Jim Kirk said from below and slightly behind
him, 'come down from there.'

Even in his odd mental state, McCoy could hear the
edge in Kirk's voice. Twenty years of friendship, and Kirk
was still perfectly capable of pulling rank. McCoy turned
and staggered. Jim grabbed his forearm and tightened his
grip more than necessary.

'Whatever possessed you to say such a thing?' Kirk said
angrily. Even the anger was insufficient to hide the pain.

'Don't know what you mean,' McCoy said. Permitting
Admiral Kirk to help him, he stepped down from the table
with careful dignity.

David Marcus had inherited his mother's tolerance for
alcohol. He had drunk several shots of some concoction as
powerful and as tasteless as everclear. Despite a certain
remoteness to his perceptions, he felt desperately sober.
His hands remained rock-steady, and his step was sure.

McCoy and Scott had insisted, cajoled, ordered, and
bullied until nearly the whole ship's company congregated
in the recreation hall for this ridiculous wake. Alone or in
pairs, people stood scattered throughout the enormous
chamber. Across the room, Dr McCoy and Admiral Kirk
exchanged words. Kirk looked both angry and concerned.
McCoy adopted a belligerent air.

They're both completely pickled, David thought. Fixed
like microscope slides. James T. Kirk, hero of the galaxy,
is drunk. My illegitimate father is drunk.

David had not yet quite come to terms with the recent
revelation of his parentage.

'Dr Marcus – '

David started. He had been so deep in thought that he had not noticed Captain Sulu's approach.

'It'd probably be easier if everybody just called me David,' he said.

'David, then,' Sulu said. 'I understand that I owe you some thanks.'

David looked at him blankly.

'For saving my life?' Sulu said, with a bit of a smile.

David blushed. He automatically glanced at Sulu's hands, which had been badly seared by the electrical shock from which David had revived him. The artificial skin covering the burns glistened slightly.

Sulu turned his hands palm-up. 'This comes off in a couple of days – there won't even be any scars.'

'I almost killed you,' David said.

'What?'

'It's true I did resuscitation on you. It's also true that I did it wrong. I'd never done it before. I'm not a medical doctor, I'm only a biochemist.'

'Nevertheless, I'm alive because of what you did. Whether you erred or not, you kept me from death or brain damage.'

'I still screwed up.' Like I may have screwed up everything I've done for the last two years, David thought.

'It might not matter to you,' Sulu said. 'But it makes some difference to me.' He turned away.

David blushed again, realizing how churlish and self-centered he had sounded. 'Captain . . . uh . . .' He had no idea how to apologize.

Sulu stopped and faced David again.

'David,' he said, carefully and kindly, 'I want to give you some advice. When we get back to Earth, you and your mother are going to be the center of some very concentrated attention. Some of it will be critical, some of it will be flattering. At first you'll think the abuse is the hardest thing to take. But after a while, you'll see that handling compliments gracefully is an order of magnitude more difficult.' He paused.

David looked at the floor, then raised his head and met Sulu's gaze.

'But I need to learn to do it?' David asked.

'Yes,' Sulu said. 'You do.'

'I'm sorry,' David said. 'I really am glad you're okay. I didn't mean to sound indifferent. After they took you to sick bay I realized I'd done the procedure wrong. I didn't know if you'd make it.'

'Dr Chapel assures me that I'll make it.'

David noticed that Sulu avoided mentioning McCoy, but thought better of saying so. He had stuck his foot in his mouth far enough for one day.

'I'm glad I could do something,' David said.

Sulu nodded and walked away. David had not noticed if Sulu drank during the toasts, but the young captain appeared to be completely sober.

He might be the only sober person on the ship right now, David thought.

But then David saw Lieutenant Saavik, all alone, watching the party without expression. He watched her, in turn, for several minutes. Back on Regulus I, she had told him that Spock was the most important influence in her life. He had rescued her from the short, brutal life that a halfbreed child on an abandoned Romulan colony world could look forward to. Spock had overseen her education. He had nominated her to a place in the Starfleet Academy. He was, David supposed, the nearest thing she had to a family. That was a delicate subject. She seldom discussed how the cross that produced her must have come about.

David walked up quietly behind her.

'Hello, David,' she said, without turning, as he opened his mouth to speak.

'Hi,' he said, trying to pretend she had not startled him with her preternatural senses. 'Can I get you a drink?'

'No. I never drink alcohol.'

'Why not?'

'It has an unfortunate effect on me.'

'But that's the whole point. It would help you loosen up. It would help you forget.'

'Forget what?'

'Grief. Sadness. Mr Spock's death.'

'I am a Vulcan. I experience neither grief nor sadness.'

'You're not all Vulcan.'

She ignored the comment. 'In order to forget Mr Spock's death, David, I would have to forget Mr Spock. That, I cannot do. I do not wish to. Memories of him are all around me. At times it is as if he – ' She stopped. 'I will not forget him,' she said.

'I didn't mean you should try. I just meant that a drink might make you feel better.'

'As I explained, its effects on me are not salutary.'

'What happens?'

'You do not want to know.'

'Sure I do. I'm a scientist, remember? Always on the lookout for something to investigate.'

She looked him in the eye and said, straight-faced, 'It causes me to regress. It permits the Romulan elements of my character to predominate.'

David grinned. 'Oh, yeah? Sounds interesting to me.'

'You would not like it.'

'Never know until you try.'

'Have you ever met a Romulan?'

'Nope.'

'You are,' she said drily, 'quite fortunate.'

* * *

11

Carol Marcus felt very much alone at Mr Spock's wake. She sat on the arm of a couch, concealed by the subdued light and shadows of a corner of the room. She felt grateful for the translucent wall that alcohol put between her and the other people, between her and her own emotions. She knew that the purpose of a wake was to release emotions, but she held her grief in tight check. If she loosed it, she was afraid she would go mad.

The pitiful gathering insulted the memory of her friends more than exalting it. Perhaps Mr Scott and Dr McCoy believed it adequate for Captain Spock and Mr Scott's young nephew. But the mourning of a few veteran Starfleet members and a surreptitiously drunken class of cadets, barely more than children, gave Carol no comfort for the loss of her friends on the Spacelab team. She kept expecting to hear Del March's cheerful profanity, or Zinaida Chitirih-Ra-Payjh's soft and musical laugh. She expected Jedda Adzhin-Dall to stride past, cloaked in the glow of a Deltan's unavoidable sexual attraction. And she expected at every moment to hear Vance Madison's low, beautiful voice, or to glance across the room and meet his gaze, or to reach out and touch his gentle hand.

None of those things would ever happen again. Her collaborators, her friends, were dead, murdered in vengeance for someone else's error.

Jim Kirk managed to get McCoy down from the table and away from the center of attention before the doctor had made too much of a fuss, and, Kirk hoped, without making a fool of either of them.

'I think you've drunk too much, Bones,' he said.

'Me?' McCoy said. 'I haven't had *nearly* enough.'

Kirk tried to restrain his anger at McCoy's juvenile behavior. 'Why don't you get some sleep? You'll feel better in the morning.'

'I'll feel awful in the morning, Jim-boy. And the morning after that, and – '

'You'll feel worse if you have to deal with a hangover *and* the results of a big mouth.'

McCoy frowned at him blearily, obviously not understanding. Kirk felt a twinge of unease. McCoy generally made sense, even when he had had a few too many. In fact, his usual reaction to tipsiness was to become more direct and pithier. Kirk glanced around, seeking Chris Chapel. He hoped that between them they might get McCoy either sobered up or asleep. Chapel was nowhere to be seen. He could hardly blame her for avoiding the wake. He wished he were somewhere else himself. He had come only because McCoy insisted. Jim supposed Chris had decided that the hard time McCoy and Scotty would give her for absenting herself would be less unpleasant than attending. Jim suspected she was right.

'Come on, Bones,' he said. Back in sick bay, the doctor might be persuaded to prescribe himself a hangover remedy and go to bed.

'Not going anywhere,' McCoy said. He shrugged his arm from Kirk's grasp. 'Going over there.' He walked slowly and carefully to an armchair and settled into it as if he planned to remain till dawn. Getting him to his cabin now would create a major scene. On the other hand, McCoy no longer looked in the mood to make proclamations. Jim sighed and left him where he was.

Jim wandered over to Carol. She was alone, surrounded by shadows. They had barely had time to talk since meeting again. Jim was not altogether sure she wanted to talk to him. He did want to talk to her, though, about her life since they last had seen each other, twenty years ago. But mostly he wanted to talk to her about David. Jim was getting used to the idea of having a grown son. He was beginning to like the idea of coming to know the young man.

'Hi, Carol,' he said.

'Jim.'

Her voice was calm and controlled. He remembered that she had always been able to drink everybody under the table and never even show it.

'I was thinking about Spacelab,' she said. 'And the people I left behind. Especially – '

'You did fantastic work there, you and David.'

'It wasn't just us, it was the whole team. I never worked with such an incredible group before. We got intoxicated on each other's ideas. I could guide it, but Vance was the catalyst. He was extraordinary – '

'Spock spoke highly of them all,' Jim said. It surprised him, to be able to say his friend's name so easily.

'Vance was the only one who could keep his partner from going off the deep end. He had a sort of inner stillness and calm that – '

'They were the ones who designed computer games on the side? A couple of the cadets were talking about them.'

'. . . that affected us all.'

'David and our Lieutenant Saavik seem to be hitting it off pretty well,' Jim said. David and Saavik stood together on the other side of the recreation hall, talking quietly.

'I suppose so,' Carol said without expression.

'She has a lot of promise – Spock had great confidence in her.'

'Yes.'

'I'm sorry I had to meet David – and you and I had to meet again – in such unhappy circumstances,' he said.

The look in her eyes was cold and bitter and full of pain.

'That's one way to put it,' she said.

'Carol – '

'I'm going to bed,' she said abruptly. She stood up and strode out of the recreation room.

14

Jim followed her. 'I'll walk you to your cabin,' he said. He took her silence for acquiescence.

With some curiosity, Saavik watched Admiral Kirk and Dr Marcus leave together. Of course she knew that they had been intimate many years before. She wondered if they intended to resume their relationship. She had observed the customs of younger humans, students, while she was in the Academy, however, and she now noted the absence of any indication of strong attraction between Marcus and Kirk. Perhaps older humans observed different customs, or perhaps these two individuals were simply shy. Mr Spock had told her that she must learn to understand human beings. As a project for her continuing education in their comprehension, she resolved to study the admiral and the doctor closely and see what transpired.

After Dr Marcus and the admiral left the recreation hall, Saavik returned her attention to the gathering as a whole. She wondered if there were something in particular she was supposed to do. Keeping her own customs after the deaths of Mr Spock and Peter Preston, she had watched over their bodies the night before Mr Spock's funeral. Only yesterday morning she stood with the rest of the ship's company and sent his coffin accelerating toward the Genesis planet. She wished she could have sent young Peter's body into space, too. He had loved the stars, and Saavik believed it would have pleased him to become star-stuff. But his body was the responsibility of Chief Engineer Scott, who had decreed he must be taken back to Earth and buried in the family plot.

Everyone assumed Captain Spock's casket would burn up in the outer atmosphere of the Genesis world. So Admiral Kirk had intended. But Saavik had disobeyed his order. Instead, she programmed a course that intersected the last fading resonance of the Genesis effect. When the coffin encountered the edge of the wave, matter had exploded into energy. Within the wave, the energy that had been Spock's body coalesced into sub-quarkian particles, thence, in almost unmeasurable fractions of a second, to normal atomic matter. He was now a part of that distant world. He was gone. She would never see him again.

She wondered how long she would be affected by the persistent, illogical certainty that he remained nearby.

'David,' she said suddenly, 'what is the purpose of this gathering?'

David hesitated, wondering if he understood it well enough to explain it to anyone else. 'It's a tradition,' he said. 'It's like Dr McCoy said a while ago, it's to celebrate the lives of people who have died.'

'Would it not make more sense to celebrate while a person is still living?'

'How would you know when to have the celebration?'

'You would have it whenever you liked. Then no death would be necessary. The person being celebrated could attend the party, and no one would have to feel sad.'

David wondered if she were pulling his leg. He decided that was an unworthy suspicion. Besides, he could see her point.

'The thing is,' he said, 'the funeral yesterday, and the wake today . . . they aren't really for the people who died.'

'I do not understand.'

'They're for the people who are left behind. People – humans, I mean – need to express their feelings. Otherwise we bottle them up inside and they make us sick.'

This sounded like the purest hocus-pocus to Saavik, who had spent half her life learning to control her emotions.

'You mean,' she said, 'this procedure is meant to make people feel better?'

'That's right.'

'Then why does everyone look so unhappy?'

David could not help it. He laughed.

The door to Carol's cabin sensed her and slid open. She stopped. Jim stopped. Carol said nothing. Jim tried to decide on exactly the right words.

'Carol – '

'Good night, Jim.'

'But – '

'Leave me alone!' she said. The evenness of her voice dissolved in anger.

'I thought . . .'

'What? That you could come along after twenty years and pick up again right where you left off?'

'I was thinking more in terms of "we".'

'Oh, that's cute – there never was any "we"!'

'There's David.'

'Do you think you're so great in bed that no woman would ever want another man after you? Do you think I've spent all these years just waiting for you to come back?'

'No, of course not. But – ' He stopped. That she might be involved with someone else simply had not occurred to him, and he was embarrassed to admit it. 'Of course I didn't mean that,' he said. 'But we were good together, once, and we're both alone – '

'Alone!' Her eyes suddenly filled with tears.

'Carol, I don't understand.'

'Vance Madison and I were lovers!'

'I didn't realize,' he said lamely.

'You would have, if you'd listened. I've been trying to talk about him. I just wanted to talk about him to somebody. Even to you. I want people to remember what he was like. He deserves to be remembered. I dream about him – I dream about the way he died – '

Jim took a step backward, retreating from the fury and

accusation in her voice. His old enemy, Khan Singh, had murdered all the members of the Genesis team except Carol and David. The people he captured refused to give him the information he demanded, so he killed them. He opened a vein in Madison's throat and let him slowly bleed to death.

Carol flung herself into her cabin. The door slid shut behind her, cutting Jim Kirk off, all alone, in the passageway outside.

David finally stopped laughing. He wiped his eyes. Saavik hoped he would explain to her what he found so funny.

She watched him intently. He looked up. Their gazes met.

He glanced quickly away, then back again.

David's eyes were a clear, intense blue.

She reached toward him, realized what she was doing, and froze. David touched her before she could draw away.

'What is it?' he said. He wrapped his fingers around her hand in an easy grip.

He could not hold her hand without her acquiescence, for she could crush his bones with a single clenching of her fist. This she had no intention of doing.

'For many years,' Saavik said, 'I have tried to be Vulcan.'

'I know.'

David was one of the few people with whom she had ever discussed her background. Though she had learned to control her strongest emotions most of the time, she never pretended to herself that they were nonexistent.

'But I am not all Vulcan, and I will never be,' she said, 'any more than Mr Spock. He said to me . . .' She paused, uncertain how David would react. 'He said I was unique, and that I must find my own path.'

18

'Good advice for anybody,' David said.

Saavik drew her hand from David's grasp and picked up his drink. She barely tasted it. The raw, unaged alcohol slid fiery across her tongue, and the potent fumes seemed to go straight to her brain. She put down the glass. David watched her curiously.

'David,' she said hesitantly, 'I am under the impression that you have positive feelings toward me. Is that true?'

'It's very true,' he said.

'Will you help me find my path?'

'If I can.'

'Will you come to my cabin with me?'

'Yes,' he said. 'I will.'

'Now?'

In reply, he put his hand in hers again, and they walked together from the recreation hall.

Jim Kirk strode down the corridor, upset, angry, embarrassed.

He nearly ran into his son and Lieutenant Saavik.

'Oh – Hi, kids.' He collected himself quickly. Long years of experience had made him an expert at hiding distress from subordinates.

'Uh . . . hi,' David said. Saavik said nothing; she simply gazed at him with her cool imperturbability.

'Got to be too much for you in there?' Kirk said, nodding toward the rec hall behind them. 'I never should have let McCoy and Scott have their way about it.'

They looked at him without replying. After a long hesitation, Saavik finally spoke.

'Indeed,' she said, 'it is not a ceremony Captain Spock would have approved. It is neither logical nor rational.'

Kirk flinched at the echoes of Spock's voice in Saavik's words. He had known Spock longer than she had, but she had spent more time working with the Vulcan in the past few years, when Kirk was tied to a desk by an unbreakable chain of paperwork.

'Perhaps you're right,' he said. 'But funerals and wakes aren't for the person who is dead, they're for the people left behind.'

'It is interesting,' Saavik said, 'that David said precisely the same thing. I fail, however, to grasp this explanation.'

'It isn't easily explained,' Kirk said. 'And I can understand why you wouldn't think of Spock in relation to a gathering where everybody was doing their best to get drunk. I was going to go to the observation deck, instead. Have either of you been up there? David, surely you haven't had a chance to see it. Would you like to come along?'

'I am familiar with the observation deck,' Saavik said.

'I'd sure like to see it,' David said, 'any other time. But Lieutenant Saavik wanted to check some readings on the bridge.'

Kirk glanced from David, to Saavik, and back. Saavik started to say something, but stopped. A blush colored David's transparently fair complexion. Kirk realized that he had put his foot in his mouth for the second time in ten minutes. He, too, began to blush.

'I see,' he said. 'Important work. Carry on, then.' He turned and strode quickly away.

Saavik watched him until he had passed out of sight around a corner.

'Nothing needs to be checked on the bridge, David,' she said.

'I had to say something,' David said. 'I didn't want to discuss our personal affairs with him. It isn't any of his business.'

'But why did he not remind you that the computer would announce any change in the ship's status?'

'I don't know,' David said, though he knew perfectly well.

'He has not commanded a starship in a long time,' she said. 'Perhaps he forgot.'

'That must be it.'

They continued down the corridor to Saavik's cabin. Inside, David blinked, waiting for his eyes to accustom themselves to the low light. The room held no decorations, only the severe furnishings standard issue in Starfleet, but the warm and very dry air carried a hot, resiny scent, like the sunbaked pitch of pine trees at high noon in summer.

Saavik stopped with her back to David.

'Saavik,' David said, 'I just want you to know – maybe we don't need to worry, but where I was raised it's good manners to tell you – I passed all my exams in biocontrol.'

'I, too,' she said softly. 'I always regarded learning to regulate the reproductive ability merely as an interesting exercise. Until now . . .' Her voice trailed off.

David realized that she was trembling. He put his hands gently on her shoulders.

'I have traveled far, and I have seen much,' Saavik said. 'I have studied . . . But study and action are very different.'

'I know,' David said. 'It's all right, it will be all right.'

Saavik reached up, and her hair fell free around her shoulders. It was thick and soft and dark, and it smelled of evergreens.

Jim Kirk did go to the observation deck. He opened the portals and spent a long time staring at the stars. After a while, the romantic in his soul overcame the admiral in his mind. The pain and grief surrounding Spock's death eased, the embarrassing encounter with David and Saavik began to seem humorous, and even his misunderstanding

21

of Carol's wishes became less lacerating in his memory. The whole galaxy lay around him.

He fancied he could still see the star of the Genesis world, far behind, a hot white star red-shifted toward yellow as the *Enterprise* raced away, an unimposing young star made fuzzy by the planetary nebula that surrounded it, by the remnants of the Mutara Nebula. The matter in the nebula had been blasted apart by the Genesis wave, blasted beyond atoms, beyond sub-atomic particles, beyond quarks, down to the sub-elementary particles that Vance Madison and his partner Del March had whimsically named 'snarks' and 'boojums'.

Khan Singh had set off the Genesis wave in an attempt to destroy Jim Kirk, an attempt that had very nearly succeeded. Thus he set in motion – what? Even Carol could not say. The resonances in the wave were designed to work upon a very different environment. No one could know what had come into existence on the Genesis world without going back and exploring it. Jim Kirk had many reasons for wanting to see that done and, what was more, for wanting to do it himself.

First he had to return to Earth. To accomplish that, he needed a crew that in the morning would be able to think of something other than their hangovers. Realizing that he had been up here all alone for nearly an hour, he decided it was about time to go back to the recreation deck and shut things down.

He closed the portals against the stars.

David dozed in the intoxicating warmth of Saavik's body. Vulcans – and, David supposed, Romulans, too – had a body temperature several degrees above that of human beings.

'Lying next to you is like lying in the shade on a hot summer's day,' Saavik said.

22

David chuckled sleepily. 'You must be psychic.'

'Only slightly,' she said. 'Vulcans and Romulans both have the ability in some measure. My talent for it is quite limited. But why do you say so now?'

'I was just thinking that lying next to you is like being in the sun on the first warm day of spring.'

She turned suddenly toward him and hugged him close. Her hair fell across his shoulders. He put his arms around her and held her. She had been raised first among Romulans who rejected her, then in the Vulcan tradition which denied any need for closeness or passion. He wondered if anyone had ever held her before.

She drew back and lay beside him, barely touching him, as if ashamed of her instant's impulse. David was not so ready to ignore the intimacy.

He traced the smooth, strong line of Saavik's collarbone with the tip of one finger. He had never been with anyone like her in his life. He caressed the hollow of her throat and cupped his hand around the point of her left shoulder. He had felt the scar on her smooth skin earlier, but just then the time had been wrong for questions. Now, though, he touched the scar in the dark and found it to be a complex, regular pattern.

'How'd you get that?' he asked.

She said nothing for so long that David wondered if his bad habit of asking questions off the top of his head had got him into trouble again.

'Sorry,' he said. 'Idle curiosity – it's none of my business.'

'It is a Romulan family mark,' Saavik said.

'A family mark!' She had told him that she did not know the identity of either of her parents, that she did not even know which parent was Vulcan and which Romulan. 'Does that mean you could find your family?'

'David,' she said, and he thought he could detect a hint

of dry humor in her voice, 'why would I want to find my Romulan family?'

Since the likelihood was that a Romulan had borne or sired her in order to demonstrate complete power over a Vulcan prisoner, David could see her point.

'I never heard of family marks,' he said.

'That is not surprising. Information about them may only be passed on orally. It is a capital crime in the Romulan empire to make permanent records of them.'

'Why don't you have the mark removed? Doesn't it remind you of – unpleasant times?'

'I do not wish to forget those times,' Saavik said, 'any more than I wish to forget Mr Spock. All those memories are important to me. Besides, it may have its use, someday.'

'How?'

'Should I have the misfortune to encounter my Romulan parent, it is absolute proof of our relationship.'

'But if you don't want to know your Romulan parent . . .'

'The family mark permits me to demand certain rights,' Saavik said. 'It would be considered very bad manners to refuse a family member's challenge to a death-duel.'

'A duel!'

'Yes. How else avenge myself? How else avenge my Vulcan parent, who surely died with my birth?'

David lay back on the narrow bunk, stunned by Saavik's matter-of-fact discussion of deep, implacable hatred.

'I never thought of Vulcans as demanding an eye for an eye and a tooth for a tooth.'

'But I am not – as Vulcans never cease to remind me – a proper Vulcan.'

'Wouldn't it be easier, wouldn't it be safer, to – I don't know, sue the Romulans for reparations?'

24

'Spoken like a truly civilized human,' Saavik said. 'But if I am only half a Vulcan, I am in no part human. Mr Spock was right – I must follow my own path.'

David moved his hand from her shoulder. The intensity of her feelings surprised him, though it should not, not any more, not after tonight.

'Don't worry, David,' Saavik said, in response to his unease. 'I am hardly going to defect to the Romulan empire in order to find a creature I have no real wish to meet. The chance of my ever meeting my Romulan parent is vanishingly small.'

'I guess,' David said. The Federation had, at best, fragile diplomatic relations with the Romulans. It was a connection like a fuse, continually threatening to burst into flame and ignite a more serious conflagration.

Saavik guided his hand back to her shoulder.

'It feels good when you touch it,' she said. 'The coolness of your hand is soothing.'

'Were you born with it? Or is it a tattoo?'

'Neither. It is a brand.'

'A brand!'

'They apply it soon after one is out of the womb.'

'Gods, what a thing to do to a little baby. Good thing you can't remember it.'

'What makes you think I cannot remember it?'

Horrified, David said, 'You mean you *can*?'

'Of course. The white glow is the first beautiful thing I ever encountered, and its touch was the first pain. Do you not remember your own birth?'

'No, not at all. I don't have any reliable memories before I was two or three. Most people don't.'

'But most people do, David,' Saavik said. 'At least, in my experience. Perhaps you mean most humans do not?'

'Yeah,' David said. 'Sorry. Bad habit.'

'No offense taken. I am always glad to learn something

new about a fellow intelligent species. The last few hours have been very rewarding. I have learned a great deal.'

David did not know quite how to take that, so he replied with an inarticulate 'Hmm?'

'Yes,' Saavik said. 'I feel that my experiments have been most instructive.'

'Is that all I am to you?' David said. 'An experiment?' He suddenly felt very hurt and disappointed, and he realized that his attraction toward Saavik was a great deal more than physical, something much deeper and much stronger.

'That is one of the things you are to me,' she said in an even tone. 'And not the least. But not the most, either. You have helped me learn that I have capabilities I believed I did not possess.'

'Like – the capacity to love?'

'I . . . . I am unprepared to make that claim. I do not even comprehend the concept.'

David laughed softly. 'Neither does anybody else.'

'Indeed? My research is unfinished – I thought I simply had not encountered a satisfactory definition.'

'It isn't something you can quantify.'

'Someone should conduct experiments.'

'Experiments!' David said, slightly shocked.

'Certainly. Perhaps we might collaborate on a paper.'

'Saavik – '

'I have heard a speculation. I am curious to know whether it is true, or merely apocryphal.'

'All right,' David said, beyond surprise. 'What speculation is that?'

Saavik turned toward him, propped herself up on one elbow, and let her hair spill over his shoulder and across his chest.

'It is,' she said, 'that Romulans are insatiable. Would you care to test this hypothesis?'

David laughed. He reached up and touched her face in the dark. He traced the lines of her lips, and found that she was smiling. She had just discovered another capability that few people would suspect her of possessing. She had a terrific sense of humor.

'Why don't we do that?' David said.

Jim Kirk strode into the recreation hall.

The wake had deteriorated even further. Cadets stood alone or in small groups, sinking into silent depression. Scott clutched a drink and talked continuously and intensely to a single captive trainee. McCoy lay sprawled in his chair. As a catharsis, this gathering was a wretched failure. It succeeded only in intensifying everyone's feelings of pain and loss and guilt. Kirk stopped by a small group of cadets.

'I think it's about time to pack it in for the night,' he said. 'You're all dismissed.'

'Yessir,' one of the cadets said. Her relieved smile, quick, and quickly hidden, was the first smile Kirk had seen all day.

The cadets, just waiting for an excuse to escape the sepulchral atmosphere, all accepted his order without objection or argument. The trainees still sober enough to be ambulatory helped their friends who had overindulged. Within a few minutes, the only cadet left was the one listening to Mr Scott's tirade. Kirk joined them. The cadet looked pale and drawn.

'Scotty – ' Kirk said, when Scott paused for breath.

'Aye, Captain, life doesna make sense sometimes, I was just sayin' to Grenni here, 'tis the good ones go before their time – '

'Mr Scott – '

' – there's no denyin' it. The boy had guts. He had potential – '

27

'Commander Scott!'

'Aye, sir? What's wrong, Admiral? Why are ye soundin' so perturbed?'

Kirk sighed. 'Perturbed, Mr Scott? Whatever makes you think I'm perturbed? You're dismissed, cadet.'

'Yes, sir. Thank you, sir.' The cadet's voice shook. He fled.

'Mr Scott, we'll reach Regulus tomorrow, and I need a coherent crew. Go to bed.'

'But my poor bairn – I wished to have all o' us sing a song for him. Do ye know "Danny Boy," Captain?'

'That's an order, Mr Scott.'

'Aye, sir.' Scott commenced to sing. '"O Danny boy, the pipes, the pipes are calling – "'

'*Mister Scott!*'

Scott stopped singing and gazed at him blearily, blinking and confused, as Kirk's tone finally got through to him.

'"Sing 'Danny Boy'" is not an order. "Go to bed" is an order.'

'Oh. Begging your pardon, sir. Aye, sir.'

Scott glanced around him, as if searching for something. Suddenly he looked very tired and old. He trudged away.

McCoy was the last member of the wake remaining. Jim sat on his heels beside McCoy's chair. The doctor snored softly.

'Bones,' Jim said, shaking him softly. 'Bones, wake up.'

McCoy flinched, muttered something incomprehensible, and lapsed back into snoring.

'Come on, old friend.' Jim dragged McCoy's arm across his shoulder and hoisted him to his feet. McCoy sagged against him and muttered a few more words. Jim froze.

'*What*?'

McCoy straightened up, swaying, and looked Kirk directly in the eye.

'Using a metabolic poison as a recreational drug is totally illogical.'

McCoy collapsed.

2

Dr Christine Chapel watched herself function efficiently. She felt very much like two different people, one performing as she should, the other separated from the world by shock. She felt numb and clumsy. That she could function at all astonished her. Yet she did what needed to be done, caring for the crew members, mostly young cadets, who had been injured during Khan Singh's attacks; dispensing hangover remedies to those who had neglected to take a preventive after Mr Spock's wake; and looking in occasionally on Leonard McCoy. She was extremely concerned about him.

She paused in the doorway of the cubicle in which she and Admiral Kirk had put him the night before. She left the lights on very low. She suspected that when Leonard woke, his headache would be a credit to its species.

He moaned and muttered something. Chris moved farther into the small room, squinting to see better in the dim light. Leonard tossed on the bunk, his face shining with sweat. His tunic was soaked. Chris felt his forehead. His temperature was elevated, not yet dangerously so, but certainly enough to make him uncomfortable.

'Leonard,' she said softly.

He sat bolt upright, staring straight ahead. Slowly he turned to look at her. He moved in a way she had never seen him move before, but in a way that was eerily familiar.

'Vulcans,' he said, in a voice much lower than his own, 'do not love.'

Chris took an involuntary step backward.

'How dare you say that to me?' she said, in a quiet, angry voice. The pain pierced through the numbness to her enclosed, repressed grief and spread like fire through her. She turned, hiding her face in her hands. She could not break down now. The ship had to have a doctor, and McCoy was in no shape to take over.

The obsession she had had with Spock for so long still embarrassed her, though it had burned out years before. She had forced herself beyond it by sheer determination and by the power of the knowledge that what she desired from him, he simply could not give. His inability to respond to her had nothing to do with Christine Chapel. He had never had the choice between 'interested' and 'uninterested'. All his training and experience required him to be disinterested, and so he had behaved.

Once Chris accepted that, she began to appreciate his unique integrity. It took a long time for her to get over her youthful fantasies, but once she did, her fondness for Spock strengthened. Losing a friend, she had discovered in the past few days, was much worse than losing a remotely potential and unrequiting lover. Accepting Spock's death, she thought, would be an even longer and more difficult task than persuading herself not that he never would love her, but that he never could.

She took her hands from her face and straightened up, under control again. This was a bad time to cry. Leonard McCoy's sense of humor was quirky, but not cruel. For him to say what he had said to her meant either that something was seriously wrong or – the simplest, if least flattering, possibility – that he was still intoxicated.

Saavik woke suddenly and sat up, startled. Mr Spock was speaking to her. His deep voice still echoed in her cabin. Saavik was not prepared to answer him. She was dazzled by strange dreams and fantasies.

'But I am not a Vulcan,' she said. 'You said to me – '

She stopped. He was not here – he had never been here. Spock was gone.

Spock's voice had sounded so real . . . but what she thought was reality was a cruel dream, and what for a moment had seemed impossible fantasy was real.

David lay sleeping beside her, cool and fair. She touched his shoulder lightly. He stirred gently but did not wake. Saavik wondered if she could be going mad with grief, or with guilt. She did not feel mad.

But Spock's voice had seemed so real . . .

Delicately, Farrendahl nibbled at the fur-covered web of skin at the base of the first and second fingers of her right paw. A bad habit, she knew it, one she had picked up from a human shipmate who bit his nails. A human's nails were such flimsy things that it hardly mattered whether they were damaged or properly sharp, but Farrendahl would never sink so low as to bite her claws. They were far too useful.

At times like these, though, she needed a nervous habit to fall back on. Her primate-type crewmates either objected to or thought amusing the more obvious forms of grooming. Never mind that she found them soothing. Farrendahl did not like to be laughed at. Primates, humanoids as they preferred to call themselves in Standard, could be astonishingly repellent when they laughed.

Farrendahl sat on her haunches in the navigator's hammock, chewing on her paw and blinking at the unfamiliar stars. Having passed out of Federation space and into the gray area between set borders some hours before, the ship now fell under the protection of no one. It had become potential prey to all. This, Farrendahl disliked intensely.

A signal came through her console. She blinked at it,

too, then in response to the new order changed the course of the ship for the third time in a single circadian. The resulting course, if left unchanged, would bring the ship face to face with the Klingons. This, Farrendahl disliked even more.

No wonder their mysterious passenger was unwilling to name a destination. No wonder the ship's grapevine sprouted rumors of an enormous payment to the captain. Great wonder, though, if the captain passed on part of his largesse in the crew's bonuses without a confrontation.

'I dislike the scent of this,' Farrendahl said. She growled softly in irritation. 'It smelled bad when we began, and its odor has become progressively more putrid.'

Her compatriot bared his teeth in that offensive primate way, and an intermittent choking noise came from his throat. In short, he laughed.

'Since when do cats learn anything useful from their sense of smell?' he said.

Compatriot. . .! A high-class word to apply to any member of this ship's crew of ill-mannered, poorly reared mercenaries.

'Since when,' Farrendahl said to Tran, 'have I been a cat?' Instead of baring her teeth, which another member of her own species would have recognized as a threat, she placed her paw on the scarred control panel. She stretched out her fingers so her paw became a hand, then slowly extended her claws. The sharp tips scratched the panel with a gradual, hair-raising shriek.

'A cat?' Tran exclaimed. 'Did I call you a cat? Who in their right mind would call you a cat?'

'I saw a cat once,' Farrendahl said matter-of-factly. 'It was digging through a garbage heap in a back alley on Amenhotep IX. I disliked it. Please explain the similarities between it and me.'

'Don't push it, Farrendahl.'

'But I desire to be enlightened.'

'All right. Both of you were in the back alley, weren't you?'

Farrendahl leapt, knocking Tran to the deck. The artificial gravity, set for economy's sake at an annoyingly low intensity, turned her attack and Tran's fall into a most unsatisfactory series of slow bounces. But they ended up as Farrendahl planned, with the human on the floor and her claws and teeth at his throat. This was a main reason she never bit her claws.

'And was there not an ugly monkey-looking creature in that same back alley, only insensible from noxious recreational drugs?'

'Probably there was,' Tran said, laughing again.

Farrendahl bristled her whiskers out, acknowledging Tran's good-humored surrender. She was about to release him when the captain walked in on them. He stopped, folded his arms across his chest, and glared at the crew members.

'If you two haven't any work, I can find some,' he said. 'We don't have time for your continual horsing around.'

Farrendahl growled softly and rose, extending her hand to Tran to help him rise. He leaped to his feet like a gymnast in the low gravity.

'A cat, a monkey, now a horse,' Farrendahl said in a low voice. 'Perhaps our mysterious mission is to transport a menagerie.'

Tran chuckled and returned to his place at the control console.

'I heard that,' the captain said. 'Ten demerits.'

'You're in a charming mood today, Captain,' Farrendahl said. She ignored the threat of demerits. She had already earned so many that ten more scarcely counted. Demerits were a source of great hilarity among the crew, ever since the time they precipitated a minor mutiny. One planetfall, on a more or less civilized world and after a long, boring journey, the captain forbade Farrendahl, Tran, and several others to leave the ship. Too many demerits, he said. Farrendahl said nothing. She simply ignored him, and she and the others went out anyway.

He could have left while they were rousting around. He could have locked them off the ship and hired another crew. But he stayed where he was, leaving the ship open to them when they returned. Apparently he preferred his tried and semi-competent, if insolent, people to a new bunch that he would have to have trained.

He continued to assign demerits, but that was the only time he ever referred to them, and he never again tried to use them for anything.

The captain ignored Farrendahl's smart remark and paused at the control console. Farrendahl despised him on every possible level. He possessed power and the title of captain not because he deserved them or had earned them but simply because he owned the ship. He knew little about running it and less about the computers that formed its guts.

'Perhaps you are concerned that we will discover what you are being paid for this trip,' Farrendahl said, putting him on notice that they all did know and that they all expected their cut.

He glared at her as she slipped smoothly into the navigator's hammock. He kept his silence. He was a bully, but he was also a coward, and he avoided any serious confrontation with Farrendahl.

'When do we find out where we are really going?'

'When you need to know,' he said.

'Waste of fuel,' Farrendahl said just loudly enough for him to hear. It amused her that he would worry the comment around in his mind, trying to find a way to conserve the fuel wasted by their roundabout route. If he had ever learned to pilot his ship himself, he would not have to depend on Farrendahl. She supposed she should be grateful for his lack of application.

The contempt in which she held him was diluted by her awareness of her own failings and limitations. She had been disappointed when, after the 'mutiny', the captain capitulated to his impertinent crew. But she might have found another berth – whatever else she was, she was an able navigator, and now and then a shipmaster turned up who was willing to waive small matters like papers and background. She could have found another place, but she did not. Inertia kept her in the same, riskless position. Beneath her contempt for the captain lurked a certain contempt for herself. Perhaps they deserved each other.

The captain remained by the console, his attitude that of one studying the readings, his eyes with the blank stare of someone who had no idea what he was looking at.

'We're on course,' Farrendahl said, 'as long as you don't have any more changes in mind. Unless you do, I am going to sleep.'

Lacking any reply, she slid from the hammock and padded away toward her cabin.

David stepped out of the turbo-lift, onto the bridge. Saavik, already on duty, glanced over her shoulder at him. A look passed between them that they innocently assumed no one else noticed or understood. Saavik returned her attention to her work as if it were easy for her. David wrestled himself back to this morning and away from last night.

It must be nice, David thought, to have the ability to control your feelings so completely. Being able to focus one's attention on a single subject gave remarkable results.

'Good morning, David,' James Kirk said.

'Uh, hi.' David could not bring himself to call Kirk 'father'. More than twenty years lay between them, years during which they could have known each other. David wondered what he would be like if he had known James Kirk as his father when it might have made a difference. He had found some reason to respect the Starfleet officer. Affection would take longer.

Kirk responded to David's unease. 'How would you feel about calling me "Jim"?'

'Okay, I guess.'

Kirk paused for a moment, then turned away again. David realized he had hurt the admiral's feelings with his lukewarm response.

'This is going to take some getting used to,' he said.

'Yes,' Kirk said. 'For me, too. We need to talk about it. In private.'

David took the hint and kept the personal matters to himself, saving them for someplace other than the bridge of the *Enterprise*.

'There it is,' Kirk said.

In the viewscreen, Regulus I hung dark and mysterious before them. The barren worldlet had always given David an eerie feeling. It had never evolved life. It had never had a chance of evolving life. It had no water and no air and too little gravity to hold either one. But Genesis had changed all that. The planetoid's interior had been turned into an entire, new, inside-out world, one with an ecosystem designed from scratch by Carol Marcus' team. It was like a Jules Verne novel brought to reality, and David was proud of his part in creating it. The memory of the short time he had spent beneath the surface of the world remained as a warm glow of pride and power. He wanted to go back inside and explore. No experiment ever turned out precisely as one planned. David wanted to discover the unexpected results. They were always the most interesting.

Spacelab drifted in its orbit, a shadowed silver flash against the limb of the planetoid. The Starfleet science ship *Grissom* lay in a matching orbit, waiting for the *Enterprise*. The ship and the laboratory satellite gradually entered the shadow of their primary, vanishing into the featureless darkness. David shivered. He had lived and worked on the research station for two years. He had called it home. Now it felt alien and threatening. If hauntings were possible, it must be haunted. On Spacelab, no one was left alive. The bodies of the people Khan Singh had murdered lay waiting to be returned to Earth and to their graves.

As the transporter beam faded from the newly material-ized form of Captain J. T. Esteban, James Kirk waited to greet him. Esteban stepped down. They shook hands.

'Welcome aboard, J.T.,' Kirk said. 'It's been a while.'

'It has that,' Esteban said. 'An eventful while, too. You folks have things in quite a tizzy, back home.'

Kirk led Esteban to the nearest turbo-lift. 'I don't believe I follow you,' he said.

'Will Dr Marcus be available, Jim?' J.T. said. 'I need to talk to the both of you.'

They stepped into the lift. 'Officer's lounge,' Jim said, and felt the faint acceleration as the lift whisked them toward their destination. 'I'll have Dr Marcus paged.' Kirk contacted Uhura. 'Uhura, Kirk here. Would you ask Dr Marcus to meet Captain Esteban and me in the officer's lounge?'

'Certainly, Admiral.'

'Thanks. Kirk out.' He turned off the intercom. He could sense the tension in the captain of the *Grissom*. 'What's going on, J.T.?'

'I just think it would save time to talk to you both at once.' Esteban was deliberately misunderstanding the question, and Jim did not push it. They tried to make small talk, but it was strained.

'The galaxy ships are already paying off,' Esteban said. 'Have you heard?'

'We've been out of touch,' Jim said drily.

'Of course. But a subspace transmission just came through – it made all the news services. *Magellan* is in Andromeda. It just completed the first close-range observation of a supernova.'

'That's very impressive,' Jim said. And for all his offhandedness, he *was* impressed. Andromeda! Another galaxy, millions and millions of light-years away. A different ship, with a different crew and a different commander, had reached it first. He made a mental note to tel Mr Sulu the news of *Magellan*, for Sulu and the galaxy ship's captain, Mandala Flynn, had been the closest of friends for a long time.

They reached the officer's lounge and went inside. Carol had not yet arrived.

'Jim?'

'Eh?' Kirk realized J.T. had spoken to him, but had no idea what he had said. 'I'm sorry, what did you say?'

'I said *Magellan* is a bit of a technological trick. It's too small to do anything but quick and dirty scouting missions. And if they encounter hostiles, what can they do but turn tail and run?'

'No doubt you're right,' Jim said. He tried to imagine something that might cause Mandala Flynn to turn tail and run. He failed.

'No, it's *Excelsior* that's the wave of the future,' J.T. said.

The door to the lounge slid open to admit Carol Marcus, accompanied by David. Carol nodded to Jim coolly; if she was not still angry at him, at best she was not yet willing to forget about last night's conversation.

'Carol,' Jim said, 'this is J.T. Esteban, commanding the *Grissom*. J.T., Dr Carol Marcus, and her son . . .' Jim paused, thinking he really should say, 'Our son,' but deciding not to because it would take so long to explain. 'Her son, Dr David Marcus.'

'Two for the price of one,' David said.

Jim chuckled and Carol smiled. Missing the joke, J.T. rubbed his jaw and frowned.

'This is sensitive information,' he said. 'I only expected Dr Marcus, senior.'

David's smile vanished. 'I can take a hint,' he said. He headed toward the door, the irritation in his voice mirrored in his stiff-shouldered walk.

'David – ' Jim said, but David kept walking.

'David, wait,' Carol said.

David hesitated, then glanced back.

'David is a full member of the Genesis team, Captain Esteban,' Carol said. 'He and I are the only surviving principal investigators. Anything you have to say about Genesis, you must say to him as well as to me.'

'The first thing I have to say is I wish you'd called it something else,' Esteban said.

'I don't understand what you mean.'

'It's too late now, but it wasn't the wisest move you could have made, in terms of p.r. Never mind that, for the moment. Dr Marcus – ' He addressed David this time. 'I apologize for my bad manners. Please come sit down with the rest of us. We have a great deal to talk over.'

They sat around one of the small tables next to the star portals, and Esteban described the circumstances they would return to on Earth.

'The news of the Genesis effect created . . . shall we say, a sensation,' J.T. said uncomfortably.

In all the years Jim had known J.T. Esteban, he had never seen him lose his composure. Anything and everything, no matter how strange, no matter the stress, he had always taken easily, even phlegmatically, in his stride. Jim had read the reports of some of his missions. Esteban had come up against extraordinarily challenging events, and he had prevailed. To see him so agitated about Genesis disturbed Jim more than anything the younger Starfleet officer could tell him.

'Of course it did,' David said. 'That's sort of the point, isn't it? We've made possible the elimination of poverty. We've made the reasons for war completely untenable – '

'You've created a device that could destroy the galaxy. That's what our adversaries perceive, not universal peace and plenty. They have demanded multilateral parity – '

'You mean they want Genesis, too,' Carol said.

'Precisely.'

'Why don't you give it to them?' David said.

'David!' Jim said, shocked. 'We didn't just go through – the last few days – so we could turn Genesis over to an enemy power. Your friends didn't die resisting Khan so you could hand over the discovery to the next person who demanded it.'

'That was different,' David said. 'Khan wanted it for revenge. Revenge against you.'

Jim scowled, but did not reply to the jab.

'I'm not talking about giving it to every crazy who comes along,' David said. 'I'm talking about making Genesis openly available for transforming lifeless worlds.'

'That is absolutely outside the realm of possibility,' J.T. said.

'But that's what we made it for!'

'My dear boy,' J.T. said.

Jim winced, seeing David bristle.

'My dear boy,' J.T. said, 'we can't give it to anyone else. That would be too dangerous.'

'The Federation is the only organization with the wisdom to decide on its use?' Carol said dryly.

'I'm glad you understand Starfleet's – the Federation's – position, Dr Marcus,' J.T. said, missing the irony the same way he always missed jokes.

'Oh, I understand it, all right,' Carol said. 'That doesn't mean that I accept it.'

'I knew it!' David shouted. 'You just can't keep your hands off any discovery, can you? You have to grab it and hoard it and twist it until you can figure out a way to use it for destruction!'

'David, relax,' Jim said.

'We would hardly have to do much figuring, now, would we?' Esteban said. 'The evidence for the destructive power of Genesis is its first deployment. It completely recreated the substance of the Mutara Nebula, a volume of space some hundred astronomical units in radius. It destroyed *Reliant* and all the people on board. It nearly destroyed the *Enterprise*, and it did cause the death of – '

'Indirectly,' Jim Kirk snapped. 'We were involved in hostilities – '

'Because of Genesis!'

'Not entirely,' Jim said. David was right: Khan Singh had intended to use Genesis to wreak revenge upon James Kirk. But he had stumbled upon the project by chance, then turned it to his purposes. He had succeeded better than he could have known.

'You're hardly being fair, Captain,' Carol said. 'The Genesis device was obviously never meant – in any form – to go off inside a ship. That particular device was never intended to go off within a nebula.'

'But that's precisely my point, doctor! After all that's happened, how can you argue that the device cannot be an instrument of terrorism?'

'But if everybody has it there isn't any need for terrorism!' David said.

Carol was touched by David's naivete, Jim was surprised by it, and J.T. thought he was being deliberately, perhaps even maliciously, dense.

'Your discovery may eliminate poverty. But it'll hardly change the natures of sentient beings. It won't eliminate greed or lust for power or simple error, and it most certainly won't eliminate ideology. The drive to convert people's minds and hearts has caused more grief, more suffering, more loss of life than any desire for property, riches, or even the necessities of survival.'

'Very eloquent, Captain,' David said sarcastically. 'I take it you mean our ideology requires us to pervert Genesis into a weapon before anybody else gets a chance to?'

'It's hardly productive to ascribe malicious motives to everybody who disagrees with you, David,' Jim said sharply.

'What has to be done with Genesis isn't up to me to say,' J.T. said. 'Or to any of us.'

'You're entitled to your opinion,' Carol said.

David jumped to his feet. 'I always said the military'd try to take Genesis away from us! I suppose if I try to call the Federation Science Network in on this, you'll throw me in the brig!'

'Sit down and shut up, David,' Jim said. 'If anybody gets thrown in the brig on this ship, it'll be by me. And you're making it mighty tempting to send you to bed without your supper.'

David glared at him with a sudden flare of resentment that surprised Jim completely.

'Try it and see how far you get!' David glared at Kirk, then at Esteban. 'I don't see any point in continuing this discussion.' He stalked away.

43

'Come back here, David,' Jim said.

'Do you think you can make me? You and who else?' He strode from the lounge.

Jim started to rise.

Carol put one hand on his arm.

'Let him go, Jim. He'll be all right when he cools down.' She smiled. 'That's another way he's like you.'

'I was never that hot-headed!'

Carol looked at him askance. Jim reluctantly sat down again.

He realized that J.T. was watching them with both curiosity and confusion. He deserved at least some explanation.

'David is my son, as well as Carol's,' he said.

'Oh,' J.T. said. 'Er . . . I didn't realize you had any children.'

Neither did I, Jim thought, but what he said out loud was, 'Just the one.'

'How did we get off on this track, anyway?' J.T. said. 'What I asked you here to tell you is that *Grissom* has been ordered to the Mutara sector to make a complete survey of the Genesis world. We can hardly discuss it, with our allies or with our adversaries, unless we know more about the effect and its consequences. Dr Marcus, I've been directed to transfer you to my ship.'

'What?' Carol said.

'Obviously, we need you to supervise the observations – '

'Forget it,' Carol said.

'I beg your pardon?'

'What the hell do you think I am? "Transfer" me? Like a crate of supplies? Do you think I'm a robot?'

'I'm sorry, Doctor. I don't follow you at all.'

'Six people died on Spacelab. I was responsible for them – and they were my friends! I owe them. At the very

44

least I owe them the courtesy of telling their families what happened!'

'Their families know of the tragedy . . .'

'What did you do – send telegrams? My gods!'

'I feel sure things were handled with more . . . more delicacy than you suspect.'

'I don't care,' Carol said. 'I'm not going back to Genesis, not now. I won't discuss it any further.'

'But –'

'The subject is closed.'

She stood abruptly and strode from the lounge, leaving Jim and J.T. together in awkward silence.

'Well,' J.T. said finally, 'I didn't handle either one of them very well, did I? Maybe if I ask her again a little later – ?'

'I wouldn't advise it,' Jim said.

Valkris knelt on the floor of her cabin, meditating. The low gravity of the mercenary's ship made the discipline very difficult. Remaining in one position for a great length of time required no strength of will, where gravity put little stress on the body.

Meditation was one of the few ways she had of passing the time during the miserable boredom of space travel when one was merely a passenger, a lone passenger at that. She had been more accustomed to flying her own ship, before her family fell upon hard times.

This mission would rebuild her family's fortune and its honor. She resisted unseemly pride: it was merely her duty to repair the damage done to all their reputations by the actions of her older brother. Kiosan had never forgiven their family for choosing Valkris, rather than him, to lead them.

In his despair and envy he set out to prove how spectacularly correct the family had been to overlook him.

He reneged on all the vows he had made when he came of age. He put aside his veil and showed his face to the world. He addicted himself to pleasure, and he showed no desire to change. Valkris offered him the opportunity to return to the family three times, and even a fourth, though the fourth offer strained her sense of aesthetics. Not only did he refuse – he dared her to break her own word and join him.

Valkris had disowned her brother with a regret so intense that to this moment she felt the pain. But Kiosan's actions had sent their family's reputation and merit into an inexorable slide that could not be reversed unless he repented or she released him. So Valkris had set him free. To all her other blood kin, he was dead. But he was still very much alive to Valkris, and when she thought of him, as she often did, she wished him well in his freedom and envied him more than a little.

She had made vows, too. Every member of each of the great families took the vows upon coming of age. Despite the example of her older brother, Valkris was unable to break them. Every action she had taken since accepting her position had been intended to benefit the family. She had never fled a duel. She had never even lost a duel, though she bore scars from wounds that would have proven her honor even had she yielded to the opponent who inflicted them. Because of her reputation for ferocious tenacity, she had not been challenged in some years. Valkris did not fight for an afternoon's entertainment. She had buried more opponents than she had permitted to be helped from the field.

It was good that the family would recover from Kiosan's foolishness. It was better that it was Valkris who designed the recovery, and who would carry it out.

She extended both her hands and clenched her fingers into fists, feeling the tension and the strength in her long, strong muscles. She rose smoothly to her feet and made a hand signal before the sensor of the intercom.

'Yes?' the captain of the mercenary vessel said after a moment.

'The gravity in my cabin is very weak. I require it to be increased.'

'There's a matter of the extra fuel to run the grav generators.'

'You will not lose by acceding to my requests, captain,' Valkris said. She was tired enough of his pettiness to consider making him a challenge. She resisted the unworthy impulse. She could gain no honor by vanquishing such a creature. He had no style.

'Very well,' the captain said disagreeably.

A short time later the gravity in Valkris' cabin began to increase. She knelt again and composed herself for meditation. When the force increased well beyond that of her home world, she simply smiled and set herself to find the discipline she had been seeking.

Saavik did her work automatically. She had practiced on the bridge of the *Enterprise* so often that the responses came without her conscious thought. Any change, any anomaly, would call itself to her attention instantly. For the moment everything was normal – as normal as it could be for a half-crippled ship – so Saavik could think of other things.

She thought about David, she thought about Mr Spock, and she thought about the strangeness of her life. Mr Spock had helped her transform herself from a starving, abandoned, illiterate child-thief into a polished, controlled, and well-educated Starfleet officer. Under most circumstances she was the very model of Vulcan propriety. That had been her goal, until her last conversation with Spock. 'You must find your own path,' he had said.

The wisdom of his words impressed her. He had told her she might find herself considering possibilities that she knew he would not approve. She should not, he said, dismiss them on that criterion alone. Instead, she should remain open to them.

The path she had chosen last night led into the unexplored regions of her Romulan heritage. Spock would most certainly not have encouraged such a journey. For that reason Saavik found even more cause to admire his insight into her character and his own.

Saavik thought about her life, she thought about Mr Spock, and she thought about – her thoughts kept coming back to – David.

'Lieutenant Saavik.'

'Yes, Admiral.' Saavik turned to face Admiral Kirk, who had just stepped onto the bridge with an unfamiliar officer: Captain Esteban of the *Grissom*, by his uniform and insignia.

'J.T.,' Kirk said, 'this is Lieutenant Saavik. Lieutenant, Captain Esteban is on a survey trip to Genesis. He needs someone along who has a scientific background, and who witnessed the creation of the world. Dr Marcus has declined to go. Would you care to volunteer?'

'Aye, Admiral,' she said. She thought of David. The words tasted bitter. She turned back to her console.

Chris Chapel paused at McCoy's bedside and felt his forehead again. His fever had receded, and she had heard him move restlessly as if he were about to wake up.

'Chris?'

'Yes, Leonard.' She tried to keep the ragged wariness from her voice, but the pain still showed. Whatever his excuse for saying a very Vulcan thing to her in a creditable imitation of Spock's voice, it had still hurt her badly.

'What's going on? What happened?'

48

'What do you mean, Leonard? Since you spoke to me last? Since last night? Since we left Spacedock? What's the *matter* with you?'

'I . . . I don't know. Everything seems so strange.'

She felt concerned enough about him to turn on the medical sensors above his bed. She had held off doing so earlier because she knew what he would say if he awoke to find them quietly talking to themselves over his head.

'What're you doing? I'm not sick. I don't need those damned blinkenlightzen interrupting my sleep.'

Chris managed to laugh. 'That's more like it,' she said. She watched the sensors through a couple of cycles. Nothing seemed amiss. Leonard's temperature had dropped to normal. His body chemistry showed no evidence of the metabolic breakdown products of alcohol. But if he had not been drunk last night . . . what had affected him? She turned off the sensors.

'What time is it?' he asked.

'Eight hundred hours.'

'Good lord.'

Without comment, Chris let him sit up. If he was well enough to help, all the better.

'Leonard,' she said.

'Hm?'

'Why did you say that to me?'

'What?'

'A little while ago you woke up, and you said, "Vulcans do not love."'

'My gods, Chris,' he said, shocked. 'Did I? I'm *sorry*. All night I've been having those horrible dreams where you can't tell if they're real or not. I can't even remember anything about them except how frightening and how real they were. I guess I must have been dreaming . . about Spock.'

'I see,' she said.

'I never would have said such a thing if I'd known what I was saying. Will you accept my apology?'

'Yes,' she said. Wanting to forget about it as soon as possible, she changed the subject. 'Are you well enough to go on duty? Someone has to accompany Carol Marcus to Spacelab. I think it should be one of us.'

'Good gods – Jim isn't going to let anybody go down there – !'

He jumped out of bed. Chris caught him when he staggered and nearly fell.

'I'm all right – just stood up too fast.'

'Uh-huh.' She helped him sit on the edge of the bed. 'You're in no condition to leave the ship – especially since I don't know what's wrong with you.'

'But – '

'Don't be an ass, Leonard. You can stay here and rest under your own authority, or you can stay under Admiral Kirk's orders. Your choice.'

'I forbid you – ' He stopped. 'Sorry. Chris, I've already been down there – I've seen . . . what happened to Carol Marcus's friends. Letting her see it would be cruel.'

'I saw the records you made – surely you didn't think I'd take Carol into *that* – ' The violence of the murders flashed unbidden into her mind. '*Grissom*'s medical officer has already taken a team into the space station,' Chris said. 'The . . . casualties . . . are in stasis. The sites are in order.' The technical words made the descriptions easier to say.

'Chris, if you're sure – '

'What I said before still holds. You're staying here, under any circumstances.'

McCoy stopped trying to hide his exhaustion. He sagged back on his bunk.

'I'm just overtired,' he said. 'Don't trouble Jim with this.'

'That's up to you.'

'I'll stay in sick bay.'

Chris nodded, relieved at his acquiescence.

The codes and the documentation for Genesis had to be retrieved from Regulus I; the bodies of Khan Singh's victims had to be formally identified and transferred to the *Enterprise*. Carol walked toward the transporter room, dreading the task that faced her. David, beside her, suddenly touched her elbow and drew her to a halt.

'What's the matter, David?'

'There's no reason for you to go down there. I can . . . take care of everything.'

'I hardly need to be protected by my own son,' Carol said. 'This is my responsibility.'

'Mother – '

'David, we both lost friends in this disaster,' Carol said. One of the ways she could hold off her grief was by reminding herself continually that she was not alone.

' – I know that Vance was more than just a friend to you.'

'I know you know it. Did you think we thought we were secret lovers?' She herself had thought it must be obvious to everyone, because she had felt as if she were walking around in a perpetual glow, a bit like the way David and Saavik looked this morning. Right after she and Vance had become lovers, David said offhand to her that he did not understand why the two of them spent so much time together. 'Del's a lot more interesting,' David had said. 'Vance is okay, but he's kind of, well, boring, I think.' And Carol, amused that David had not caught on, replied, 'Then you don't know Vance very well.' Vance was quieter than his partner, more reserved, and steadier. Del possessed a fragile ego and a quick temper, and Carol, for all that she acknowledged his brilliance, thought he was a little crazy. Vance, though . . . Vance was the sanest person she had ever known. Del might be interesting to be around – as in the old Chinese curse, 'May you live in interesting times.' Being with Vance was simply and purely fun.

David had seemed to catch on, eventually, though now was the first time they had directly discussed it. Far from being jealous, as certain psychological theories would have made him, he had subsequently become much better friends with Vance, which had pleased Carol tremendously.

'I just thought,' David said, 'if you didn't have to see him . . .'

Carol took his hand and held it between hers. 'David, losing Vance is the most painful thing I've ever experienced. I still don't believe he's gone. Because of our work, I *have* to go down to Spacelab. But even if I didn't, I'd have to go anyway. Do you understand?'

'I don't think so,' he said.

'If I don't . . . If I don't see him, I'll never be able to believe he's dead. I have to accept it.'

David hugged her suddenly.

'I'm so sorry,' he whispered. 'I'm so damned sorry. When you and he were together, you looked happier than I ever saw you before. It just isn't fair – !' His voice broke, and he did not try to say more.

Carol hugged him, then drew back and scrubbed her sleeve across her eyes.

'We'd better go,' she said.

3

Carol Marcus and Christin Chapel materialized within the stasis room of Spacelab. The blue glow of the stasis fields leaked eerily from the edges of five of the chambers. Carol hesitated a moment, then opened the first one. She looked down at the shrouded figure, then drew the cloth from the pale face of a very young man, who had died with an expression of terror.

'This is Jan.' She said his full name and his i.d. number for the identification record that Chris was making. 'He was our steward. He hadn't been on Spacelab for long. A freighter stopped by a few months ago, and when it left he stayed behind. He said he was working his way across the galaxy. He wanted to see everything there is to see. "I know that's impossible," he told me, "but it's too good a line to pass up." He wrote poetry, but he would never let anyone read it.' She covered his pale face again, closed his chamber, and opened the second one, which protected an older man with flecks of gray in his black hair. After identifying him for the record, Carol said, 'Yoshi, our cook, shouldn't have been here at all. He was due for leave, with the rest of Spacelab's staff. But when he found out a few of us were staying, he said he would, too, because otherwise we would all forget to eat and make ourselves sick with malnutrition. I think, though, that he stayed because he was as fascinated by Genesis as the rest of us. He didn't want to miss the second phase of the experiment.'

Carol glanced at Chris. 'Is the machine getting this? I want you to get it all.'

Chris nodded. Carol was well aware that nothing was needed beyond a formal identification, but Chris recognized the private eulogies to be a facet of Carol's grief. 'Yes,' she said. 'I'm getting it.'

The third chamber held a fair, handsome young man who looked completely at peace.

'Delwin March,' Carol said. 'He and Vance Madison were partners. They practically invented a whole field of physics. They called it "kindergarten physics" because it dealt with sub-elementary particles. They used to go to conferences and drive their older colleagues to distraction by refusing to take anything seriously. As far as we know yet, the two particles they discovered are the basis of the whole universe – and they named them "snarks" and "boojums," out of a Lewis Carroll poem. I didn't get along very well with Del March. There was a streak of fury and pain in him that frightened me. I didn't understand it. I couldn't do anything about it and I couldn't do anything to help him. The only person who could reach him when he began to sink into that anger was his partner, and all Vance could do was keep him from hurting himself too badly.' She brushed a lock of light brown hair from March's forehead and covered his face with his shroud.

The fourth chamber held the body of a Deltan woman. Her face was stately and elegant and extraordinarily beautiful. 'Zinaida Chitirih-Ra-Payjh was one of the finest mathematicians in the Federation. We couldn't have gotten past stage one of Genesis without her.' Carol smiled sadly. 'All the boys, Jan and David and Del – poor Del, particularly – and some of the young women on the station – fell desperately in love with her, of course. Almost every human here fell in love with her or her partner or with both of them.' She glanced at the recorder. 'Jedda Adzhin-Dall isn't here. He died by phaser,

54

down inside Regulus I.' She sighed. 'Deltans have a powerful effect on humans. Zinaida and Jedda handled it beautifully. They were polite and cool and amused. They knew, I think, that nothing will douse a crush quicker than amusement. Everybody wondered what they did in their cabin together. I doubt anybody ever got up the nerve to ask. I think they laughed – not cruelly, but just because human beings must have seemed so silly and immature to them.' She put the palm of her hand along the side of Zinaida's face. 'Dear Zinaida . . .' Carol glanced at Chris. 'Leonard said he could not find a cause of death,' she said matter-of-factly.

Chris hesitated, disturbed by Carol's eerie calm. But refusing to answer would be close to lying.

'Deltans can will themselves to die,' she said. 'If they find themselves in intolerable conditions. I think she wouldn't have felt any pain.'

'She wouldn't have been frightened of pain,' Carol said. 'She would have seen it as a challenge – maybe even as an opportunity to experience something she hadn't chosen to encounter before.' She replaced the shroud carefully. She opened the last chamber.

'This is Vance Madison.' Her hands shaking, she uncovered his face. It was strong, intelligent, determined. The light glinted like jewels in his very curly black hair. 'I used to tease Del and him by calling them "twins," because they were so completely different. Fair and dark, white and black, short and tall, quick-tempered and serene . . . crazy and sane.' Her calm voice suddenly broke. 'Oh, damn, Chris, now I have to believe he's dead . . .'

Chris Chapel turned off the recorder, went to Carol, and put her arms around her while she cried. 'I know,' Chris said. 'I understand.'

* * *

After Carol and Chris beamed down to Spacelab, Saavik and David stepped up on the transporter platform to beam into Regulus I's new ecosystem.

'Energize,' Saavik said.

'Lieutenant,' the cadet said hesitantly, 'I can't find a clear place to beam you to.'

'What?' David said. 'It's full of open spaces in there.'

Saavik joined the cadet at the console and inspected the readings.

'It is true, David. The surface in range of the beam is covered with some amorphous material. Even the tunnels are filled.' The readings were completely different from what she had expected. She scanned further until she found a relatively empty spot. 'Beam me here, cadet,' she said. 'I will report what I find.'

'Saavik, wait a minute –' David said.

She returned to the platform. 'I will either return immediately or send for you. Energize.'

The cadet obeyed.

Saavik experienced the brief disorientation of dematerialization. She arrived on Regulus I, beneath the planetoid's surface and within one of the tunnels dug as a staging area for the second phase of the Genesis project. She held her communicator open and her phaser ready, should the changes threaten her.

She found herself in a very small clearing left by the random arrangement of a tangled mass of undergrowth. Vines completely filled the tunnel in which Dr Marcus and her team had hidden the Genesis records.

'Saavik to *Enterprise*. I have reached the surface. David, the flora has grown into the tunnels and filled them. Is this what you intended?'

'No. Not at all – but like I told you, things always happen that you don't expect. I'm coming down.'

'Wait a moment. I will clear a place for you.' First she

tried to push aside the beautiful flowering tendrils, but they sprang back into place. In trying to move them, she crushed some of the stems and blossoms. The damaged foliage released a pungent and entrancing scent.

Saavik set her phaser to very-short-range disintegrate. She had checked the phaser out precisely because David had told her that the Genesis experiment was so complex that its outcome could not be predicted in every detail. She had not, however, expected to be attacked by the vegetation.

The scarlet-edged green leaves withered and vanished before the beam of her phaser. The sweet, spicy fragrance intensified. She opened her communicator.

'Saavik to *Enterprise*. Cadet, can you lock onto the cleared area?'

'Aye, Lieutenant.'

David materialized beside her. He looked around and whistled in surprise.

'I take that to mean you did not expect anything like this,' Saavik said.

'It's even more viable than we thought! My gods, look at the growth, even under artificial light!'

Saavik forbore to puncture his enthusiasm by pointing out that the ball of glowing plasma deeper inside the planetoid gave light no more 'natural' than did the overhead fixtures illuminating the tunnels. The mass of reacting gases was held to the proper density by magnetic fields and kept in place by stress fields. It and the surrounding shell of the planetoid existed in an essentially unstable relationship.

'I would call this "overgrowth," David. And we still must reach the Genesis records. We do not have much time.'

'Hey, I designed these vines – at least give me a chance to admire my own handiwork for a minute, will you?'

'Admire the ones behind us. I must destroy some of the ones in our path. Please do not take it personally.' Before she fired her phaser she added, 'They are very beautiful. And the scent is aesthetically pleasing.'

'Thanks.'

Through the intertwining foliage, Saavik could just see the great pile of portable memory banks that held the Genesis research. As she cut a path in that direction, David plucked a spray of leaves from a vine, crushed them, and inhaled the scent.

'They'll grow berries in a couple of months. Ought to make great wine.'

Saavik reached the cache of Genesis records. She focused her phaser to a tight beam, powered it down to its minimum level, and used it like a scalpel to remove the undergrowth from the boxes. As she finished, David approached. He put his arms around her from behind and rubbed the leaves together between his hands. The refreshing perfume rose up around her face.

'Wouldn't you like to try some wine that tasted like these smell?'

Saavik holstered her phaser and took David's hands between her own. She stroked the backs of his hands with her fingers and grasped his wrists, feeling the cool throb of his pulse.

'The scent requires nothing more,' she said. 'It is complete in itself. It is perfect, very much like its designer.'

He let the leaves fall to the ground and hugged her more tightly, burying his face in her hair. She wanted nothing more than to respond to his caress.

Her communicator beeped.

'I'd never design a bird that made a silly noise like that,' David whispered in Saavik's ear. 'Must have been my mother, she was never very good at music. Let's ignore it.'

'It would merely make more silly noises,' she said. 'And when it stopped, a whole flock of its comrades would come looking for it, accompanied by a whole flock of cadets playing at being security officers.' She kissed him quickly and pulled out her communicator. Chuckling, David brushed the last remnants of his vines from the storage boxes.

'Saavik here.'

'How long will you be, Lieutenant?' Admiral Kirk said. 'Captain Esteban wants to leave for the Mutara sector as soon as possible.'

'A few more minutes, Admiral,' Saavik said. 'We have located the Genesis records and are preparing to beam them up.'

'Very well. Shake a leg. Kirk out.'

With a curious frown, Saavik closed the communicator. '"Shake a leg"?' she said to David. 'How would that be of benefit? Is it an exercise?'

'It's an idiom, it means hurry up. Why did he tell you Esteban's plans?'

'Because he has ordered – ' She stopped, and then, to be fair, she said, 'Or, rather, he strongly invited me to volunteer to accompany *Grissom* to Genesis. Such invitations are not wisely declined.'

'What? Damn! So he's trying to cut me and mother out of the follow-up! Saavik, do you know what this means?'

'It means he is under the impression that you do not care to go – he said you had declined.'

'The hell I did!'

'But he said – Oh. Perhaps he meant Dr Marcus, senior.'

'He didn't even ask *me!* Son of a bitch!'

'Surely if you tell him you wish to go – '

'He'll probably think of some way to stop me. He'll try, anyway. Especially now that you're going.'

David made Saavik acutely uncomfortable when he referred to the admiral in such an angry, abusive tone.

'Why do you speak of him like this, David? I was under the impression that you and he had found reason to accept each other.'

'So was I. For a while. But maybe I was wrong. Maybe we're too different.' He blew his breath out in exasperation, then suddenly grinned. 'I have an idea. Let's let him wait. Let's blast a trail to the interior and see what's going on there.'

Saavik put her hand on her phaser and very nearly drew it. She was so tempted by his invitation that the strength of her desire shocked her.

'I would like that very much,' she said.

'Great. Let's go.'

'What I would like is very far from what I must do.'

'Oh, come on – a few minutes won't hurt.'

'It would take hours to clear a trail through the tunnels.'

He snatched playfully at her phaser. She avoided him easily, and not at all playfully.

'Spoilsport,' he said. 'I thought you were different, but you're just like everybody else in Starfleet.'

'I am like no one else at all, in Starfleet or outside it,' she said.

'Indoctrinated in the military mind.'

'You are provoking me, David.'

As she pulled out her communicator, David grabbed again for her phaser, this time with more determination. Reacting automatically, she grasped his hand in a move Captain Sulu had taught her in a self-defense class. The phaser went flying.

'Let go! Geez, what are you doing?'

'The technical term is "*kotegaeshi*," ' Saavik said.

'I don't give a shit what it's called – will you let go!'

He dug the nails of his free hand into her fingers to try

60

to make her release him. She put enough twist on his wrist to hurt if he resisted.

'Okay, okay!' he said.

Before she could put the communicator away and retrieve her phaser, the *Enterprise* signalled again.

'*Enterprise* to Saavik,' Admiral Kirk said. There was a definite edge to his voice. 'Will you get a move on, Lieutenant?'

'Immediately, Admiral,' she said. 'The Genesis records are cleared of foliage. The transporter beam may now lock onto them.'

'Preparing to beam up,' the cadet in the transporter room said through the communicator.

'Think you can cut me out of my own project, do you, you filthy warmonger?' David shouted before Saavik could close the channel.

'David? What are you talking about?' Kirk's tone was hurt and surprised.

'I'll tell you what I'm talking about – '

Saavik snapped the communicator closed and slapped it back in place on her belt.

'What is wrong with you?' Saavik had begun to get used to David's impulsive actions. Until now he had never seemed maliciously irresponsible.

The transporter beam glowed; the boxes of Genesis records sparkled and disappeared.

Saavik dragged David around till she could reach her phaser. It had fallen into a tangle of vines. She had to rip it loose from the tendrils that had curled around it. The pungent scent rose up to enclose her.

She felt dizzy. She shoved the phaser against her belt and fumbled for the communicator.

'Saavik to *Enterprise*. Beam us up.'

'One moment, please, Lieutenant. We have to clear the platforms.'

'Quickly!' She slipped to her knees. The stone floor of the tunnel felt very hard and cold. Tiny tendrils of David's beautiful vines dug into the solid rock. Saavik struggled to her feet. Her grip on David's hand loosened and he came toward her, reaching again for her phaser.

The transporter beam enveloped and dematerialized them.

Jim Kirk stormed into the transporter room just as Lieutenant Saavik and David appeared on the platform among the piles of boxes that the cadet had shoved untidily aside.

David and Saavik were holding hands.

Charming, I'm sure, Kirk thought, but hardly the place or time – and damned foolish to do while being transported. Lucky neither had lost an arm.

'I take it you have something to say to me, young man,' Kirk said to David.

The young scientist pulled his hand free of Saavik's and strode forward to meet his father.

'You bet I do.'

Behind them, Saavik took one step forward and felt her knees begin to buckle. Before she could fall, she sat down quickly on the edge of the platform. David and the admiral argued, David resentfully, the admiral indignantly, neither listening to the other. Saavik stopped listening to both of them.

'Saavik, are you okay?' The cadet crouched beside her, concerned.

'Yes . . . of course.' She had to draw on all her Vulcan training to find enough strength to rise. She had not had much sleep in the past several days, but she should be able to function effectively for much longer without rest. She had done so before, in practice. She felt ashamed and embarrassed.

'Admiral,' she said. Neither he nor David heard her.

62

'Admiral Kirk!' she said more loudly, breaking into the argument.

Kirk swung around to face her. 'What *is* it, Lieutenant?'

'May I be dismissed? I must prepare to transfer to the *Grissom*.'

'All right, yes. Dismissed.'

Saavik sat in her cabin, grateful for its dry warmth and the dim, scarlet-tinged light. Her preparations remained incomplete, but she needed a moment to collect herself and to think about her own and David's inexplicable behavior.

Absently she drew her phaser and plucked away the delicate pink tendrils. Many climbing plants have the ability to coil themselves around whatever solid object they contact. This species moved quickly, but she had seen others that were faster. Its ability to probe into solid rock was exceptional – if she had seen what she thought she saw. She wished for time to explore Regulus I. She was, she thought, nearly as anxious as David to know the full results of the Genesis programs.

Saavik lifted a crushed vine-leaf to her nose to experience again the dazzling scent. The fragrance twined around her like the tendrils around her phaser.

Dizziness hit her. Saavik jerked the leaf away. She gazed at it, frowning. She put it aside, went to the synthesizer panel, and requested the ship's computer to send her a sampling envelope. When it appeared, she swept together all the bits of David's vine. Repressing the wish to inhale their redolent essence, she sealed them within the clear plastic.

Jim Kirk folded his arms across his chest. 'David, I don't understand what you're so angry about. Carol said she didn't want to go back to the Mutara sector – naturally I assumed you didn't want to go, either.'

'You should have asked me,' David said stubbornly. He felt tremendously relieved that his mother was not willing to return yet, and terrified and angry that he might be forbidden to do so. 'I'll tell you why you expect me to do exactly what she does – it's because everybody you know has jumped when you said "frog" for so long that you don't think anybody has a mind of their own!'

Jim chuckled. 'You don't know the people I know, if you think that. Look, I've apologized – I don't see that there's much else I can do, if you're determined to sulk.'

'You can send me out on *Grissom*.'

Jim hesitated. 'Are you sure that's wise?'

'Why isn't it wise?'

'I just thought . . .'

David glared at him belligerently. Jim took a moment to sort through his own feelings.

'I'll be honest with you, David. I was hoping you'd stay on board the *Enterprise*. I've wanted a chance to talk to you. I can't make up for all the years that I didn't know you – '

'No,' David said coldly. 'You can't.'

Taken aback by David's reaction, Jim said, 'Whether you like it or not, I am your father.'

'You can't spend twenty years ignoring my existence – '

'David, I didn't – '

' – and just waltz in and expect me to shower you with filial piety!'

'All I want is for us to try to be friends.'

'It's too late! It's too damned late for you to come along and try to make friends with me!'

They were getting nowhere; they were succeeding only in antagonizing each other. Jim decided to try to defuse the argument until they both could cool down.

'I hope you're wrong, David,' he said. 'But I think I understand why you're angry and disappointed. I hope someday you can forgive me, or even accept me. In the meantime let's try at least to be civil to each other. For your mother's sake.'

'For my mother's sake! Since when did you give a damn about my mother?'

'You aren't going to let up, are you?' Jim was both angry and hurt. Every concession he had tried to make, David had thrown back in his face. 'Get your things together – *Grissom* warps out of orbit in an hour.'

He stalked out of the room.

David knocked softly on the door of his mother's cabin. He waited, then knocked again. The door finally slid open. Darkness faced him.

'Mother?'

'Yes, David.' Her voice was very quiet.

'Your things that were down inside the cave – I brought them back up with me.'

'Thank you.' She turned on a light.

'They told me you didn't want to go back to the Mutara sector.'

'No,' she said. 'Not now. I can't, not now.'

'I volunteered to. I think it's important that one of us be in the reconnaissance party.'

She looked at him in silence.

'I understand why you want to go back to Earth,' David said. 'I should, too, probably.'

'I'd hoped . . .' she said softly.

'Mother, this is essential. *Somebody's* got to keep an eye on Starfleet. To be sure they tell the truth about what happened out there. We can't just let them have free rein, not after everything that's happened.'

'I know,' she said. 'You're right that one of us should go. Probably both of us should.'

'No!' he said quickly, then forced his voice back under

control when she reacted to his intensity. 'It isn't going to be anything but a fast survey. Somebody's got to keep them honest, but it won't take both of us. Mother, I'm leaving you to do the hard job all alone – '

'I have to do it alone,' she said. 'It's only that I've been afraid . . .'

'Of what?'

'There's a reason I never told you Jim Kirk is your father, David. There are a lot of reasons, but the main one was selfish.'

'I don't understand.'

'I was afraid that if you found out that your father was a starship captain, you'd be off on the next ship, flying around the galaxy, and I'd never see you again.' She sighed. 'I told Jim I want you in my world, not in his. But I should have let you make the decision.'

'What decision?' He laughed. 'Mother, can you really see me on the crew of this ship?' He jerked to attention. 'Yessir. Aye-aye sir. I'll be glad to swab the poop deck, sir.' Slowly and deliberately, he crossed his eyes.

Carol could not help but laugh. 'I don't think starships have poop decks, David.'

'They'd probably invent one just for me to swab. I'd never make it in the military.'

'Only . . .'

'What?'

'You've met your father, and you're about to go off on a starship.'

'Yeah, but note carefully that it isn't *his* starship. Honest, Mom, I'm not going to up and join Starfleet.' He hugged her. 'I won't even be gone very long. Promise.'

'I know.'

'They're leaving soon. I better go.'

'Good-bye, David. Be careful.'

'I almost forgot – ' He reached under his shirt and drew

out a folded piece of drafting fabric. 'Our Starfleet friends sealed the Genesis records, but I insisted on checking them over before they locked them away. I didn't know if they'd let either of us in there again. Who knows who they'll turn everything over to, back on Earth. So . . .' The shiny, silvery material slipped out of its folds and lay soft and unwrinkled in his hands. Dark blue lines and stippling marked it. 'I stole this for you when nobody was looking.' He handed her the map of the second phase of Genesis.

After drawing the map of the ecosystem for Regulus I, Vance Madison had made a copy for each member of the team. They had all contributed to the plan, and they had all been looking forward to comparing the map with the eventual outcome. The vines in the staging area hinted at greatly divergent results. David wondered if he – if anyone – would ever get the chance to explore Regulus I's interior.

Carol took the map from him and smoothed it out across her lap.

'David . . . thank you.' She touched the outer reaches of the map, near the north pole. Inside the shell of the world, centrifugal acceleration created an artificial gravity. But as one curved around toward the poles, the force would become more acutely angled to the surface. The radius of spin would shorten. Thus one would seem to be climbing up an increasingly steeper hill, against a steadily decreasing force.

The team had left the odd environment of the poles almost uncolonized by their creations, for they had primarily been interested in inventing life forms that would be useful on a new world. Carol was rather pleased with her silk heather, and Yoshi had suggested the cornucopia tree, which produced several different kinds of fruit at each season. Vance had invented a small carnivore that he fancifully named the white rabbit, and Del responded by designed the March hare. Its main distinction, he claimed, was complete lunacy. The way he described it, it sounded like a cross between a howler monkey and a gecko. Carol smiled, thinking that it was characteristic of the two young men to design a 'rabbit' that was not a rabbit, and a 'hare' that was not a hare. When they presented their creations at the weekly design meeting, Carol had laughed and threatened to make up something they could call the mad hatter.

None of those creations lived out toward the poles. At the very top of the map, in spidery script, Vance had written 'Here be dragons.'

'I wonder if there really are dragons,' Carol said softly.

Saavik arrived in the transporter room, ready to beam on board *Grissom*, but found herself all alone. As she was punctual, she felt it safe to assume the others had not left without her.

Waiting in the empty, dim transporter room, she sought something to occupy her mind. Someone spoke her name.

'Captain – ?' She turned around, looking for the speaker.

No one else had yet entered the room. The deep shadows offered no hiding places.

'Who is there?' she said.

It occurred to her that someone might be trying to play a joke on her, though no one had ever done so before. No one had ever even told jokes to her. Until a few days ago she had considered them completely frivolous, and thus beneath notice. Jokes could be based in cruelty, she knew, but it was usually a sort of benign cruelty.

Cruel it would be, and not the least bit benign, to play a joke on Saavik by calling out her name, in Mr Spock's voice.

'*Saavikam* –'

She clapped her hands over her ears. The voice spoke in Vulcan, using a Vulcan form of address.

'*Saavikam*, why did you leave me on Genesis?'

The voice was audible only to her.

It was not a joke.

'Mr Spock,' she whispered, 'why are you not at peace? I watched over you, and I sent your body into the new world. I thought that would please you . . .'

She heard voices in the corridor. Bringing herself back to some semblance of composure, she pulled her hands from her face and straightened her tunic.

Admiral Kirk and Captain Esteban entered.

'Hello, Lieutenant,' the Admiral said. 'I see you're on time. Think how much we could get done, J.T., if we were as organized and imperturbable as Lieutenant Saavik.'

Nothing Kirk had said to Saavik required a reply, so she remained silent. She felt neither organized nor imperturbable.

This time she did feel as if she were going mad.

Saavik had experienced mind-meld several times during her life, most often with Spock. The touch of his mind was the first civilized experience she had ever had. The touch of a mind was unique. It was impossible to mistake the mind of a person one had touched for that of any other sentient being, strange or familiar. Yet the voice Saavik had felt, the consciousness that had just cried out to her, had felt like Mr Spock's. Which it could not have been.

'You're very quiet, Lieutenant. Are you having second thoughts about this mission? You did volunteer, you know – you can change your mind.'

'No!' she said more forcefully than she had intended.

He gave her a quizzical look, not precisely a remonstration, but not approval either.

'No, sir,' she said in a more collected tone. 'I believe it is extremely important for me to go on this mission.'

'Very well. Where the devil is David?'

'He'd better hurry along if he's coming,' Esteban said. 'I can't wait all day.'

'*Is* David coming, Admiral?' Saavik asked.

'He better be,' Kirk said. 'He read me the riot act about not asking him in the first place.'

At that moment David strode in, a small pack slung over his shoulder.

'We were just about to give up on you,' Kirk said.

'I was saying good-bye to my mother,' David said. 'Any objections?'

'None at all,' Kirk said mildly.

Kirk shook hands with Captain Esteban.

'Good to see you again, J.T. Let's not leave it so long before we cross paths again.'

'We'll be back in a month or six weeks, Jim.'

'We'll plan to get together then.' Kirk turned to Saavik and, to her surprise, extended his hand to her. She shook it gingerly.

'Good luck, Lieutenant. Take care of my son.'

'Aye, sir,' she said, and wondered how many layers a human being, accustomed to the ambiguities and 'little jokes' of Standard, would find in his order.

'David.'

Kirk reached out to his son. When David warily grasped his hand, Kirk drew the young man toward him and into a bear hug.

'Take care of yourself, son,' he said.

David extricated himself rather less gracefully than he might. David's mercurial character, Saavik thought, was not ready to forgive what had passed between him and the admiral.

'Don't worry,' David said. 'There's nothing dangerous in the Mutara sector anymore. Nothing dangerous at all.'

Kirk watched the young people – Esteban, David, and Saavik – vanish from the transporter platform. Off into the unknown. He did wish he were going with them.

Instead, he called the bridge and asked Captain Sulu to warp out of orbit and head back toward Earth. Then Kirk himself headed for sick bay.

McCoy was up and working. His façade was excellent, but Kirk could tell it was only a façade. To Kirk, McCoy appeared pale and fragile and distracted, despite the gentle joke he made with an injured young cadet, despite the steadiness of his hands and the certainty of his voice.

'Good morning, Bones,' Kirk said. 'Talk to you in your office?'

'Hi, Jim. Sure. One minute.'

McCoy joined him in the office as soon as he had finished with his patient.

'What's up? Need a good hangover remedy?'

'I might ask you the same question.'

McCoy gave up his jocular pose. 'But I wasn't – ' He stopped. 'Never mind. It doesn't matter. I owe you an apology anyway. Scotty wanted to have a wake for his nephew, and I thought, Why not include Spock? All I can say is it seemed like a good idea at the time.'

'It's over and done,' Jim said. 'If I'd thought about it I probably would have put my foot down before the whole thing got up any momentum. My only excuse is I had other things on my mind. But I'm worried about you. Last night, you were acting . . . odd.'

'Odd?' McCoy chuckled. 'I'm not surprised. The synthesizers aren't quite up to decent liquor.'

Kirk frowned, detecting a false note in McCoy's dismissal of last night's events.

'I don't mean drunk. You didn't act drunk.'

'I didn't?' McCoy exclaimed, all too heartily. 'I must be out of practice.'

'Don't you remember what you said?'

'About what?'

'You stood up on a table and said "Grief is not logical" in a pretty damned good imitation of Spock's voice. That isn't your usual sort of . . . humor.'

'That isn't humor of any sort,' McCoy said. 'I must have been farther gone than I thought.'

'Tell me what's wrong,' Jim said. 'Bones, let me help.'

'Sure – you can help by accepting my apology and forgetting what it is I'm apologizing for.'

When McCoy wanted to avoid interrogation, he could sidestep with the best of them. Jim had not quite reached the point of trying to get an answer out of his old friend by pulling rank. Besides, when had it ever done him any good, with McCoy, to assert his authority as a starship captain?

'Apology accepted. Forgetting – that's going to take a little longer. If you want to talk, you know where to find me.'

Kirk returned to the bridge, still disturbed about McCoy, and feeling that his visit to sick bay had been very nearly futile.

On board *Grissom*, Saavik thanked the duty officer for giving her a cabin assignment. The young Vulcan did not bother to stop by her room. She had nothing with her to drop off, and a more pressing matter to attend to than observing the decor of *Grissom*'s cabins.

She felt the faint shift in the ship's gravity fields that indicated they had warped out of orbit. *Grissom*, a small, fast ship, could travel between Regulus and the Mutara sector much more quickly than the crippled *Enterprise*.

Saavik entered the main laboratory and stopped short.

Before her stood a being like a column of rippled crystal. Saavik had never met a Glaeziver before. They were very rare. They intended and planned to be extinct within a hundred Standard years. Their planet had been destroyed in the nova of its star. They possessed such strong ties to their world that they never found another on which they felt anything but alien. And so they disbanded, scattering throughout the Federation and perhaps even beyond.

It occurred to Saavik that if Genesis could be programmed to copy their lost world closely enough, they might change their collective decision to die. If they possessed a world to return to, they might choose to live.

'Hello,' Saavik said formally. 'How may I address you?'

The utter motionlessness of the being gave Saavik the impression of enormous potential energy preparing to translate itself into motion. When the Glaeziver stirred, it did so with a controlled power that belied the delicacy of its form. The many transparent strands making up its substance brushed together with a chiming like jewels in the wind.

'You're well-mannered for an opaque being,' the Glaeziver said. Its voice was like a cymbalon. 'If you can pronounce my name, you may use it.' It spoke a beautiful word like a song, which Saavik reproduced as best she could.

'Not bad,' the Glaeziver said. 'You may call me that, if you like. I prefer it to Fred.'

'"Fred"?' Saavik said.

'One of my co-workers fancies that my name sounds like a phrase of Chopin's. How may I address you?'

'My name is Saavik.'

'How do you do, Saavik. What can I do for you?'

'I wish to analyze a sample from the interior of Regulus I. May I use your equipment?'

'Can you talk and work at the same time?'

'Certainly.'

'In that case, I'll make you a deal. We will analyze your sample on my equipment while you tell me what has been going on out here – inside Regulus I, and in the Mutara.'

'That appears a fair trade to me,' Saavik said.

'Great. What kind of analysis do you want – macroscopic, molecular, atomic, sub-atomic?'

'Molecular, please.'

'You got it.'

Glaezivers had a reputation for being very formal and stand-offish. Saavik found it quite interesting that the being had held to formality during their introductions, but spoke very casually otherwise. It was very easy to think of it as 'Fred.'

Saavik's cabin was standard for a Federation ship, designed and intended for a human being. The lighting imitated the spectrum of Earth's star, and the temperature conformed to the temperate regions of their home planet. Saavik glanced around the room, approving of its lack of extraneous decoration and its communications terminal, disapproving of the heavily padded furniture. She preferred hard chairs and a sleeping mat.

She reprogrammed the environmental controls. The light dimmed and reddened, and the temperature began gradually to rise. Saavik sat down for the first time since arriving on *Grissom*. Preparing for the survey of Genesis and analyzing the sample from Regulus I had given her plenty of work, for which she was grateful. It took her mind off the fears she had had for her own sanity.

But since leaving the *Enterprise*, she no longer sensed Spock's presence. If she still believed in ghosts – as she had when she was little, for things happened on Hellguard that an uneducated and unsophisticated child could explain no other way – she would have believed Spock's shade to be haunting the *Enterprise*. But she did not believe in ghosts anymore. She believed that for a short while she had been at least a little bit insane.

And now? To test herself, to test the silence, Saavik took the risk of opening her mental shields. She closed her eyes and reached out, seeking any resonance, real or imagined, of Spock.

After some minutes she opened her eyes again. She had found nothing.

The echo of her teacher had vanished. He was gone, and Saavik grieved for him. But at least she was not mad.

She picked up the printout of the Regulus I sample and reread the analysis.

Someone knocked on her door.

'Come.'

David entered, smiling. 'Hi. Guess what. I'm right next door. Great, huh?'

'That depends. Have you come to your senses?'

'What? Are you talking about what happened down in the Genesis cave?' He shrugged it off. 'Yeah, sure, sorry – I don't know what got into me. I guess I was overexcited.'

'That is your explanation?'

'What's the matter? I'm sorry I tried to take your phaser – that was dumb. If it's any comfort, you twisted the hell out of my wrist. I can still feel it. And, look, there's a bruise there on my hand where you put your thumb.'

'You should not have resisted,' Saavik said. 'You injured yourself with your own violence.'

'And you got your revenge.'

'Why do you assume I want revenge? Or that I would take pleasure in hurting you? That is beside the point. You know that I do not use recreational drugs. Even if I did, I was on duty when we beamed down to the Genesis caves. How could you not warn me?'

'Saavik, what are you talking about?'

Saavik was prepared for a laugh and a claim of 'a little joke'. She was not prepared for deliberate obtuseness. She handed him the printout.

He scanned it.

'Interesting organic make-up. What is it?'

'You should know. You designed it.'

'I never did. I never saw this set of molecules before in my life.'

'David, that is an analysis of the Genesis vines – the vines you created.'

'It's nothing like. Well, superficially, maybe. But this whole subset of molecules – '

'I ran the samples twice,' Saavik said. 'I am hardly infallible, but this summary *is* accurate.'

'But it shouldn't look like this. I don't even know what half the stuff is.'

'This,' Saavik said, pointing to a heterocyclic compound, 'is an extremely potent psychoactive alkaloid.'

'What!' David looked at it more closely. 'My gods, it could be, couldn't it?'

'It is. It is also the reason we behaved as we did – why we nearly abandoned our tasks to go exploring, like two irresponsible children – '

'"We"?' David said, rubbing his wrist. 'You could have fooled me, if you were about to do anything out of line.'

'I came very close to it,' Saavik said. 'The active ingredient in those vines is a narcotic.'

'I designed it so you could brew tea out of the leaves if you wanted. I put a lot of caffeine in it, that's all.'

Saavik could see the resemblance between the molecule in question and caffeine, but it had gone through considerable mutation to become what it was.

'I think you would not want to brew tea out of this plant,' Saavik said. 'Or make wine of its fruit.'

'You never know,' David said.

Saavik raised one eyebrow.

'Just kidding,' David said.

4

Phase three of Genesis spun like a mobile drifting in the breeze. David watched the newly-formed star system on the *Grissom*'s viewscreen. Despite his calculated calm, he was astonished that the new world was his creation. So far it looked like the programs had worked perfectly. The lack of a sun for the world to orbit had enabled the star-forming subroutine. The great dustcloud of the Mutara Nebula had provided plenty of mass to form a small, hot star.

David leaned against the bridge rail. He felt out of place and in the way, despite the ship's being there at least partly because of him. Behind him, at the main sensor station, Saavik seemed to David very much in place, cool and controlled.

She had forgiven him for the incident in the Genesis caves back on Regulus I. David truly had not designed a plant containing a chemical of the potency they found. They had talked about what might have gone wrong. The changes in the experiment's outcome were of a far greater magnitude than David had expected. He was still trying to convince himself that everything really had evolved nearly the way the Genesis team intended, only a little more so. He was not ready to admit any serious doubts to himself, much less discuss them with anyone. Even Saavik.

Saavik completed the current log entry.

'. . . We are approaching destination planet at point zero three five. So noted in ship's log.'

She removed the data cube from the recorder and delivered the log to Captain Esteban to certify and seal.

'Very well, Lieutenant.' To the helm officer, he said, 'Execute standard orbital approach.'

'Standard orbit, aye.'

'Communications. Send a coded message for Starfleet Commander, priority one . . .'

He paused for a moment. David decided, with a smile, that the captain was thinking over his message to be sure it would not include a single informal word.

'"Federation science vessel *Grissom* arriving Genesis planet, Mutara sector, to begin research. As ordered, full security procedures are in effect. J.T. Esteban, commanding."'

'Aye sir, coding now.'

David found the security on *Grissom* restrictive and a little scary. Genesis had always been, in theory, a secret project. Acceding to the security requirements had been the only way they could get the research funded. The whole team had taken a rather lackadaisical attitude toward the rules, mostly by thinking about them as infrequently as possible. They had all been certain that the first implementation of the project would make secrecy impossible.

That's one thing we were right about, David thought. But now the authorities wanted to try to clamp the lid back down.

On *Grissom*, dealing with Starfleet directly instead of one step removed, David had the distinct impression that they wished he knew nothing about the project, and that they would have denied him clearance if they could have done so without looking ridiculous.

Captain Esteban turned toward him. 'Dr Marcus,' he said, 'it's your planet.'

Astonished, and pleased despite himself, David grinned. 'Thank you, Captain. Begin scanning, please.' He joined Saavik at the science station as she activated the macroscopic scanner. It glowed into life, forming a schematic of the world before them. The schematic showed a stable sphere, with core, mantle, crust, and oceans, absolutely indistinguishable from a naturally evolved world.

Well, what did you expect? David asked himself. That it would be flat?

Suddenly he laughed, and all his doubts and fears evaporated in the sheer pleasure of inspecting his handiwork.

'This is where the fun begins, Saavik!' he said.

She replied, *sotto voce*, 'Like your father . . . so human.' Then, turning on the recorder, she took the irony and humor out of her voice. 'All units functional, recorders are on . . . Scanning sector one. The foliage is in a fully developed state of growth. Temperature, twenty-two point two degrees Celsius.'

'Sector two . . . indicating desert terrain,' David said. 'Minimal vegetation, temperature thirty-nine point four.'

At several team presentation meetings the discussion had centered on whether to include desert or any other severe climates at all. Vance said he was not interested in working on anything 'so beautiful it's sappy,' Del (as usual) agreed with Vance. Zinaida persisted, as Deltans often did, in quoting the Vulcan philosophy, 'infinite diversity in infinite combinations.' David wondered how Vulcans liked being quoted by the Federation's most renowned sensualists. He himself had pushed for trying to make Genesis a shirt-sleeve environment from pole to pole. That would have been quite a challenge. He was, however, outvoted.

'Sector three,' Saavik said. 'Sub-tropical vegetation.'

David glanced across the bank of sensors. They must be scanning a region where several different ecotypes blended into one another.

'Temperature – ' Saavik said. She stopped and checked her readings again. 'Temperature decreasing rapidly.'

My gods, look at that, David thought. Infinite diversity indeed.

'It's snow,' he said. 'Snow in the same sector. Fantastic!' He could not get a topographical map off the sensor he was using, but he assumed they must be looking at a snowcapped mountain upthrust in the midst of subtropical forest edged by desert.

'Fascinating,' Saavik said.

'All the varieties of land and weather known to Earth within a few hours' walk!' David knew he was exaggerating, just a bit, but for a time the team had engaged in a sort of informal competition to see who could design the most complicated conditions within the smallest area. Nobody had quite come up with a workable way to juxtapose arctic and equatorial climates, but everyone had developed a different method of coming close. Some of the schemes were positively Byzantine. The trouble was, Carol eventually declared the competition out of hand and said she would not include any of the results in the Genesis device.

Maybe she changed her mind, David thought.

'You must be very proud of what you and your mother have created,' Saavik said.

David gazed at the sensors and felt some of his doubts and fears beginning to creep back.

'It's a little early to celebrate,' he said.

One of the sensors erupted into frantic beeping. Saavik started, then covered her surprise by bending intently over the monitor.

'Same sector,' she said evenly. 'Metallic mass.'

'Underground, right?' David said. 'Probably an ore deposit.'

'Negative,' Saavik said. 'It is on the surface, a manufactured object.'

Manufactured! David thought. Debris from Khan's ship? The Genesis torpedo? But that was impossible – anything in range of the Genesis wave had disintegrated into a plasma of sub-elementary particles. Then he realized –

'There's only one thing it could be!' he said.

He glanced at Saavik. Surely the same answer must have occurred to her. She gazed intently at the sensors.

'Short range scan,' David said.

Esteban joined them at the console and glanced over the readings.

'Approximately two meters long,' Saavik said. 'Cylindrical in form . . .'

'A photon tube – !'

Saavik continued to avoid David's look.

She's upset, David thought, and she's embarrassed about being upset. I don't blame her – If I thought I'd buried a friend, and then his coffin turned up . . .

'Could it be Spock's?' Esteban asked.

David had noticed that the captain did not much like being surprised.

'It has to be,' David said. There were several ways it could have reached the surface of the Genesis world without burning up in the atmosphere like a shooting star. 'The gravitational fields were still in flux. It must have soft-landed.'

'In code to Starfleet,' Esteban said. '"Captain Spock's tube located intact on Genesis surface. Will relay more data on subsequent orbits."'

'Yes, sir,' said the communications officer. 'Coding your message.'

Saavik continued to stare at the changing sensors. David neither questioned nor challenged her. Instead, he reached out and put his hand over hers. Still she said nothing, but she did not draw away from him, either.

As the ship passed over the surface of the new world,

crossing the terminator into darkness, the sensor's beeps grew fainter and fainter. The ship moved out of line-of-sight of the torpedo tube and the signals cut off abruptly.

J. T. Esteban thoughtfully stroked his thumb under his jaw and considered what to do. Spock's coffin was supposed to have been launched in a standard burial orbit, one that should have resulted in complete ablation. There should be nothing at all left of it. That it had landed intact created all sorts of problems, from the possibility of contamination to the responsibility for retrieving the casket and either re-launching it (J.T. would send it into the star, so there could be no mistake), or holding a formal interment on the surface of Genesis. Technically, Spock's most recent C.O. should make the decision. But with any luck, someone at Starfleet HQ would give the word. Jim Kirk could do without going through the wringer again over the death of a friend.

Under any other circumstances, J.T. might have taken it upon himself to decide what would be done, but not this time – not when it involved something as important as Genesis.

Personal log of James T. Kirk:

With most of our battle damage repaired, we are almost home. Yet I feel – uneasy. And I wonder why. Perhaps it is the erratic behavior of ship's surgeon Leonard McCoy, or the emptiness of the vessel. Most of our trainee crew have been reassigned. Lieutenant Saavik and my son David are exploring a new world. The *Enterprise* feels like a house with all the children gone . . . No, more empty even than that. The news of Spock's tube has shaken me. It seems that I have left the noblest part of myself back there, on that newborn planet.

Jim Kirk stalked the bridge of the *Enterprise*. Sorting out his thoughts in his personal log had failed to diminish his unease.

83

He paused next to the science station, where Spock always sat. He put his hands on the back of the chair.

The transmission from Esteban, on Genesis, troubled him. He felt unreasonably angered and betrayed at the news that Spock's coffin had soft-landed. Kirk had ordered a trajectory that should have burned the tube to ashes in the upper atmosphere of Genesis. Whether Spock's body returned to its constituent atoms quickly, in fire, or slowly, in the earth of a new world, surely did not matter to the Vulcan any longer. But Kirk, who wished the flames for himself when he died, had made a decision and given an order, and some unforeseen and unknown conspiracy of the universe had served to defy him.

Starfleet had sent the medical rescue ship *Firenze* out to meet the *Enterprise* and to transport all but a few of its trainee crew, injured and healthy alike, back to Earth, so at least he no longer had a boatload of children to worry about.

The *Enterprise*, though patched and limping, was out of immediate danger. It could easily have made it to Alpha Ceti V to rescue *Reliant*'s crew, whom Khan marooned when he hijacked their ship. But before the light of *Firenze*'s engines had fairly red-shifted out of the visible spectrum, Starfleet recalled the *Enterprise* to Earth and sent another ship to Alpha Ceti V. 'The *Enterprise* is fully capable of carrying out this mission,' Kirk had said, and HQ replied, with a fine disregard for irony, 'But, Admiral, your ship is dangerously short-handed.' By then Kirk did not know whether to laugh, cry, or blow his stack. He decided, instead, to make the best of it.

David's decision to return with *Grissom* to the Genesis world disappointed Kirk. Carol was barely speaking to him. One relationship that had started well and one that he had thought to resume were dissolving into nothingness.

And finally, there was Leonard McCoy. Kirk *was* worried about him. Kirk could have understood grief; he could even have understood a refusal to admit to grief. He could not comprehend McCoy's disjointed conversation, his brief episodes of intense activity, and his speaking Spock's words in Spock's voice.

For a while Kirk had felt good about having his ship back, but the price of regaining it was far too high.

Get hold of yourself! he thought. He turned away from Spock's station.

'Status, Mr Sulu?'

'On course, Admiral,' Sulu said. 'Estimating Spacedock in two point one hours.'

'Very well.' Kirk returned to his own place on the bridge. 'Mr Chekov, I need a pre-approach scan. Take the science station, please.'

Chekov hesitated. Kirk understood his reasons, but the ship could not function without the science station. Someone had to take Spock's place. The sooner Kirk and Chekov and everybody else got used to that, the better.

'Yes, sir,' Chekov said. He stood, left the helm, and moved to the science station.

'Uhura,' Kirk said, 'any response from Starfleet on our Project Genesis inquiries?'

'No, sir,' Uhura said. 'No response.'

'Odd . . .' Kirk murmured. He was accustomed to having his questions answered without delay. Esteban had been infuriatingly obscure about the public reaction to the Genesis effect. He had piqued Kirk's curiosity. Apparently, though, Kirk was just going to have to wait until he got back to headquarters to find out what was going on.

He opened an intercom channel to the engine room.

'Scotty, progress report?'

'We're almost done, sir,' Scott replied. 'Ye'll be fully automated by the time we dock.'

'Your timing is excellent, Mr Scott,' he said. 'You've fixed the barn door after the horse has come home.' Scott's jury-rigged automation would help relieve the ship's short-handedness . . . for about the last hour of the return trip. 'How much refit time till we can take the ship out again?'

'Eight weeks, sir – '

Kirk started to protest, but before he could get a word out, Scott spoke again.

' – But ye dinna have eight weeks, so I'll do i' for ye in two.'

Kirk had the feeling the Scot had been waiting for a very long time to spring that line on him. In the same spirit, he said, 'Mr Scott – have you always multiplied your repair estimates by a factor of four?'

'Certainly, sir. How else would ye expect me to keep my reputation as a miracle worker?'

'Your reputation is secure, Scotty.' He turned off the intercom. 'Captain Sulu, take the conn. I'll be in my quarters.'

'Aye, sir,' Sulu said.

Kirk climbed the stairs to the upper level of the bridge. Before he got within range of the turbo-lift's sensors, one of the few trainees who had remained on board half-rose.

'Sir – I was wondering – ?'

The cadet was an electronics specialist who had kept the navigational computer going during and after the battle, when Spock was no longer able to do so. Ignoring the breach of protocol, Kirk dredged in his memory and came up with the youth's name.

'Yes – Foster, is it?'

'Aye, sir,' Foster said. The pleasure and embarrassment at being recognized brought a red blush to his dark face. 'I wondered, when we get home – what should we expect? Does anybody back on Earth know what happened out there?'

'Will they give us a hero's welcome?' Kirk smiled gently, for some of the youngsters, Foster among them, had behaved extraordinarily well for being half-trained and inexperienced. 'Lord knows, son, they ought to. This time we paid for the party with our dearest blood.'

He took the last step into the turbo-lift's sensor field. The doors opened, and he disappeared between them.

When the doors closed, cutting him off from the bridge, he let the mantle of command fall away from his shoulders. He slumped against the wall. The respite would be short, but at least during the ride to his quarters he could be free of responsibilities.

The lift slowed and stopped, and the doors slid open. Almost as a reflex, Kirk straightened up.

McCoy stood in the doorway. He looked as if he had not slept in days, and as if, when he tried to sleep, he had lain down in his clothes. The beard repressor he used had worn off at least twenty-four hours ago. He needed a shave.

He entered the elevator, turned to stand side by side with Kirk, and gazed nonchalantly at the ceiling. The lift hummed into motion again.

'Bones,' Kirk said, a greeting with a hint of a query in it.

'Jim,' McCoy said stiffly, ignoring the implied question.

Kirk waited, hoping McCoy would offer some explanation for his appearance, hoping he would show some sign of snapping out of his strange behavior.

McCoy continued to stare at the ceiling.

'Are you planning,' Kirk said with irritation, 'to shave today?'

'*Quo vadis*, Admiral?' McCoy said.

'What is *that* supposed to mean?' Kirk searched McCoy's face, hoping to find – what? A flash of his friend's intelligence and good sense pushing him beyond the guilt he felt for Spock's death? There was nothing

McCoy could have done, nothing any of them could do. If Spock had not behaved as he had, the Vulcan would not have been the only one to die. They all would be dead. But McCoy regarded any death as a personal failure.

'What is our destination?' McCoy asked. He articulated each word precisely, without contractions. No trace of his southern accent showed, though usually it was strongest when he was under stress.

'We'll be orbiting Earth in two hours,' Kirk said.

'Then we are headed in the wrong direction.' He spoke as if to the air, without turning toward Kirk, without taking his gaze from the ceiling.

'Bones, don't do this! This is me, Jim. Your friend.'

When McCoy spoke, his voice took on a peculiar, low timbre. 'And I have been, and always shall be, yours.'

Kirk suddenly shivered. The chill of fear infuriated him. He wanted to grab McCoy and shake him back to his senses.

'Damn it, Bones! Don't quote Spock to me! I have enough pain of my own. I don't need your – your self-indulgence.'

McCoy slowly turned toward him. His eyes were glazed. 'You left me,' he said in a completely matter-of-fact tone. 'You left me on Genesis. Why did you do that?'

'What the hell are you saying?'

McCoy blinked slowly, then suddenly reacted to what he himself had just said.

'I don't know . . . I just . . .' He stopped. 'Why did we leave Spock?'

'Bones! You must deal with the truth. He's gone.' Kirk gripped McCoy's upper arms. His intensity increased. 'Spock is *gone*. We both have to live with that.'

McCoy stared at him a moment, then lifted his hands

and grasped Kirk's forearms in a gesture of understanding and gratitude. They stayed like that only a split second before McCoy pulled away.

The turbo-lift stopped; the doors opened. McCoy took one hurried step out, then swung back to face Kirk.

'I can't get him out of my head, Jim! I'd give the whole state of Georgia if someone could tell me why.'

The doors slid closed again, shutting Kirk off, alone, angry, and confused.

Valkris rose to her feet, taking only detached notice of the smoothness with which she moved. The high gravity, the hours in one position, had no effect on her. She had never meditated in such an intense gravity field before. She wished she had discovered its beneficial properties much sooner.

The cabin held all her material possessions, which were honorably few in number. Valkris' wealth resided in the holdings of her bloodline, in her responsibilities, and in the duties she had carried out for her family. It resided particularly in the duty she had carried out toward her brother.

'Kiosan, dear brother, may you drink and carouse and gamble for all time,' she said softly, without a trace of irony or anger.

She picked up her headcloth, put it on, and drew the sheer fabric across her face. She could see perfectly, and felt comforted to know that the material was opaque from the other side, opaque to the barbarians with whom she must treat.

Then she left her cabin for the first time since the voyage had begun.

Valkris strode through the corridors of the ship, as repelled now by the shabby, dirty vessel as she had been when first she boarded. The trip were better made on a sturdy, high-powered ship of Valkris' family's own production, but, alas, that was not to be. Not in this region of space.

A shadow moved.

Valkris stopped short, reaching for the dueling knife that hung almost, but not quite, concealed at her side.

The shadow stepped forward, resolving itself into the feline form of the ship's navigator. Farrendahl glided toward her, stalking four-legged, calmly inspecting her.

'Milady passenger,' Farrendahl said softly, a purr in her voice. 'To what event do we owe the honor of your company?'

'Milady navigator,' Valkris said. 'Does a simple constitutional qualify as an event?'

'I wonder,' said Farrendahl.

The single most exciting thing Valkris had ever seen was a performance of a hunt by a troupe of Farrendahl's people. One of the reasons Valkris had chosen this ship above another was her research into the crew. She had hoped to speak with Farrendahl and to learn more about her civilization and her people, who had been in space thousands of years longer than any other known species. Farrendahl's kind did not claim planets, they did not colonize, they did not take territory. They only explored, and hunted, and made their homes beyond the frontiers of space. Perhaps, to them, the exploration and the hunt were the same.

These were the first words the two had exchanged. When Valkris had come on board, she realized she could not take time to socialize. She had much to think over, much to work out. She preferred action to meditation, but her meditation had brought her to certain conclusions, and now she rather wished she had chosen not to hire this particular ship.

'Perhaps milady passenger would care to divulge our

90

destination? I am the navigator; I must know it eventually.'

'I think not,' Valkris said. 'As we are nearly there.'

'But there's no star system within a parsec!'

'Nevertheless,' Valkris said.

Farrendahl bristled out her whiskers and growled softly, a thoughtful sound.

'A rendezvous, then,' she said.

'I did not say so.'

'You did not have to.'

Farrendahl's presumption amused and delighted Valkris. It also made her very sad.

But then she thought, If one were worthy . . . if one were sufficiently perceptive . . .

The handle of the dueling knife still lay cool in Valkris' hand, but now she had no thought of drawing the blade.

The sheath of the knife was encrusted with flakes of minerals, so finely-cut they appeared as gemstones. The sheath ended in a heavy mass of fringe that was also thickly hung with cunningly milled discs of mica in all the colors of the spectrum. Each frequency of color meant something different, some honor or remembrance. Many – her dueling records – were transparent and colorless, the representation of emptiness, nothingness, death. She chose to carry only one that was black; her disinclination to carry a disc for each member of her family was the only fault her bloodline could hold against her.

She unfastened the length of fringe and drew it from beneath her robe.

'Milady navigator,' she said to Farrendahl, 'I wish to give you a gift.' She slid the sparkling strands across her palm. The sharp discs touched together with a sound as silver as water. 'This might benefit you, one day. It has no intrinsic value. It is . . . symbolic.' She offered it to Farrendahl. 'Be careful,' she said. 'The edges are quite sharp.'

91

The navigator accepted the decoration gingerly. 'Milady passenger . . . why do you honor me?'

'You might,' Valkris said, 'call it a whim.'

'But I might not.' Farrendahl stroked the strands so gently that she did not need to fear the razor edges. Her delicate, clawed fingers singled out the black shard of mica. 'Who is this?' she said.

Valkris felt pleased beyond reason and dignity. Few in this region of space would understand, as the navigator did, what she had been given, much less the significance of its details. If anything she had underestimated Farrendahl, not overestimated her.

'It is my brother, Kiosan,' she said. 'He, or any member of my bloodline, would recognize what you hold, and honor it.'

Farrendahl looked up at her, seeking the explanations that Valkris could not speak aloud.

'Milady passenger,' Farrendahl said, 'your hand is bleeding.'

'Yes,' Valkris said. 'It does not matter.'

She strode down the passageway without looking back.

Farrendahl watched the mysterious passenger glide away. The ceremonial fringe, with its adornment of electronically readable glass-chip records, hung heavy in her hands.

Farrendahl did not understand why the passenger would wish to warn her, a stranger. She did not understand why she had offered the warning in a symbolic and obscure way rather than directly. But she did understand what the warning was. At least she thought she did. And if she was right, she had to make a decision instantly.

Farrendahl attached the fringe to her belt, for she carried no knife to which to fasten it. Then she sprang into a run, four-legged, and loped down the corridor.

She slid to a stop at Tran's cabin and raked her claws

92

across the surface of the door, scratching the paint and the metal underneath. Like the passenger's bleeding hand, that did not matter any more.

'What is it?' Sleep slurred Tran's voice. Like most primates, he woke slowly. But for a primate he was all right.

'Let me in,' Farrendahl said.

The door opened, and she paced into the darkness. In a moment she could see. Tran sat in a tangle of blankets, blinking the sleep from his eyes.

'What's the matter?'

'Get up. Hurry. We're leaving.'

'Leaving – ?'

'Do you trust me?'

'In what context?' he said, sounding more awake.

Farrendahl growled and turned on the computer terminal on the wall of Tran's cabin.

'I have no patience for discussions of anthropoidal philosophy,' she said. She reproduced a security-breaching program she had developed long ago, tunnelled into the ship's computer, and disabled certain alarms. 'I am leaving this ship. I am leaving now. I have good reason. You may come, or you may stay. It is of no moment to me which you choose.'

Tran threw off the blankets and reached for his pants. 'Then why are you bothering to tell me?'

Farrendahl did not bother to reply. She hid her tracks in the computer with a flimsy cover that would break down under any scrutiny, but she doubted anyone would have the chance even to begin an investigation.

'I guess if I've been promoted from pithecanthropoid to anthropoid – ' Tran fastened his belt and reached for his shirt.

'No time for all that foolishness!' Farrendahl said. She grabbed his wrist and dragged him out of his cabin. He snatched up his shirt and his boots and carried them with him. Farrendahl raced down the corridor, pulling Tran behind her.

Valkris swept into the control room.

'We're nearly there,' the captain said when he noticed her.

'We are there,' she said. 'Kill all velocity.'

The captain frowned, then nodded to the crew member at the control console, giving assent to his passenger's order.

'Where the hell's Farrendahl?' he said.

The ship vibrated faintly as it decelerated to counteract the forward momentum. And – was that a slight sideways shudder, as of a small craft exiting its mother ship? Valkris could not be certain.

'We have no more need of a navigator, captain,' she said evenly.

'Delta-vee zero.'

'Scan the area,' the captain ordered.

Valkris smiled to herself as the scanning began. It continued for some minutes. Valkris retired to shadows in the back of the chamber, rather enjoying the curious and very nervous glances of the disreputable rogues around her.

'Nothing, captain,' the crew member said.

'Steady . . . steady, boys. Keep scanning.' The captain gave Valkris a poisonous glance. 'I thought you people were reliable. Where the hell is he?'

'He has been here for some time. I can feel his presence.'

'Don't give me your Klingon mumbo-jumbo! There ain't another vessel in this whole damned sector!'

Valkris noticed the reaction among the crew to what their captain had said, and by it she understood that none but he, on this nominally Federation ship, had known till now who or what she was.

'Put me on the hailing frequency,' Valkris said, ignoring his impertinence. Nothing could affect her or offend her now.

'Sure,' the captain said, sourly and sarcastically, 'whatever games you want to play.' He opened the channel for her, and nodded that it was ready.

Valkris grasped the end of her headcloth, using her uninjured right hand, and drew it slowly aside.

The crew reacted uneasily to her appearance, their recent suspicions confirmed, new fears engendered. Renegades they might be, but they were renegades within the Federation, still a part of it. Valkris' people were their antagonists, unknown and dangerous.

Approaching the transmitter, Valkris moved from shadows into light.

'Commander Kruge, this is Valkris. I have obtained the Federation data, and I am ready to transmit.'

'Well done, Valkris. Stand by.'

Everyone in the control room, even the captain, started at the rough, powerful voice that crashed out of the speaker. The voice spoke a few words which only Valkris recognized, for they were in a Klingon language. Now knowing precisely what Kruge planned, she turned toward the viewport, watched, and waited.

'Oh, my gods,' one of the crew members whispered.

Like a ghost, like a creature of mist and fog, the Klingon fighter glowed into existence before the renegade merchant ship, very close, threatening. The Klingon craft had the same effect as its master's powerful voice.

'What the hell . . . ?' the merchant captain said.

Valkris herself had never seen the cloaking device in action before. It impressed and fascinated her. She watched carefully until the ship had taken complete and solid shape.

'Transmit data,' Commander Kruge said.

Valkris withdrew the data record from an inner pocket of her robe and inserted it into the transmission enclosure. The monitor blurred with the high-speed transmission. Valkris could not resolve the images, but she knew every frame of what she was sending.

'Transmission completed, Commander. You will find it essential to your mission.'

Valkris's hot blood streamed down her slashed wrist and palm and between her fingers, soaking the inner folds of her robe, growing cold. She was beginning to feel the effects of loss of blood.

In the language of Kruge and Valkris, which possessed an almost limitless number of forms and variations, every utterance had many layers, many meanings. When Kruge spoke again, he switched to the most formal variation. Valkris understood it, as did all well-born members of their society, but she had never spoken it, or had it spoken to her, outside the classroom. She felt honored, and she knew for certain that Kruge would keep the vows he had made to her.

'Then you have seen the transmission,' Kruge said, implying regret and inevitability.

'I have, my lord,' Valkris replied, granting permission in the second stratum and offering forgiveness as the third.

'That is unfortunate,' Kruge said, accepting what she gave him and affirming that it was neither frivolously given nor lightly accepted.

'I understand,' Valkris said. She made all three strata the same, for she wanted him to know that she understood what she was doing and why, that she understood what he was doing and why, and that she understood that he would make certain the promises made to her would be kept.

'Thrusters,' Kruge said, in the form of their language used by commanders to subordinates.

In the viewport, the Klingon fighter changed. The wings of its aft armament section swung from neutral into attack. The vessel rotated, arcing around until its bulbous command chamber thrust toward the merchant ship.

The merchant captain turned on Valkris in a fury.

'What's going on? When do we get paid off?'

'Soon, Captain,' Valkris said. 'Quite soon.' She spoke again, in formal tongue, to Kruge. 'Success, Commander. And my love.' She did love him, indeed, as the instrument of her bloodline's redemption.

She felt curiously lightheaded and happy. Happiness had deserted her for far too long. She was glad to experience it this one last time.

'You will be remembered with honor,' Kruge said. Then he switched dialects again. Valkris knew he was speaking so she would be sure to hear his command: 'Fire!'

The Klingon fighter swept toward them like a hunting falcon. Valkris did not see the beams of energy, for their destructive force reached the merchant ship at the same instant as the coherent light that formed them. The ship quaked. People shouted, then screamed. Valkris smelled the acrid smoke of burning insulation and flash-burned computer circuits. She heard the terrible hiss of escaping air.

I have shown my face to the world long enough, she thought. It is time to return to the customs of my family.

Her left hand was dark with blood. It marred the whiteness of the veil as she covered her face for the last time.

'For gods' sake!' the merchant captain cried. 'Make him help us! We'll keep your damn secrets, just don't let him space us!'

Valkris closed her eyes.

The bulkhead imploded upon her.

The merchant ship exploded into slag. A shock wave of pure energy battered its scout ship, which Farrendahl had gentled out into space and concealed against the side of the larger craft. At the instant of the explosion, Farrendahl hit the acceleration hard, cut it just as abruptly, and fired all the steering rockets at once. The maneuver blasted the scout out of its hiding place along the merchant's flank and put so much roll, pitch, and yaw on the scout that it would look like merely another bit of exploded debris.

Tran shouted an inarticulate curse.

The scout was far too small to carry gravity, so the spin had its full effects on the occupants. Farrendahl struggled to keep her bearings and her consciousness. When she could stand the erratic tumbling no more, she gradually engaged the steering rockets and brought the scout to a steadier course. She dared not do it quickly lest the attacker notice that this bit of the ship moved under its own power.

'So "we may have to just turn around and go back inside," huh?' Tran said, still stunned and dizzy. That had been the only explanation Farrendahl would give him, till now, and now the explanation was obvious.

She used the aft scanners. Through the expanding, thinning cloud of debris, Farrendahl saw the Klingon ship send one last blast of energy against the destroyed merchant, then turned away from its kill and head toward Federation territory.

'Where did it come from?' Tran said.

'Out of the ether,' Farrendahl said.

The scout ship carried too little fuel to reach the nearest inhabited star system. She plotted a low-fuel course toward the nearest shipping lane, where they stood an excellent chance of being picked up. It would take them a while to get there. Just as well: before they were rescued, they would need to fabricate a believable and innocuous explanation for their plight.

Commander Kruge watched the ramshackle merchant ship go violently and silently to pieces under his fire. He stroked the spiny crest of his mascot, Warrigul, who sat by his side whining and hissing with excitement.

The demise of an opponent offered more satisfaction if the death came slowly, but the merchant was too easy a catch to be treated as an opponent. Besides, Kruge deigned to give Valkris a clean finish.

He nodded to his gunner, who reacted to the unusual order without question or hesitation. He fired the beams and blew the merchant ship beyond atoms.

The few remaining bits of debris tumbled away. Kruge felt completely satisfied. His only regret was never meeting Valkris face to face. He had heard much of her, both before her bloodline came to grief and after. Her information would win for him a great triumph; her death would return her family to its previous place in their society's hierarchy. Kruge doubted that the family had another member to choose who would be the match of the formidable Valkris. He wondered if he himself could match her. He was good, but she was renowned as a duelist. Now he would never have the chance to test himself against her.

Kruge rose and surveyed the work pit. His command chair stood at a level that put him well above the heads of the crew members. None looked at him. Each bent intently over the task at hand, fearing a charge of laziness and the resulting discipline. Kruge could find some breach of regulations under almost any circumstances, but having just asserted his dominance over the merchant ship, he felt no need to assert his complete authority over his crew.

He removed the data plaque from the recorder and slipped it under his belt.

Warrigul rubbed its head against Kruge's knee. Its spines scraped against the heavy fabric of the commander's trousers. Kruge reached down and scratched behind his pet's ears. Warrigul leaned harder against him. It was the only creature on board about whose loyalty the commander had no doubt whatsoever. Everyone else might be a spy, a challenger, a traitor.

Kruge glanced at his assistant. As usual, Maltz reacted badly to ambush. The officer was deplorably sensitive to violence. Kruge kept him on because he was an excellent administrator and follower-of-orders, because Maltz seldom thought for himself, and because while he might betray Kruge – anyone might become a betrayer – he would never challenge his commander. It was inconceivable that any of their superiors would consider Maltz a suitable replacement for Kruge. Maltz not only supported Kruge's position, he insured it. Therefore Kruge pretended never to notice behavior that some less devious commander might not have tolerated.

'I'll be in my quarters,' Kruge said. 'Execute a course to the Federation boundary.'

'Yes, my lord!' Maltz said, and hurried to do his bidding.

Kruge started away. Warrigul trotted after him, growling. One of the crew members in the work pit flinched. He glanced away from his work long enough to be certain Warrigul was not growling at him, then looked quickly down at his console again. Kruge stopped. His boots were on a level just above that of the crew member's head. The crew member reluctantly raised his head when he realized Kruge was not going to move.

100

Kruge gestured casually at Warrigul.

'You may have the honor of feeding my pet,' he said.

Struggling to keep the fear from his expression, the underling nodded vigorously. Kruge was so amused that he decided not even to discipline him for failing to answer properly.

The commander strode toward his quarters, where he kept a secure data-viewer. He was exceedingly anxious to watch what Valkris had obtained for him.

5

Federation science ship *Grissom* sailed out of the darkness
and into sunrise, crossing the terminator of the brand new
world. David was excited and pleased by what he had seen
so far. For a first try, Genesis was a smashing success.
Saavik, as usual in public, showed no emotion. He wished
they could go off somewhere and talk so he could find out
what she really thought.

'New orbit commencing,' she said. 'Coming up on
sector three.'

She was upset by their discovering Captain Spock's
coffin down on the surface, David knew it, but she hid the
fact well. David decided to try to persuade Captain
Esteban to send some people down to bury the tube.

'Short range scan,' he said.

Saavik studied the sensors. 'As before, metallic mass.
Verifying triminium photon tube. No new data.'

'Check for trace radiation. Infrared enhancement.'
David had observed Captain Esteban's tendency toward
overcautiousness. He would surely want to have proof
that the tube was safe before he permitted anyone to
approach it.

'Residual radiation only,' Saavik said. 'The level is
minimal.'

The sensor output changed abruptly. David started
violently and hurried to Saavik's side. Studying the monitor intensely, she adjusted the controls. But the new
sound meant more than simple interference. Instead of
fading, it sharpened and strengthened.

'I don't believe it,' David said.

Captain Esteban, who had been hovering around them for the whole two hours of the first orbit, leaned over his shoulder to see the screen.

'What is it?'

'If our equipment is functioning properly,' Saavik said, 'the indications are . . . an animal life form.'

Esteban folded his arms. 'You said there wouldn't be any,' he said to David.

'There *shouldn't* be any. We only enabled the plant forms in the Genesis matrix.'

Captain Esteban seemed unwilling to accept what David had tried to tell him several times: that Genesis was an *experiment*. Besides being a prototype, the torpedo had detonated in an environment completely different from the one it had been designed to affect. And who knew what Khan Singh might have done while he possessed the device? However obsessed he was, he had to have been a brilliant man. He could surely have discovered how to turn on the programs the team had disabled for the first use of Genesis.

That must be what happened, David thought, if this reading isn't just a sensor gremlin. If Khan was going to use Genesis to create a world for his people to live on, he would have wanted the complete ecosphere, animals included. He would have known he couldn't import any species from Earth – that's for damned sure!

But David had to wonder why it had taken a full orbit to find the first animal life form.

He pushed away his worries. Animal life was decidedly not a symptom of the things David had most feared might go wrong.

Good grief, now you're sounding like Esteban, David said to himself. You're demanding a complete analysis to ten decimal places before you have enough information for a first approximation. Go ahead and form a hypothesis if you want, but don't turn it into a natural law before you've collected any data.

Then he thought, Holy Heisenberg, what if Vance's dragons really are down there? That would please mother.

Saavik had been working while David daydreamed and Esteban hovered.

'Cross-referenced and verified,' she said. 'An unidentified animate life form.'

Saavik had been trying to analyze her own reaction to the discovery of Spock's coffin. At the time of Spock's funeral, sending his body to intersect the Genesis wave, to disintegrate into its sub-elementary particles and be incorporated into the very fabric of the new world, had seemed to Saavik an elegant solution, one Spock would have approved. Disobeying Admiral Kirk's orders so flagrantly had troubled her slightly, but her loyalty to Spock was of a higher order entirely. In truth, she believed she was the only person who could understand him and appreciate his life.

Now, having disobeyed Admiral Kirk's instructions, having chosen an orbit of her own design, she must take the responsibility for what had happened. But – what *had* happened? She was dealing with forces that no one yet completely understood. Again and again David had stressed the potential for unexpected events. Perhaps the potential reached as far as inexplicable occurrences . . .

For something – or *someone* – was down there on that planet.

Saavik glanced at David and saw that he was as perplexed as she, yet both delighted and excited. She wished they could go off in private and discuss what they had found.

Esteban rubbed his jaw.

'Do you wish to advise Starfleet, sir?' the communications officer said.

'Wait a minute,' Esteban said. 'We don't know what we're talking about here.'

'Why don't we beam it up?' David said, just to watch Esteban react.

'Oh, no, you don't!' Esteban said sharply. 'Regulations specifically state, "Nothing shall be beamed aboard until danger of contamination has been eliminated." Can you guarantee that?'

David reflected that it was no fun to pull someone's leg if he never eventually realized his leg was being pulled.

'Not from here, no,' the young scientist said.

'Captain,' Saavik said, 'the logical alternative is obvious. Beaming down to the surface is permitted – '

'"If the captain determines that the mission is vital and reasonably free of danger." I know the book, Lieutenant Saavik.'

'Captain, please,' David said. He was getting sick and tired of having Starfleet regulations quoted at him in regard to his own project. 'We'll take the risk. We've got to find out what's down there!'

'Or who,' Saavik said, very softly.

David glanced at her, startled.

Esteban nodded thoughtfully to David. 'All right,' he said: 'Get your gear. I'll put you down next time around.'

'Thank you *sir*,' David said.

Starfleet Cadet R. Grenni awoke in the trainees' dorm. He felt groggy, and his head ached. He had slept too much. He had nothing else to do. Whenever he slept, he had nightmares – but even the nightmares were better than the things he remembered.

He wished he were back on the *Enterprise*. At least there he would have work to do. He had volunteered to stay, but he had been transferred to *Firenze* along with most of his other classmates. Only a few essential cadets had been left on board the *Enterprise*. Obviously, Commander Scott had not considered Grenni essential.

When *Firenze* reached Earth, Starfleet gave all the trainees several weeks' leave. If they had deliberately planned to torture Grenni, they could not have chosen a better way.

His message light was glowing. He stumbled to the reception panel. Hands trembling, heart beating violently, he accepted the communication. They had caught up to him, they had realized their mistake. This must be his summons to a court-martial –

A small packet fell into the slot. Reluctantly, he opened the door. The envelope bore the seal of Starfleet in gold and blue. He picked it up and fumbled at the flap until it came loose.

'By order of Admiral James T. Kirk,' he read, 'you are presented with the gold star of valor, jeweled . . .'

The gold star was for conspicuous bravery. The jewel signified an engagement in which lives had been lost. Humans received a ruby. It stood for blood. Grenni's hands started to shake. He blinked rapidly, forcing away tears. He barely made it through the rest of the message. It commanded him and the rest of his class to appear at Starfleet headquarters a few days from now, for the formal presentation of the medal.

The delicate gold star, with ruby, fell out of the envelope and into his hand.

On the bridge of the *Enterprise*, Jim Kirk leaned back in the captain's seat. Before him, Spacedock grew slowly larger. The ship was nearly home. Kirk felt almost as he had in the old days. He could almost forget the *Enterprise* was running on automatic because it had even less than a skeleton crew. He could almost forget that the ship was patched and scarred and battle-worn. He could almost forget the empty chair behind him.

Almost.

'Stand by, automatic approach system,' he said. 'Advise approach control.'

'Approach control, this is USS *Enterprise*,' Uhura said. 'Ready for docking maneuver.'

The controller came back with a crisp, clear voice. '*Enterprise* is cleared to dock.'

'Lock on.'

Sulu transferred control to Spacedock. 'Systems locked.'

'Spacedock,' Kirk said, 'you have control.'

'Affirmative, *Enterprise*. Enjoy the ride, and welcome home.'

'*Enterprise* confirms. With thanks.'

The ship approached the dock in a huge curve, arcing around its flank and spiraling in to approach threshold number fifteen. The great enclosed docking bay allowed people to work outside the ship, yet it protected them from the free radiation of space. The *Enterprise* sailed closer and closer to Spacedock, heading straight at the closed radiation-shield doors.

Kirk never liked having to give up direct control of his ship.

Finally, at what seemed to him the last second, the massive doors parted silently. The *Enterprise* coasted in and moved slowly and silently into the bay. It passed ships under construction and ships under repair, ships in storage, and decommissioned ships only waiting to be dismantled.

The enormous bay stretched off into darkness, with only a single pool of light in its entire length. The *Enterprise* came abreast of the lights, where NX 2000, USS *Excelsior*, floated among its acolytes as they readied it for its first voyage. It was a beautiful ship, sleek and new, its burnished hull untouched by radiation or micrometeorites or battle.

'Would you look at that?' Uhura said.

'My friends,' Kirk said, 'the great experiment: *Excelsior*, ready for trial runs.'

Kirk glanced at Sulu, approving of his restraint. *Excelsior* was Sulu's next assignment, his first command. In many respects, Sulu was Kirk's protégé. The admiral was proud of the young captain. Kirk searched his heart for envy and found none. *Excelsior* belonged to Sulu. Kirk's ship was the *Enterprise*, and he wanted none other.

'It has transwarp drive,' Sulu said matter-of-factly.

'Aye,' Scott said, 'and if my grandmother had wheels, she'd be a wagon.'

'Mr Scott,' Kirk said with mild reproof.

'I'm sorry, sir, but as far as I'm concerned, there's nothin' needed for space travel that *this* old girl doesn't already have.'

'Come come, Scotty,' Kirk said. 'Young minds. Fresh ideas.' His voice grew dry. 'Be tolerant.'

Sulu smiled to himself, refusing to be baited by the conversation. Behind his calm façade he glowed with pride. *Excelsior* was *his* ship, the ship he had worked so hard and waited so long to command. He knew its lines by heart. He had had considerable say in its design. He was so proud of the ship that even Mr Scott's criticisms could not get very far under his skin.

He had been around and around about *Excelsior* with Scott. Scott thought *Excelsior* was a kludge, full of extraneous bells and whistles. Sulu was beginning to think that Scott was turning into a sort of high-tech Luddite, wanting to go just so far and no farther, afraid of any more advances.

The engineer would change his mind if he ever got a

chance to work inside those engines. Sulu gazed at his ship, and the sight of it gave him nearly enough pleasure to overcome the tragedies of the past few days, nearly enough pleasure to overcome his natural reserve and make him laugh aloud.

After the *Enterprise* passed *Excelsior*, Sulu noticed movement behind the row of small ports along the upper level of Docking Bay 15, the ports that opened out from the cafeteria. Sulu looked more closely.

Everyone sitting up there, drinking coffee, shooting the breeze, relaxing, saw the *Enterprise*'s approach. As the great ship limped its slow, stately way to its berth, all along the line the people rose in silent acclamation.

Jim Kirk, too, grew aware of the homage. He fought with powerful and conflicting emotions. When the controller demanded his attention, he felt glad of the distraction.

'*Enterprise*, stand by for final docking procedure.'

'Standing by. Mr Sulu, activate moorings. Stand by umbilical and gravitational support systems.'

'Aye, sir. Moorings activated. All systems standing by.'

'Admiral!' Chekov exclaimed. 'This is not possible!'

'What is it, Mr Chekov?'

'Energy reading from C deck . . . from inside Mr Spock's quarters.'

'Mr Chekov, I ordered Spock's quarters sealed!' Kirk said angrily.

'Yes, sir, I sealed room myself. Nevertheless, I am reading life form there.'

'Mr Chekov,' Kirk said, his voice angry and quiet, 'this entire crew seems on the edge of obsessive behavior concerning Mr Spock.' Chekov opened his mouth to protest. Kirk cut him off with a sharp gesture. 'I'll have a look. Mr Sulu, continue docking procedure.'

Kirk strode from the bridge. As the doors closed behind

him, Chekov shrugged fatalistically. He saw what he saw. In an assertion of Vulcan logic that had seemed completely illogical to Chekov, Spock had always refused to lock his cabin, or even to go through the security procedures with the computer that would permit it to be locked if he chose. Vulcans never used locks. It was a matter of principle with Spock. Because of the damage to the electronic systems of the *Enterprise*, Chekov had not been able to initiate the procedures himself when Kirk ordered the cabin closed off. Instead, Chekov secured the door mechanically, that is, with an alarm, with sensors, and with a lead seal and stamp from the ship's archives. Consequently, someone *could* have broken in.

And unless the sensors had gone completely wonky (which was also possible), apparently someone had.

Kirk strode toward Spock's room, his temper frayed and just short of breaking. If one of the cadets had entered Spock's room, if this were some tasteless and thoughtless practical joke – then Kirk would soon be giving someone a lesson in the uses of black humor.

An alarm was ringing softly. Kirk broke into a run, then slowed abruptly so as to come upon the intruder unaware.

At Spock's door he stopped short. A violent force had ripped away the seal and wrenched open the door, as if an intruder of enormous strength had been too distressed, too desperate, to try any method but direct force.

Kirk touched the alarm, and it faded to silence. He squinted, but saw nothing through the darkness. He stepped cautiously forward, waiting for his eyes to become acclimated to the low light.

'Jim . . . help me . . .'

Kirk gasped. The voice was Spock's.

'Take me up . . . up the steps . . . of Mount Seleya through the hall of ancient thought . . .'

110

Kirk clenched his fists. His hands were shaking with anger and shock. He peered more deeply into the shadows and saw –

The indistinct form plunged toward him out of the darkness, knocking him aside. Kirk grabbed it and wrestled with it. Its strength was enormous. Somehow he got a judo hold on his opponent and wrenched him down and into submission. They both fell to the floor and into the lights from the corridor.

McCoy struggled against him.

'Bones! What the hell are you doing? Have you lost your mind?'

McCoy stared at him blankly. 'Help me, Jim. Take me home.' His voice rasped, totally drained of strength.

'That's where we are, Bones,' Kirk said gently. 'We are home.'

'Then . . . perhaps there is still time . . . Climb the steps, Jim . . . Climb the steps of Mount Seleya . . .'

'Mount Seleya? Bones, Mount Seleya is on Vulcan! We're home! We're on Earth!'

McCoy's empty stare continued. Kirk loosed his hold on the doctor's arm.

'Remember!' McCoy said.

In Spock's unmistakable voice.

'*Remember!*'

Kirk knelt on the cold deck, frozen with shock.

'Admiral,' Uhura said through the intercom, 'docking is completed. Starfleet Commander Morrow is on his way for inspection.'

McCoy shuddered, tried to rise, and fainted. Kirk caught him before he hit the floor.

'Uhura! Get the medics down here! Get them now!'

He held McCoy, feeling the doctor's pulse race frantically, thready and weak.

'Bones, it's all right,' he said. 'It will be all right.'

111

But he wondered, Will it? What in heaven's name is happening to us all?

The skeleton crew of the *Enterprise* assembled in the docking chamber in preparation for Starfleet Commander Morrow's review.

'Tetch-hut!'

The botswain's pipe wailed eerily, the doors slid open, and 'fleet Commander Morrow stepped on board, his aide close behind.

'Welcome aboard, Admiral.'

Morrow grasped Kirk's shoulders. 'Welcome home, Jim,' he said. He tightened his hands. 'Well done.'

He embraced Kirk. The sincere affection between them was of long standing. Morrow had been Kirk's first commanding officer. He had sponsored him for his captaincy, and again for his promotion to the general staff.

'Thank you, sir,' Kirk said, as Morrow stepped back. To break the tension he said wryly, 'I take it this is not a *formal* inspection?'

A ripple of half-repressed laughter spread through the small group.

'No. At ease, everyone.' Morrow glanced around. 'Where's Dr McCoy?'

Kirk hesitated. 'Indisposed, sir.'

'Ah,' Morrow said, 'too bad.' Taking the hint, he dropped the subject. 'Well. You have all done remarkable service under the most . . . difficult . . . of conditions. You'll be receiving Starfleet's highest commendations. And more important – extended shore leave.'

The youngsters, particularly, reacted with pleased surprise and anticipation.

'That is – shore leave for everyone but you, Mr Scott. We need your wisdom on the new *Excelsior*. Report there tomorrow as Captain of Engineering.'

'Tomorrow isna possible, Admiral,' Scott said, 'And forbye, with all appreciation, sir, I'd prefer to oversee the refitting of the *Enterprise*. If it's all the same to ye, I'll come back here.'

'I don't think that's wise, Mr Scott.'

'But, sir, no one knows this ship like I do. The refit will take a practiced hand. There's much to do – ' He glanced at Kirk. 'It could be *months*.'

'That's one of the problems, Mr Scott.'

'Well, I *might* be able to do i' for ye a little quicker – '

'You simply don't know what you're asking.'

'Then perhaps the admiral would be so kind as to enlighten me.'

'I *can* cut you new orders to stay and oversee the *Enterprise* – ' he said.

'I'd thank ye for that.'

' – but the orders would have to be for you to oversee the ship's dismantling.'

Jim Kirk felt the blood drain from his face. He could hear exclamations of shock from the crew around him.

'I'm sorry, Mr Scott,' Morrow said. 'There isn't going to be a refit.'

'But ye canna do that!'

'Admiral, I don't understand,' Kirk said. 'The *Enterprise* – '

'Is twenty years old. Its day is over, Jim.' His sorrow was sincere, but he made no pretense that the order was anything but final. 'The ship is obsolete. We kept it on as a training vessel, mainly because you insisted. But after this last trip . . . well, it's clear just by looking at the ship that it's seen its last encounter.'

'Ye've no e'en done an inspection!' Scott cried. 'Ye canna just look at a ship and condemn it to the scrap heap! All ye need do is gi' me the materiel I requisitioned – '

'Your requisitions have been through a thorough

analysis. We gave the ship every point we could – I made sure of that. But it simply isn't cost-effective to bring it back to optimum.'

'"Cost-effective"!' Scott muttered angrily. '"Optimum"! What d'ye – '

'Scotty,' Kirk said gently.

Scott opened his mouth, saw the look on Kirk's face, closed his mouth, and resentfully subsided.

'Scotty, go on over to *Excelsior* for the time being – '

'Nay!' Scott said. 'Do ye no' understand? It isna possible!'

'Indeed?' The frost in Morrow's single word lowered the temperature ten degrees. He was not used to having his orders questioned, much less directly refused.

'My nephew Peter is still on board the *Enterprise*,' Scott said. 'His body is. I must take him home, to my sister. To his grave.'

The admiral relented. 'I see. Of course, you must go to Earth. But Mr Scott, the preliminary test of the engines is urgent. You're the best man for the job. In a day or so – '

'I canna promise. I *willna*. Some things there be that are more important than starships, and one of them is family, one of them is ties of blood.'

He hurried from the docking bay.

Kirk turned to Morrow.

'Admiral, I requested – I'd hoped to take the *Enterprise* back to Genesis.'

'Genesis!' Morrow exclaimed. 'Whatever for?'

'Why – a natural desire to help finish the work we began. Dr Marcus is certainly going to want to return – '

'It's out of the question. No one else is going to Genesis.'

'May I ask why?'

Morrow sighed. 'Jim . . . in your absence, Genesis has become a galactic controversy. Until the Federation

114

Council makes policy, you are all under orders not to discuss Genesis. Consider it a quarantined planet . . . and a forbidden subject.'

Morrow's expression forbade argument in general, and argument before the assembled ship's crew in particular.

'Dismissed,' Kirk said.

Sulu broke off from the rest of the crew of the *Enterprise* before they reached the transporter room. He had no reason to return to Earth immediately, and no desire whatever for shore leave. All he wanted was to get back to *Excelsior*. He had gone on the *Enterprise* training cruise as a favor, out of courtesy to James Kirk. He should have been back on board his own ship days ago.

'Captain Sulu,' Morrow said.

Sulu turned back. 'Yes, sir?'

'Where are you going?'

'To *Excelsior*, sir. I'm several days late as it is.'

'Would you come with us, instead, for the time being?'

Sulu hesitated, but Morrow had given him, however subtly, a direct order if he had ever heard one.

'If you please,' Morrow said.

'Yes, sir.' Sulu followed, trying to ward off a deep feeling of apprehension.

Morrow did not speak to him again until they had beamed back to Starfleet headquarters on Earth. The Starfleet Commander bid good-bye to Kirk and the others. Sulu waited for an explanation. When everyone else had gone, Morrow motioned to Sulu to accompany him. They went into his office, and he closed the door.

'Please sit down, Captain,' he said.

Sulu complied.

'I appreciate your patience,' Morrow said. 'I have a delicate situation here that I hope you can help me out with.'

Sulu resisted the obvious invitation to offer to do anything he could.

'How much do you know about Genesis?' Morrow asked.

'I know who developed it, I know what it does. I've seen it work.' He knew a few of its technical details, for though he had not seen Carol Marcus' fabled proposal tape, he hardly needed to. The ship's grapevine had described it quite thoroughly.

'Do you know what its effect back here has been?'

'No, sir.'

'The uproar has been . . . well . . . considerable. There's going to be a Federation inquiry, and a summit meeting. I'm afraid I'm going to have to ask everyone who was on board the *Enterprise* during this recent . . . incident . . . to keep themselves available to offer testimony. This will pose no difficulties for the others. But in your case . . .'

Sulu saw where this was all heading. He rose in protest.

'Please sit down, Captain,' Morrow said.

'May I assume that the Admiral has already rewritten my orders?' Sulu said stiffly. He remained standing.

'Yes. I'm sorry.'

'Permanently?'

'I sincerely hope not, Captain. In a few months, when this has all blown over . . .'

Sulu held back his protest. He knew that it would do no good, and furthermore that he could only humiliate himself by making it.

'So many factors are involved,' Morrow said. 'The ramifications of the Genesis incident complicate matters beyond any of our expectations. But above that, our investment in *Excelsior* precludes our keeping it in its berth indefinitely. The shakedown cruise must occur as scheduled. Captain Styles will take over for you while you're otherwise occupied.'

'I see,' Sulu said. Anger made his words tight and hard, but he did not raise his voice. He also did not say, What about afterwards? Do you really expect me to believe that afterwards, after Styles has had a chance to command that ship, that he'll turn *Excelsior* over to me without a protest?

All this was equally obvious to Morrow, who at least had the good grace to look embarrassed. 'Captain, after all the turmoil has died down, I promise you Starfleet will make this up to you. Even if things don't turn out quite as we expect, you'll find your cooperation well rewarded.'

No ship existed, no ship was even planned, that came close to *Excelsior*. Sulu feared that once he lost it, he lost it forever. Being told that something could make up for that was so outrageous, so absurd, that Sulu nearly burst out laughing.

'I will find that reward quite fascinating to contemplate,' Sulu said bitterly. 'If the Admiral will pardon me, I have – absolutely nothing to do.'

Morrow frowned at him, not knowing how to interpret what Sulu said.

Without waiting to be dismissed, Sulu turned and strode from the lavishly appointed office.

Dannan Stuart awakened at sunrise, in her mother's house. The young starfleet pilot could smell the new-cut hay from the field beyond the horse pasture. The bird that had been singing all night, confused by the huge full moon, twittered into silence. Dannan flung off the bed-clothes and wrapped herself in her silken. It clasped itself around her.

The floor creaked beneath her bare feet. She leaned on the sill of the small window and looked out across the valley. The wall of the house was half a meter thick, for Dannan's mother's house was five hundred years old and more. Its massive walls insulated the interior against the occasional summer heat of northern Scotland, and against the continual damp cold of winter. Today would be a perfect day, cool and sharp, the sun bright. A better day for saying hello than saying good-bye.

The valley glowed with dawn. Dew lay thick on every surface. Dannan could see a darker path through the silvered grass, where her little brother's old pony had made its way to the creek to drink. Dannan remembered coming home from school on vacation and looking out on mornings just like this, to see young Peter riding Star bareback and bridleless at a gallop across the field. She remembered all the times she had been mean and impatient, when the prospect of taking care of a pesky child had been too much to bear. Often she had been too busy to pay him much heed. She had been so eager to go off drinking and carousing with her friends that she had pushed Peter aside. All he had ever wanted, since he was old enough to understand what Dannan planned for her life, all he had ever wanted from her was to hear her tell her stories.

Poor kid, she thought, poor brother. We did have some fun, in the last few years, but I regret all the times I closed you out and went my own way. I hope you found it in your heart to forgive me.

She whistled from the window. A few minutes later Star trotted slowly over the crest of the hill. He was old and stiff, and he had been retired since Peter went away to school. The bay pony's black muzzle was speckled with white.

Dannan climbed down the steep, twisty stairs to the main floor of the house, grabbed a carrot and a piece of bread from the kitchen, and ran through the back yard to the pasture fence. The dew was cold on her feet, but the water beaded up on the silken. The motion of her running spun the droplets sparkling into the sunlight.

Star whickered at her and reached his head over the

fence for the treats she brought. He nipped up the bread with his soft, mobile lips and crunched the carrot in two bites. Dannan rubbed his cheek, then traced the unusual five-pointed marking of white on his forehead.

When Peter came home and whistled, Star whinnied like a colt and galloped to him, age and arthritis forgotten.

'Poor old boy,' Dannan said. 'You're lucky, you never have to understand he isn't coming back. Maybe you'll even forget him.'

She gave the pony one last pat and trudged back across the wet grass. The house peered at her from beneath eyebrows of thick willow thatch, where the edge of the roof had been trimmed in graceful curves to leave the upstairs windows open to the light.

In the kitchen she made a pot of coffee and put the morning's bread in to bake, though she did not feel very hungry. She had not, since hearing the news of Peter's death on board the *Enterprise*.

The kitchen led into her mother's studio. Dannan could smell the heavy odor of wet clay and the sharper electric tang of ozone from the kiln. Dannan rubbed her fingers around the fluid shape of the mug from which she drank her coffee. Her mother sent her sculptures and commissions into the city to be fired in her co-operative's radioactive kiln. The radiation interacted with the glazes she used, producing an unusual depth and patina. But the things she threw for use around the house, she fired in the traditional way in her studio.

She had spent all day, and most of the night, in the studio. Dannan had left her alone. It was her mother's way, in bad times, to close herself off with her work. Dannan would have liked to talk about what had happened and about Peter, but she knew her mother would not be able to do that for some while yet.

Dannan heard a brief, shivery sound from the street

outside, a sound she knew well but seldom heard in her mother's house. Dannan preferred traveling here by more ordinary means, by train or ground car. The time gave her a chance to make the transition from high tech to countryside. Beaming in, besides being too expensive to use very often for personal business, was terribly abrupt.

But the sound of a transporter beam was unmistakable. The loud knock at the front door confirmed her assumption.

She hurried into the hallway and opened the door just as her uncle, Montgomery Scott of Starfleet, raised his hand to rap insistently again.

'Hush, uncle,' she said. 'Mother's asleep – don't you know what time it is?'

'Nay,' Uncle Montgomery said. 'I dinna think to look.'

'It's just past dawn.' Even thirty years on a starship should not have taken his ability to glance at the height of the sun and realize it was early; but, then, even thirty years on a starship had not changed his indifference to the subtler niceties of social interaction.

Montgomery stood on the doorstep just off the deserted cobbled street. One of the things Dannan loved about this house was that its front door led directly into the village and its back into the countryside. She had grown up here, she was used to it, but friends she had brought home from school for a visit, when she was in the Academy, never failed to find it surprising.

'Well?' said Uncle Montgomery. 'Are ye going to let me in or are ye going to stand in the street all day in thy skivvies?'

'Don't insult my clothing,' Dannan said. 'It's sensitive to discourtesy.'

'I knew I should ha' beamed straight in,' he muttered.

Dannan stood aside to let him pass. Even Uncle Montgomery had better manners than to beam directly into a private home, whether it belonged to his sister or not.

He tramped to the kitchen and looked at the coffee-pot with distaste.

'Is there no tea?'

'You know where it is as well as I do,' Dannan said. She sat down and hooked her bare feet over a rung of the chair.

'I'm in no mood for thine impertinence, young lady,' he said.

'We're not on Starfleet ground now,' she said. She resisted pointing out that even when they were on Starfleet ground, she was only one grade in rank beneath him and thus rated being treated as a colleague rather than as a subordinate. 'We're both guests in mother's house, and I think we should call a truce.'

He shrugged and sat down without getting himself any tea. He fidgeted in silence for some minutes.

'When is the funeral?' he finally asked.

'Ten o'clock,' Dannan said.

He lapsed again into silence. Dannan could not think of any subject to bring up that would not cause one or the other or both of them pain. They had never got along very well. He had opposed her joining Starfleet, saying she was too spoiled and undisciplined ever to succeed. When she did succeed, he never acknowledged it. He never said a word to indicate that he had been wrong. Dannan assumed he was still waiting for her to fail.

The message system chimed softly and the reception light turned on. Grateful for the diversion, Dannan rose to check it.

The message was addressed to her. This surprised her. No one but Hunter, her commanding officer, knew where she had gone. She turned it on.

Dannan immediately recognized the image that formed

before her. Peter had described Lieutenant Saavik in his letters more than once. She was just as beautiful as he had said. She had great presence; she gave the impression of strength, intelligence, and depth. Dannan began to understand why Peter had spent so much time talking about her when he wrote.

'Please forgive me for intruding upon your privacy,' the young Vulcan said. 'My name is Saavik. I cannot convey my message in person, as I am unable to accompany the *Enterprise* to Earth. I knew your brother, Peter Preston. He spoke of you often, with admiration and with love. He was my student in mathematics. He was quick and diligent and he found great satisfaction in the beauty of the subject.' The image of Saavik hesitated. 'Though I was the teacher, he taught me many things. The most important lesson was that of friendship, which I had never experienced before I met your brother. I may discover other friends, but I will cherish the memory of Peter always. I would not have been able to speak of these feelings had I never met him; that is one of the things he taught me. He was a sweet child, a wholly admirable person, and he saved many lives with his sacrifice. This is perhaps as little comfort to you as it is to me, but it is true.' Saavik paused, collecting herself, Dannan thought, fighting to keep her emotions hidden, as her culture demanded. 'I hope that someday we may meet, and speak of him to each other. Farewell.'

The image on the tape faded out. Dannan removed the message disk and slid it inside her silken, which obediently formed a pocket for it.

Dannan returned to the kitchen.

'What was that?'

'Just a message,' Dannan said, trying to keep her voice steady. 'Uncle, what happened?' When she asked the question, her voice did break.

'I canna tell ye,' he said. ''Tis all top secret.'

'But everybody already knows about Genesis,' Dannan said. 'Trust Starfleet to put something everybody already knows under seal! But I don't care about that. I just want to know what happened to Peter!'

'I'll not have you maligning Starfleet – '

'What was he doing on the *Enterprise*, anyway? Why was he under your command?'

'Because ye wouldna take him under yours!'

'I'm his sister! It wasn't proper for either one of us to train him!'

'Proper! Who says it isna proper? I'll not be accused of favoritism by an impudent – '

'Favoritism!' She laughed angrily. 'I'll bet you demanded three times as much from Peter as you did from anyone else! Favoritism! Others might accuse you of that, but your family knows better!'

' 'Tis for the family that I arranged to teach him! I didna want him to be ill-taught – '

'Is that why you won't tell me what happened? Did you push him beyond his abilities? Did you put him where he shouldn't have been?'

'None o' the bairns should ha' been where they were,' he said so sadly that Dannan felt a twinge of pity through her grief. 'They were all pushed beyond their abilities.'

'By Admiral James Kirk,' Dannan said bitterly, softly. 'Admiral Kirk, who – '

'I willna tolerate slander!'

'I'm not saying anything everybody else hasn't been saying for days,' Dannan said. 'The last two times he got his hands on the *Enterprise*, the captains died. First Decker, now Spock. If I had command of a ship I wouldn't let him within a light-year of it!'

'Ye dinna know anything about the situations! And ye'll never get wi'in a light-year of command if any friend o' the admiral hears ye speaking like that!'

'Or if you have anything to say about it?'

''Twillna take a report from me for thy superiors to see ye are too hot-headed for command.'

What happened to the truce? Dannan thought. Did I start this? I didn't intend to, if I did.

'All I wanted to know was what really happened to my brother,' she said.

Uncle Montgomery stood up, stalked out into the yard, and would not speak to her again.

Later that morning, Dannan endured the memorial for Peter. She barely listened to it. Today was the first time in years that she had been in a church. She sat next to her mother, holding her hand.

The pastor described Peter as an obedient and dutiful little boy – a boring creature, not very similar to what he had been as a child, and nothing at all like the sharp and independent young man he had been well on his way to becoming. Dannan wanted to jump up and push the clergyman aside and read everyone her last letter from Peter, written just before he died, received after she knew he had been killed. She smiled, thinking of the practical joke he had played on Admiral Kirk. That took nerve, it did, to face down a general officer.

The last line in his letter was, 'Lieutenant Saavik says we are friends. I'm glad. I think you would like her. Love, Peter.'

She thought he was right. She hoped she had a chance to meet Saavik someday, face to face.

The eulogy ended. Everyone rose and filed out to the churchyard. The raw pit of Peter's grave gaped open in the hard, cold autumn ground. A few dead leaves scattered past, rustling against Dannan's boots. They came from the oak grove that encircled the top of the low hill behind the church. The grove was sacred, or haunted, or cursed, depending on whom one asked about it. Dannan

124

remembered winter nights long ago in front of the fireplace, and summer nights around a campfire, telling deliciously scary stories about the creatures and spirits who lived among and within the trees.

In the oak grove, a dark shape moved. Dannan started.

It was nothing. Just the wind, shaking a young tree (but there were no young trees in the grove, only ancient ones that did not quiver in the wind), or a dust-devil (but weather like today's never produced dust-devils). Who would hide up in the grove? Who would come to a funeral and fear to attend it? Who would prefer the solitary strangeness of the grove to the company of friends?

At the side of the grave, Dannan's mother bent down, picked up a handful of the cold, stony earth, and scattered it gently onto the coffin of her youngest child. Dannan followed, but she clenched her hand around the dirt until the sharp stones cut into her hand. She flung it violently into the grave. The rocks clattered hollowly on the polished wood. The other mourners looked up, startled by her lack of propriety.

She did not give a good god's damn for propriety. She wanted to bring her brother back, or she wanted to take revenge on the renegade who had killed him, or she wanted to punch out her uncle's lights. These were all things she could not do.

Tears flowing freely, Uncle Montgomery scooped up a handful of dirt and dropped it into Peter's grave.

'Ashes to ashes, dust to dust . . .'

'To fully understand the events on which I report,' James T. Kirk said, 'it is necessary to review the theoretical data on the Genesis device.'

Kruge leaned back in the command chair, contentedly rubbing Warrigul's ears as he contemplated his prize.

The image of Admiral James Kirk dissolved into the simulated demonstration of the Genesis device.

The translator changed the words from the standard language of the Federation of Planets into Kruge's dialect of the high tongue of the Klingon Empire.

'Genesis is a procedure by which the molecular structure of matter is broken down, not into sub-atomic parts as in nuclear fission, or even into elementary particles, but into sub-elementary particle-waves.'

The torpedo arced through space and landed on the surface of a barren world. The rocky surface exploded into inferno. The planet quivered, then, just perceptibly, it expanded. For an instant it glowed as intensely as a star. The fire died, leaving the dead stone transformed into water and air and fertile soil.

Kruge casually transferred his attention to his officers, Maltz and Torg. A few minutes before, alone in his cabin, he had watched the recording that Valkris sacrificed her life to acquire. Now, playing it again for his two subordinates, he was more interested in observing their reaction to the presentation.

'The results are completely under our control. In this simulation, a barren rock becomes a world with water, atmosphere, and a functioning ecosystem capable of sustaining most known forms of carbon-based life.'

Torg watched intently, all his attention on the screen. The young officer was in a state of high excitement, indifferent to any potential danger. Maltz gazed at the screen with wonder and admiration.

The human narrating the tape thanked her listeners. Kruge smiled to himself at that, wondering what she would say to *this* audience. He made the tape pause.

'So!' he said. He looked at Torg. 'Speak!'

'Great power!' Torg said eagerly. 'To control, to dominate, to destroy.' He scowled. '*If* it works.'

Kruge made no response. He scratched Warrigul beneath the scaly jaw. The creature pressed up against his leg, whining, sensing the tension and excitement.

Kruge turned his ominous gaze on Maltz.

'Speak!'

'Impressive,' Maltz said thoughtfully. 'They can make planets. Possibilities are endless. Colonies, resources – '

'Yes,' Kruge said gently. He noticed with satisfaction Maltz's chagrin at his tone, and his surprise. 'New cities, homes in the country, your mate at your side, children playing at your feet . . .' As Kruge's voice grew more and more sarcastic, Maltz's expression changed from one of satisfaction to one of apprehension. '. . . And overhead, fluttering in the breeze – the flag of the Federation of Planets!' He fairly growled the last few words, and Warrigul snarled in support. 'Oh, charming!' Kruge said. He sneered at Maltz. 'Station!'

'Yes, my lord,' Maltz said quickly, knowing better than to try to defend himself when he had so completely lost his ground. He hurried to his post and made himself very inconscpicuous.

Kruge regarded Torg. 'It works. Oh, yes, it works.' He touched the controls of the player to let the tape continue.

'It was this premature detonation of the Genesis device that resulted in the creation of the Genesis planet.' On the screen, a constellation-class Federation starship fled the expanding wave that turned the dust and gases of a nebula into a mass of energy and sub-elementary particles, thence into a blue new world.

Kruge turned off the machine, removed the information insert, and slipped it beneath his belt.

'Tell this to *no one*,' he said to Torg. He glanced significantly across the control room at Maltz.

'Understood, my lord.'

'We are going to this planet,' Kruge said. 'Even as our

emissaries negotiate for peace with the Federation, we will *act* for the preservation of our people. We will seize the secret of this weapon – the secret of ultimate power!'

Torg nodded, nearly overwhelmed by the magnitude of what he had seen. 'Success,' he whispered. 'Success, my lord.'

'Station!'

'Yes, my lord!'

Torg returned to his position. At Kruge's side, Warrigul whined and slavered, reacting to the emotions of its master. Kruge dropped to one knee to soothe the creature.

'My lord,' said the helm officer, speaking carefully in the tongue of subordinates. 'We are approaching Federation territory.'

'Steady on course,' Kruge snapped, easing his impatient first stratum with a second stratum of approval. 'Engage cloaking device.'

'Cloaking device – engaged.'

From within the ship, it was a most odd and satisfying sensation. The ship and all its contents and all its occupants became slightly transparent. Voices grew hollow, like echoes.

Warrigul howled in protest. Lower subordinates shuddered at the keening cry, knowing that the cloaking device put the creature's temper on a thin edge. It had a similar effect on people. Once in a while it would, without warning, drive someone mad. But this time everyone survived the transition sane. Kruge smiled and stroked his beast, satisfied in the knowledge that outside the cloaking field, his ship was completely invisible.

6

Saavik stepped onto the transporter platform beside David.

'Transporter room,' Captain Esteban said through the intercom. 'Stand by to energize.'

'Transporter room standing by.'

'Energize.'

The beam caught Saavik up and dissolved her. A moment later it reassembled her, atom by atom, on the surface of the world David had helped to create.

From her point of view, the world solidified around her. She had no real sensation of being torn asunder and put back together. Throughout the entire process she could feel sensations from her body, feel the weight of the backpack on her shoulders, hear and see and think.

The Genesis world lay wreathed in silver haze. Great primordial fern-trees reached into the air then drooped down again with the weight of their own leaves. The fronds had captured miniature pools of glittering rainwater.

David appeared beside her and looked around with wonder.

'It really is something, isn't it?' he said.

'It is indeed,' Saavik said. She took her tricorder from her belt and turned it on. David did likewise. The bio readings were what she had expected, similar to the long-range scans. The animate life signals matched nothing she had ever seen before, but they definitely existed.

David set off through the forest as Saavik switched the emphasis on her tricorder and scanned again. She raised one eyebrow in astonishment.

'This is most odd, David,' she said.

He glanced impatiently back.

She frowned and took out her communicator. 'Saavik to *Grissom*.'

'*Grissom* here.'

'Request computer study of soil samples for geological aging.'

'I'll handle that later,' David said.

Saavik wondered why his voice was so sharp and tense. She, too, was anxious to proceed, but not to the point of recklessness.

'My readings indicate great instability.'

'We're not here to investigate geological aging, we're here to find life forms!' He scanned around with his tricorder. The signals changed and strengthened. 'Come on!' He hurried off between the trees.

Saavik felt an intense uneasiness, but she followed David.

'*Grissom* to landing party.' Even through the communicator, Saavik could hear the worry in Captain Esteban's voice. 'We show you approaching indications of radioactivity. Do you concur?'

'Affirmative, Captain. But our readings are well below the danger level.'

'Very well. Exercise caution, Lieutenant. This landing is "captain's discretion". *I'm* the one who's out on a limb here.'

Saavik stood in the midst of a profoundly unknown world and replied, straight-faced, 'I will try to remember that, Captain.'

She strode after David, who had hurried several hundred meters ahead of her. He paused to take readings, and she caught up to him. Her tricorder showed strange and fluctuating life-signs. She flipped the setting quickly from bio to geo and got the same disturbing readings of

130

instability. At the very least this area would be prone to severe earthquakes.

Reluctantly Saavik changed the sensor again.

The metallic mass she had detected from on board *Grissom* lay very near. She glanced in the direction of the reading. Before her the trees thinned out into a blaze of sun. The air was very warm and very humid. Saavik could not see beyond the sun's dazzle in the steamy haze.

She walked toward the source of the readings. Before her, just out of sight, lay a casket that held the body of her teacher. She did not need to see it to be certain he was dead. Because now, she *was* certain. Her speculations in response to the life-sign readings had been fantasies, dreams, wishes. She felt nothing of the neural touch that had disturbed her so deeply back o he *Enterprise*. If Spock were nearby, if by some incredible action of the Genesis wave, or some unsuspected ability of the Vulcan-human cross, he had returned, Saavik would perceive him. Of that she felt quite sure.

David pushed his way through the thick fronds of the fern-trees and into the glade beyond. The sunlight burst upon him and he stood still, blinking.

Saavik moved more slowly out of the green shade, giving her eyes the few seconds they needed to adapt.

'It *is* Spock's tube!' David said. He squinted at it, trying to screen out the light.

'David . . .' She pointed to the base of the tube.

A mass of pale, moist worms writhed and wriggled in the shadow of the casket. A few fell from the cluster into the sunlight and frantically burrowed into the dark loam.

His eyes now accustomed to the brightness, David saw what she was pointing at. He took one step toward the slimy creatures and stopped. A muscle along the side of his jaw tightened, and he swallowed hard.

'Well,' he said bitterly. 'There's our life-form reading.

It must have been microbes, caught on the surface of the tube. We shot them here from the *Enterprise*.' His voice was tinged with irony and disappointment. 'They were fruitful, and multiplied.' He looked around the otherwise peaceful glade. 'Probably contaminated the whole planet.'

Saavik could think of several other explanations for the presence of the worms, but as the casket appeared still to be sealed, she hoped David's explanation was correct.

'But how could they have changed so quickly . . . ? Did you program accelerated evolution into Genesis?' Perhaps the creatures were far more complicated than they appeared at first glance. She focussed her tricorder on them, but could not reproduce the reading that had brought her here.

David approached the torpedo tube. His tricorder bleated and clicked, registering the increased radiation flux and confirming the torpedo tube as the source. Nevertheless, the level was well below the danger point.

David grimaced, then forged ahead, kicking his way through the worms. Saavik followed until she realized what he intended to do. She stopped, unwilling to see again the terrible burns on Spock's sculpted face, preferring not to consider the effects of climate.

She started despite herself when David slowly raised the lid of the bier. He stared down into the casket.

'Saavik . . .'

Pushing a path through the worms with her boots, Saavik joined him.

'. . . He's gone,' David said. He reached into the empty coffin and drew out the black shroud. 'What is it?' he asked.

She took the silvery, silky piece of heavy black fabric from his hands.

'It is Spock's burial robe,' she said, her voice even, but her thoughts in disarray.

Saavik heard a low, threatening rumble. The ground shook gently beneath her feet. Merely a temblor, not a true quake, but a precursor to and a promise of events more violent.

As the quivering of the earth faded away, a frightened cry echoed through the forest. A mammal? A predatory bird? A creature unique to this world? David spun toward the sound, that lonely shriek of pain, then, when the echoes had faded and the cry came no more, he looked back at Saavik.

She felt sure he was thinking, as was she: No highly evolved microbe screamed that scream.

Dannan fidgeted on the sofa in the living room. It was early evening, and beginning to grow dark outside. The day seemed to have stretched on forever.

Uncle Montgomery sat on the other side of the room, in silence and in shadows.

Dannan's mother had vanished back into her studio. Everyone in the family knew better than to disturb her when the door was closed. That was one of the things Peter's father had never been able to get through his head; it was the final bit of selfishness Dannan's mother could not tolerate. Dannan returned from school once to find, rather to her relief, that the elder Preston had packed up his things and departed, muttering about eccentric artists and heading for – he said – a Federation colony, on the first available ship. Dannan had smiled to hear that, for if he thought an artist who did not like to be interrupted when she was working was eccentric, wait until he met the people who shipped out to colonies. He had not been a bad person, just a self-involved one who should perhaps never have tried to join a family. Dannan wondered if anyone knew where he was, to let him know about Peter.

Dannan rose, crossed the living room, and took in one

stride the three steps up to the foyer. She slipped into her boots and went out the front door, into the village. She made her way down the steep cobbled street to the river's edge, thence through the town and back to the churchyard, the cemetery, and the old oak grove.

The evening was extraordinary. In the west, the sun lined the horizon from below in a thick ochre gold. The color shaded upward into a soft, intense, and glowing mauve. Dannan could not describe the sky in terms of clear spectral colors, only in mixes and delicate hues. What color did one name the region where the sky shaded from predominantly gold to predominantly violet? She could not answer. In the east, the enormous blood-red harvest moon began to glide above the horizon. The just-set sun and the just-risen full moon combined to create a lavender twilight.

Tonight was the autumn equinox. Dannan spent most of her life on starships, where every day was the same length and one counted one's time by the artificial measurement of star dates. When she came home, to a place where seasons still mattered and time was more subjective, she experienced the days and nights and dawns and evenings, the colors and sounds and scents, as a brand new discovery.

Twilight remained when she reached the graveyard, though the livid gold horizon had faded and the sky had changed from lavender to deep blue. Stars glinted here and there, bright and steady in the cold, still air. They were never as clear as they were in space. She was glad Peter had at least had a chance to see them from above the atmosphere.

Dannan sat on her heels by Peter's grave. Beneath the flowers that lay thick and fragrant upon it, the raw earth smelled of rocks and ripped turf. She could make out his name, and the summation of the short years of his life,

134

carved into gray granite. He lay among ten previous generations of his family, the first of his generation to die. Because of the family's tradition of taking the name of one's parent of the same gender, her brother was the only Preston among many Scotts, more Stuarts, a scatter of MacLaughlins, and one Ishimoto, a great-uncle Dannan remembered with great fondness.

She wished she had some memento of space to leave on Peter's grave, some alien bloom to put down to remind everyone that he had dreamed of and sought after and loved the stars.

As the moon rose higher, Dannan saw a hard glint among the flowers littering Peter's grave. She reached between the soft petals and picked up the bit of gold. It was a medal, the star of valor, with ruby. She wondered for an instant if it were Peter's, if her mother or her uncle had put it here, but in the same instant she recognized it as the wrong form for a posthumous medal. It was not engraved with name or place, so it had not yet been formally presented. It had to belong to one of Peter's classmates.

A sound broke the silence that lay easily over the graveyard.

At first Dannan identified the noise as a dog, a lost puppy. She stood up and waited to hear it again.

It came from the oak grove.

Dannan strode toward the trees. Fallen leaves crunched beneath her boots. All the scary childhood stories about ghosts and changelings passed through her mind, though she knew the sound came from someone who was merely flesh and blood.

Besides, she thought, I'm a Starfleet officer, remember? With citations for bravery of my own.

Big deal.

She heard the sound again: a sob.

'Come on out,' she said.

The usual silence of the grove was one of calm. This was the breathless quiet of concealment and apprehension.

'Come on,' Dannan said. 'It's cold out here.'

The young man scuffed out of the trees, the red coat of his uniform black in the moonlight. He stopped before her, hanging his head.

'Who are you?'

'One of Peter's shipmates.'

He was several years older than Peter; he must have been a third or fourth year student, while Peter was only first.

'Is this your medal?'

'Yes.'

'Why?'

He still did not look up.

'I thought Peter deserved it more than I did.'

'Because he's dead and you're alive?' Dannan was about to tell him how brutally often the difference came down to nothing but chance.

'No!' he said before she could continue. 'No!' He hung his head lower, if that were possible. His voice was muffled and reluctant. 'Because he stayed . . . and I ran.'

Dannan stepped toward him with a flare of shock and surprise and anger. She wanted, quite simply, to kill him. She was perfectly capable of doing it with her bare hands.

But then the boy did raise his head, as if baring his throat to accept her revenge. He made no move to defend himself. The utter defeat was all that saved him.

She understood why he had lurked in the grove during the funeral, and why he had not shown himself. She did not understand why he was still here.

'Get out of here,' she said. 'Why don't you just go home?'

His shoulders slumped. 'I can't,' he said. 'I'm AWOL,

for one thing . . . and I used up all my money getting here. I don't know how to get back.'

'That shows great foresight,' Dannan said. 'Is that what they teach you at the Academy these days?' She sighed. 'You'd better come with me.'

Dannan took Grenni back to her mother's house wondering what the devil to do with him.

Uncle Montgomery had not moved from his place in the corner when Dannan returned, and the door to the pottery studio still was closed.

'I believe you know this gentleman,' Dannan said sarcastically to her uncle as Grenni followed her into the living room. 'He came . . . for Peter's funeral.'

Uncle Montgomery greeted Grenni with every indication of pleasure and gratitude for his presence.

'"Tis good o' ye to come pay thy respects to our bairn – '

'Stop it!' Grenni cried. 'Why do you keep being so nice to me? You know where my station was – you must know Pres is dead because of me!'

Scott stared at him.

'You know he was the only one in our section who held his post! I was cadet commander, I should have ordered him out of danger!'

'He'd no' ha' gone,' Scott said.

'Then neither should I.'

'Perhaps not,' Scott said. 'Then we would have two funerals to attend today, instead o' one.' He rose and approached the boy, took him by the shoulders, and looked him in the eye. 'Dinna get me wrong, boy. Ye did a cowardly thing. Now ye must decide if ye are fit for the career ye've chosen. If this is thy character – '

'It isn't!' Grenni said. 'I don't know what happened – I don't understand why it happened. I never did anything like that before in my life!'

Montgomery Scott nodded. 'Ye hadna been properly

prepared for what we faced. 'Tis at least as much my fault.'

'Are you saying – you forgive me?'

'Aye.'

Grenni looked at Dannan. 'Do you forgive me too, Commander?'

'Not bloody likely,' Dannan said.

Her uncle and the cadet both looked at her, shocked.

'Dannan – ' her uncle said, raising his voice in protest.

'But I'm sorry!' Grenni cried. 'I didn't mean it! If I could make it up – '

'Make it up? Make up for the death of my brother?' Her voice was cold with contempt. 'I don't think so.'

'I know there's nothing I can do, that's what makes it so awful – '

'Ye dinna want to be vengeful, Dannan,' her uncle said.

'No,' she said, surprised to find that vengeance was not what she wanted. 'You're right, uncle. But so are you, cadet. There's nothing you can do . . .'

Uncle Montgomery stood up angrily. 'Ye always were a cold-hearted little – '

'. . . and that's what makes it so hard,' Dannan said.

Her uncle put his arm over the boy's shoulders. 'Come along, cadet. 'Tis time to go home.' He sent one quick glare at Dannan. 'Tell thy mother farewell, I canna wait any longer for her to come out.'

He and Grenni left the house. A moment later Dannan heard the electric sparkle of a transporter beam. The window next to the front door glowed briefly, and then turned dark again.

Jim Kirk stared out the window of his apartment at the night and at the bridges on the bay, lines of light leading out of and into an infinity of fog. Reflections overlaid the distant city. Jim turned to them and raised his glass.

'To absent friends,' he said.

Uhura, Chekov, and Sulu raised their glasses in response. They all drank.

'Admiral, is it certain?' Hikaru said. 'What's going to happen to the *Enterprise* – ?'

'Yes,' he said. 'It's to be decommissioned.'

'Will we get another ship?' Pavel said.

We? Jim thought. Is there a 'we' anymore? The ship to be dismantled, the crew dispersed, McCoy in shock and doped to the gills, and . . . Spock dead.

'I can't get an answer,' he said. 'Starfleet is up to its brass in galactic conference. No one has time for those who only stand . . . and wait.'

'How is Dr McCoy, sir?' Uhura said.

'That's the "good" news,' Jim said dryly. 'He's home in bed, full of tranquilizers. He promised me he'd *stay* there. They say it's exhaustion.' He sighed. 'We'll see.'

His doorbell chimed.

'Ah,' Jim said. 'It must be Mr Scott, fresh from the world of transwarp drive. Come!'

The door responded to his voice and whirred open.

Expecting Scott, Jim started at the sight of a much taller figure standing cloaked and hooded in a Vulcan robe, half hidden by the shadows in his foyer. Jim felt panic brush against him, bringing the fear of madness. He thought for an instant that, like Leonard McCoy, he was beginning to perceive the ghost of Spock in every patch of darkness, in dreams and wakefulness alike.

The figure reached up and drew back its hood.

'Sarek!' Jim exclaimed.

Ambassador Sarek strode into the light. He looked as he did the first time Jim had met him, well over a decade before. He had not aged in that time. He would by now, Jim reflected, be nearly one hundred twenty years old. He looked like a vigorous man of middle age, which, of course, was precisely what he was. But a Vulcan of middle age, not a human being. He had many years left to look forward to, just as Spock, his son, should have had over a century.

'Ambassador,' Jim said, feeling flustered, 'I – I had no idea you were on Earth . . .' His words trailed off. Sarek said nothing. 'You know my officers, I believe,' Kirk said.

Sarek showed no inclination to acknowledge the others. He moved to the window and stared out, his back to the room.

'I will speak with you alone, Kirk,' he said.

Kirk turned toward his friends. They regarded him with questioning expressions, each clearly uneasy about leaving him alone in Sarek's intimidating presence.

'Uhura, Pavel, Hikaru – perhaps we'd better get together again another evening.' Kirk put into his tone a confidence of which he was far from certain. With a gesture he silenced Pavel's hotheaded objection before it started; he shook Hikaru's hand, appreciating his equanimity, and he returned Uhura's embrace as he showed his three compatriots to the door.

'We're here,' she said, 'when you need us.'

'I know,' he said. 'And I'm grateful.'

He let them out, watched the door close behind them, and turned back to Sarek with considerable apprehension.

Sarek remained at the window, silhouetted black against black. Kirk approached him. He stopped a pace behind him, and the silence stretched on.

'How . . . is Amanda, sir?' Kirk asked.

'She is a human being, Kirk. Consequently, she is in mourning for our son. She is on Vulcan.'

'Sarek, I'm bound here to testify, or I would have come to Vulcan, to express my deepest sympathies. To her, *and* to you – '

Sarek cut off Kirk's explanation and his sympathy with

a peremptory gesture. 'Spare me your platitudes, Kirk. I have been to your government. I have seen the Genesis information, and your own report.'

'Then you know how bravely your son met his death.'

'"Met his death"?' Sarek faced Kirk, and the cold expressionlessness of his eyes was more powerful than any grief or fury. 'How could you, who claim to be his friend, assume that? Why did you not bring him back to Vulcan?'

'Because he asked me not to!' Kirk said, rising to the provocation.

'He *asked* you not to? I find that unlikely in the extreme.'

Sarek stopped just short of calling Kirk a liar, which did not serve to improve the admiral's temper.

'His will states quite clearly that he did not wish to be returned to Vulcan, should he die in the service of Starfleet. You can view it – I'll even give you his serial number.'

'I am aware of his serial number,' Sarek said with contempt. 'I am also aware that Starfleet regulations specifically require that any Vulcan's body be returned to the home world. Surely this would override the dictates of a will.'

'The trivial personal wishes of an individual?' Kirk did not give Sarek a chance to reply to his barb. 'I'll tell you why I followed Spock's request rather than the rules of Starfleet,' he said bitterly. 'It's because in all the years I knew Spock, never once did you or any Vulcan treat him with the respect and the regard that he deserved. You never even treated him with the simple courtesy one sentient being owes another. He spent his life living up to Vulcan ideals – and he came a whole hell of a lot closer to succeeding than a lot of Vulcans I've met. But he made one choice of his own – Starfleet instead of the Vulcan Academy – and you cut him off!'

141

He stopped to catch his breath.

'My son and I resolved our disagreement on that subject many years ago, Kirk,' Sarek said mildly.

Kirk ignored the overture. 'For nearly twenty years I watched him endure the slights and the subtle bigotry of Vulcans! When he died, I was damned if I would take him back to Vulcan and give him over to you so you could put him in the ground and wash your hands of him! He deserved a hero's burial and that's what I gave him – the fires of space!' He stopped, his anger burned to ashes, yet he thought, And I can think of a few dogs I would have liked to put at his feet.

Sarek behaved as if Kirk's outburst had never occurred, as if he believed that by refusing to acknowledge it, he caused it not to exist.

'Why did you leave him behind? Spock trusted you. You denied him his *future*.'

Jim felt entirely off balance and defensive. He had no idea what Sarek was talking about. If Kirk had hoped to accomplish anything by exposing to Sarek the anger he had built up over the years, he had failed, miserably, spectacularly, completely.

'I – I saw no future!'

'You missed the point, then and now. Only his body was in death, Kirk. And *you* were the last one to be with him.'

'Yes, I was . . .' My gods, Jim thought, is Sarek trying to tell me that if I had behaved differently – Spock might still be alive?

'Then you must have known that you should have come with him back to Vulcan.'

'But – why?'

'Because he asked you to! He entrusted you with . . . with his very essence, with everything that was not of his body. He asked you to bring him to us, and to bring that which he gave you, his *katra*, his living spirit.'

Sarek spoke with intensity and urgency that served merely to disguise, not to hide, his deep pain and his loss. Jim had received the response he intended to provoke. He wished he had been gentler.

'Sir,' he said quietly, 'your son meant more to me than you can know. I'd have given my life if it would have saved his. You must believe me when I tell you he made no request of me.' If there was a chance for him to live, Kirk cried out in his mind, why *didn't* Spock ask me for help?

'He would not have spoken of it openly.'

'Then, how – '

Sarek cut him off. 'Kirk, I must have your thoughts.'

Jim frowned.

'May I join your mind, Kirk?'

Jim hesitated, for the Vulcan mind-meld was not the most pleasant of experiences. The human perception was trivial, Vulcans claimed, compared to the discomfort Vulcans underwent in order to mingle their refined psyches with the disorganized thought processes of human beings. It was clear, however, that Sarek needed information that Jim did not possess in his own conscious mind. Acceding to the mind-meld was the one thing Jim could do, perhaps the only thing, that might give Sarek some peace.

'Of course,' he said.

Sarek approached him and placed his hands on Jim's face, the long forefingers probing at his temples. His gaze never met Kirk's. He seemed to be looking straight through him. Kirk closed his eyes, but Sarek's image remained.

The sensation was as if Sarek's slender, powerful hands reached straight into his brain.

Kirk travelled back through time. The recent message from *Grissom* brought a strong resonance of hope from

143

Sarek: My son's body may yet exist – perhaps there is still time! Time to save him for the Hall of Ancient Thought . . .

And James Kirk understood that even if Sarek found what he sought, Spock was lost to the world he had lived in. Only a few individuals, trained for years in Vulcan philosophic discipline, could communicate with the presences that existed in the Hall of Ancient Thought. If Sarek found what he was looking for, he would give Spock a chance at immortality . . . but not another chance at life.

Sarek's powerful mind forced Jim farther back in time. Jim's memories of Spock's death, which had barely begun to ease, returned with the cruel clarity of dream.

'He spoke of your friendship.'

Jim could not tell if Sarek uttered words or communicated through the mental link. Likewise he could not be sure if he himself replied aloud, or in silence.

'Yes . . .'

'He asked you not to grieve . . .'

'Yes . . .'

'The needs of the many outweigh . . .'

'. . . the needs of the few – '

'Or the one.'

The image of Sarek faded from Jim's mind. Spock appeared, horribly burned and dying.

'Spock . . .' Jim said.

'I have been . . . and always shall be . . . your friend,' Spock said. 'Live long . . . and prosper.'

'No!' Jim shouted, as if by force of will he could twist the dictates of the universe and mortality to his wishes.

The illusion drained away like a spent wave, leaving Jim soaked and shaken. He experienced one last, hopeless thought from Sarek: What I thought destroyed, my son's body, is found; but his soul is irrevocably lost.

He broke the contact between them.

Jim's knees buckled. Sarek caught and supported him. Jim pressed the heels of his hands against his closed eyes, trying to drive back the sharpened memories.

'Forgive me,' Sarek said. 'It is not here. I assumed he had melded his mind with yours. It is the Vulcan way, when the body's end is near.'

'But he couldn't touch me! We were separated!'

'Yes,' Sarek said. 'I see, and I understand.' He turned away, weariness – even age – apparent in the set of his shoulders. 'Everything that he was, everything that he knew, is lost. I must return to Vulcan, empty-handed. I will join Amanda. We will mourn our son. We will mourn for the loss of his life, we will mourn for the loss of his soul.' Without a word of farewell, he started toward the door.

'Wait!' Kirk cried. 'Please . . . wait.' Like a man trying to scale a crumbling cliff he clutched at fragile branches, and they pulled loose from the rock. 'Sarek, surely he would have found a way! If there were so much at stake, Spock *would have found a way!*'

Sarek strode toward the door and Kirk feared he would sweep out of the room without a backward glance, hinting at possibilities, abandoning them.

Sarek slowed, hesitated, turned. 'What are you saying, Kirk?'

'What if he melded his mind with someone else?'

7

The flight recorder from the *Enterprise* lay under seal and under guard. Even Admiral James T. Kirk had to do some fast talking and some throwing around of his authority to see it, much less to bring in an outside observer. Though Sarek knew all there was for any diplomat to know about Genesis and about the last voyage of the *Enterprise*, whoever had cleared him for those reports had not thought to include the flight recorder. This caused what seemed to Kirk like an endless delay. However esteemed Sarek might be within the Federation, he was not a member of Starfleet. Then, when the ambassador finally received special clearance to view the data, Kirk was absolutely refused permission to transmit the recording anywhere outside the records storage center. He and Sarek had to go to it.

Kirk arrived at the center chafing under the limitations of surface travel. He found it incredibly frustrating to be forced actually to traverse the distance from one point to another, rather than to have a convenient transporter beam at his beck and call.

Finally all the distance had been covered, all the permissions had been granted, all the forms had been signed and sealed and retina-printed, and he and Sarek entered a viewing cubicle that would display data from the *Enterprise*'s flight recorder.

Ordinarily the recorder would lie essentially suppressed, quiescently tracking only the routine mechanical functions of the ship. An alert increased its powers of observation and set it to making a permanent record of the ship's crucial areas. The engine room monitor had watched Khan's attack and Spock's last moments of life.

Jim Kirk had already relived Spock's death once today, in an all too realistic fashion. He wondered, as he keyed into the player the star date he wished to observe, why he had fought so hard to be permitted to see it again. He could leave Sarek alone with it and let the Vulcan make of it what he would. But in the end Kirk could not abandon his responsibilities to Spock or – if his suspicions proved true – to McCoy.

'Engine room, flight recorder, visual,' the computer voice announced. 'Star date 8128 point seven eight.' It froze at the decimal he had chosen. 'Point seven eight . . . point seven eight . . .'

On the screen, Spock lay dying against the glass of the radiation enclosure, frozen in time.

'Back!' Kirk snapped. 'Point seven seven.'

The random access search skipped to the last words between James Kirk and Spock.

'Back! Point six seven.'

'Flight recorder, visual. Star date 8128 point six seven, point six seven – ' The tape had reached the point before Kirk left the bridge, before Spock entered the radiation chamber, a time when the *Enterprise* was still in imminent danger of being caught up in Khan Singh's detonation of the Genesis device. Spock was poised in freeze-frame at the radiation chamber control console.

'Go.'

Spock's image flowed into life. McCoy entered the picture, intercepting Spock before he reached the chamber. They argued in eerie silence. Spock guided McCoy's attention toward Mr Scott, who lay half-conscious on the floor. As soon as McCoy turned his back, Spock felled him with a nerve pinch.

And then . . . Spock knelt down and pressed his hand

to Dr McCoy's temple. Spock's lips formed the silent word:

'Remember.'

'Hold,' Kirk said. The image froze. 'Augment and repeat.' The scene scrolled smoothly back. The central image expanded. 'Audio,' Kirk said.

Spock guided McCoy's attention toward Mr Scott, who lay half-conscious on the floor. As soon as McCoy turned his back, Spock felled him with a nerve pinch.

Spock knelt down and pressed his hand to Dr McCoy's temple.

'Remember!' Spock said.

'Freeze!' Kirk said. He struggled against hope and excitement to retain his composure. 'Bones . . .' Kirk said softly. All the doctor's tortured behavior, his confusion –

'One alive, one not,' Sarek said. 'Yet both in pain.'

'One going mad from pain!' Kirk said. 'Why – *why* did Spock leave the wrong instructions?'

'Do you recall the precise words, Kirk?' Sarek cocked his eyebrow at Kirk and saw that he did not. He repeated a phrase from Spock's will as he had plucked it from Kirk's mind. '"Failing a subsequent revision of this document, my remains are not to be returned to Vulcan – "' He paused. 'Spock did not . . . did not believe that his unusual heritage would permit the transfer of his *katra*. He did leave the possibility open.'

'But he never made a revision. He left only – '

' – The good Dr McCoy,' Sarek said. 'Who, if the process had worked properly, would have known what to do. Perhaps Spock was correct. Perhaps he was unable to transfer . . .'

'He transferred *something!* And it's driving McCoy insane!'

'Had Dr McCoy ever experienced the mind-meld before?'

'A couple of times, in emergencies.'

'How did he react?'

'He didn't like it. To put it mildly.'

Sarek raised his eyebrow again but forbore to remark upon the comment. 'Did he become physically ill, afterwards?'

'I don't know. He wouldn't necessarily have said so if he did.'

'He is undergoing an allergic reaction.'

'*What*?'

'It is unusual, but not unprecedented. McCoy's mind is rejecting what Spock gave to him.'

Kirk fought an impulse to laugh. He lost.

'You find this amusing?' Sarek said stiffly.

'No – yes, I'm sorry, Sarek, I can't help it. McCoy would find it hilarious, if he were in any shape to appreciate it. Come to think of it, Spock would, too.'

'I find that highly unlikely,' Sarek said. 'Since the result is that McCoy was unable to assimilate the new information even so far as to rescind the provision of Spock's will that may now destroy both of them.' He shook his head. 'It would have been better if Spock had been near another Vulcan when he died. He did not prepare well, Kirk. He left too many factors open to chance – '

'This is hardly the time to criticize Spock!' Kirk said angrily. 'Or to deplore Murphy's Law, for that matter.'

'What is "Murphy's Law"?'

'"Whatever can go wrong, will go wrong."'

'How apropos.'

'What do we do to make things right?'

'It may already be too late.'

'Sarek – !'

Sarek gazed at the frozen screen in silence.

'The fact that Dr McCoy retains even a semblance of sanity gives me some cause for hope. You are fortunate

149

that you failed in your plan to burn my son like a barbarian chieftain. Had it succeeded, McCoy would surely be lost to us by now. The mind and the body are not a duality, they are parts of a whole. If one is destroyed, the other must disintegrate. If they are separated . . . the greater the distance, the greater the strain, until it becomes intolerable.'

'The strain on McCoy, you mean.'

'Precisely.'

'What must I do?'

'You must recover Spock's body from the Genesis world,' Sarek said. 'You must bring it, and Dr McCoy, to Mount Seleya, on Vulcan. Only there is the passage possible. Only there can both find peace.'

'What you ask,' Kirk said, 'is difficult.'

'You will find a way, Kirk. If you honor them both, you must.'

Kirk glanced again at the frozen image of his two closest friends.

'I will,' he said. 'I swear it.'

Even before Jim Kirk and Sarek had left the records storage center, the questions the ambassador had left unanswered began to trouble Jim.

'Sarek,' he said, 'if I succeed in what you ask . . . will Spock know? I mean – will he be aware of himself? Will he retain his individuality?'

'He will not be as you knew him,' Sarek said.

'I understand that!' Kirk said. The lessons of the mind-meld remained fresh in his consciousness. 'That wasn't my question.'

'Your question is one that cannot be answered in a few simple words, Kirk. There is no time – '

'I'll take the time!'

Sarek regarded him coolly. 'Will you take ten years of

your life? First you must learn to speak Vulcan, and then you must dedicate yourself to study. In ten years you might approach the simplest questions of this philosophy . . . and the question you have asked is far from the simplest.'

'Ambassador, with all due respect – that explanation is getting pretty stale! "I cannot answer your question because humans are too immature to understand. Humans are too uncivilized – "'

'I said nothing against humans. Do you forget that Spock's mother is human? She has studied the discipline of ancient thought these many years. She has earned a place among the adepts and the teachers. Granted, she is extraordinary. But even you might reach a moderate level of comprehension – '

'I get the picture,' Kirk said, irritated. 'It still comes down to, "None of your business". Is that what I'm supposed to say to Harry Morrow, when I ask him to bend regulations into the fourth dimension?'

'You must say what you think best,' Sarek said, without irony.

Hikaru Sulu leaned forward in his leather armchair.

'Admiral, I – '

'No!' Kirk said sharply. 'Don't answer me now. I want you to think it over first.'

The image of James Kirk faded abruptly from the 'phone screen.

On the surface, what Kirk had asked Sulu to do was not very difficult. A volunteer mission, a few days out, a few days back. But if worse came to worst, the consequences could be grave. Kirk had not softpedaled the most severe of the possibilities.

Kirk's intensity troubled Hikaru. It was Kirk who had first commented on the crew's obsession with the death of

Spock, and now he himself seemed obsessed and driven. What he hoped to accomplish was not entirely clear to Hikaru – who had the definite impression that Kirk was not clear on the details, either.

But it was certain that Kirk felt responsible for Spock's death, and that he could not accept it. Hikaru believed Kirk had taken on this mission to expiate the guilt he felt, and he understood Kirk well enough to know that he would never be free of the guilt, or of his grief, until he completed what he had sworn to do.

Cold rain skittered against the window. Hikaru sat in the dark for an hour, thrashing questions around in his mind.

He admitted to himself that he feared for James Kirk's sanity.

The house was very quiet. He shared it with four other people, but tonight he was the only one home. He was, in fact, the lone member of the household on Earth. Only rarely was everyone home at the same time, but even more rarely was everyone else gone.

I shouldn't be home, either, he thought. Dammit!

He got up and went out the back door into the garden. Without his noticing, the rain had stopped and the sky had cleared. The full moon was risen halfway to its zenith. The wet lawn felt cold against his bare feet and the air was ozone-washed. In the near distance, the sea rushed against the shore and away.

His mind chased itself around in circles. He needed to think about something else for a while, or better yet to think of nothing at all. He began to move in a *bo* routine, *bō-no-ikkyo*, though his *bo*, his wooden staff, was back in the house along with his *gi*, and the black belt and *hakama* he had only recently earned when he passed his *shodan* test.

Tsuki, deflect, *tsuki, yokomen, yokomen* –

152

Over the years he had studied a number of martial arts. He was an excellent fencer, and he had progressed to the first of the several degrees of brown belts in judo. But his interest in judo had always had more to do with the fact that he was learning it from Mandala Flynn (he believed she had the same feeling about fencing, which he had taught her). Aikido was different. It was a martial art dedicated to non-violence, to demonstrating to one's opponent the futility of violence. He had been training for some years now. The thrill of being promoted to *shodan*, of putting on for the first time the black belt and the *hakama*, the long wide pleated black trousers, was just as intense as what he had felt when he received the orders giving him command of *Excelsior*.

Yokomen, kakushibo, sweep, reverse, thrust, *dogiri* –

Usually he could lose himself in the motions, but tonight the question he had been asked and the decision he had still to make remained uppermost in his mind, spoiling the flow and the peace of the routine.

James Kirk planned to return to Genesis, whether he got help and the *Enterprise* from Starfleet, or merely a blind eye turned when he departed.

If he were denied permission, or expressly forbidden to go . . .

Sulu thought of his magnificent new ship, up in spacedock, waiting for him, nearly ready to fly. That was where he should be, not down here Earthbound, waiting for debriefings, waiting to testify, waiting to find out from Starfleet whether he had kept his nose clean enough to rate being given back his command.

They had no right to take it from me in the first place, he thought. But they did, and they made very clear the conditions under which I might hope to regain it.

Yokomen, tsuki, yokomen, sweep and turn –

He lost the rhythm and the pattern. He stopped. He

153

blotted the sweat from his forehead, from the sides of his face.

He weighed *Excelsior* against what James Kirk had asked of him. He weighed his ambitions against his allegiance; he weighed the future and the past.

He made a decision, without regret and without reservation.

He swirled back into the routine, moving lightly over the springy wet grass while the last fall roses perfumed the air. The pattern of his motions was smooth and pure, the way he hoped and tried to form his life.

Saavik ran through the steamy, humid glade, pushing aside rain-laden fronds that doused her with cascades of sun-warmed water. She followed the sound of the cry, pierced to her center by its despair. The tricorder in her hand beeped and clicked with life-sign readings, but she hardly glanced at it. Its data were superfluous.

She burst from the forest. It ended so abruptly that she stopped. David hurried up behind her, breathing hard.

'Not so fast,' he said between gasps. 'We don't know what that scream was.' He bent over to catch his breath. 'It might be a predator – it might be one of Vance's dragons.'

Saavik wondered who had designed this section of the landscape. Enormous cactuslike trees stretched bulbous fingers to the sky. On the rocky surface, gray, leathery succulents spread their thick leaves like wounded wings, soaking up the sun.

The ground quivered gently beneath Saavik's feet. It was like a caress – but the illusion shattered when the pain-filled cry came again. Whatever made that sound experienced no pleasure from the trembling land.

Saavik strode forward, the gravel of the desert crunching beneath her boots and sliding beneath her heels.

The rounded, waterworn stones made the surface treacherous and slippery and difficult to negotiate.

'Was this a "little joke"?' she said to David.

'What?'

'Waterworn stones, in a desert that has never seen water? False history, false geology.'

'We wanted to make it seem real,' David said. 'Layered. Not as if everything were brand new.'

'In that, you certainly succeeded.' The cacti might each have been a thousand years old. The succulents might have been left over from an earlier age, living fossils of the beginnings of evolution.

She continued deeper into the forest of cacti. The dryness was a relief after the oppressive humidity of the glade, but what glimpses she could get between the gnarled and looming trunks hinted at other abrupt change of climate.

A hundred meters farther on, the ground was covered with snow.

The rumble of a tremblor surrounded her. She tensed – and the cry came yet again. She had been expecting it –

We hear the cry whenever the ground quakes, she thought. As if there were some direct connection . . . But she amended her hasty deduction. She did not have enough data to draw a significant conclusion, and besides, the creature, the being, might simply be frightened by the earthquakes.

'*Grissom* to ground party. What's going on down there?'

Saavik stopped and flipped open her communicator.

'Saavik here, Captain. We have strong life sign readings, bearing zero-one-five. We are proceeding to investigate.'

'All right, Saavik, I concur . . . But be advised that we *are* tracking a severe and unnatural age curve for the planet. The harmonic motion of the core is increasing in amplitude at a rate that is making me *very* nervous.'

Saavik covered the microphone of the communicator. David was staring in the direction of the snow, apparently ignoring her conversation with Captain Esteban.

'Do you have an explanation?'

'Later,' he said with an intensity that belied his outward indifference to Esteban's information. He gestured impatiently. 'Let's *go!*' Without waiting, he started toward the snow-covered bluffs beyond the desert, moving away from her in more important ways than simple distance.

Saavik uncovered the communicator pickup. '*Grissom*, your message acknowledged. Will advise. Saavik out.'

She snapped shut the communicator and followed David across the desert. He had already passed beyond the limits of the twisted cactus trees. A breeze ruffled his curly golden hair. With every step he took the wind grew stronger. By the time Saavik reached the edge of the forest, the wind had begun to swirl flakes of dry snow against David's feet. He was only about fifty meters ahead of her. She stepped out of the shelter of the cacti, into the whine of the wind. The temperature dropped precipitously, perhaps thirty degrees in as many paces. The wind howled past them.

David reached the first patch of solid snow, stopped, and gazed down at something. Saavik joined him. A trail of small, blurry footprints led from the edge of the snow and up the white-blanketed slope. The wind had obscured their outlines. A sudden flurry of snow threatened to bury them entirely.

The sky held no clouds. The snow was not falling; it was, rather, being carried by the wind from some other source. The icy, stinging flakes cut the visibility to almost nothing.

Saavik sat on her heels and looked closely at the vanishing footprints. She shook her head and rose to her feet.

'Those are not, I think, the tracks of *Sauriform Madisonii*,' she said. Neither, though, were they the tracks she had hoped to find.

In the Starfleet officers' lounge, Jim Kirk feigned calm as he waited for Harry Morrow's reply. Morrow stared silently out into the night, his reflection black on black against the wide expanse of the window that stretched seamlessly from one side of the lounge to the other. The Starfleet commander's expression remained unreadable. Kirk forced himself not to clench his fists.

'No,' Morrow said finally. 'Absolutely not, Jim. It's out of the question.'

All the repressed tension fueled Kirk's words. 'Harry – Harry, I'm off the record now. I'm not speaking as a member of your staff. I'm talking about thirty years of service. I have to do this, Harry. It has to do with my honor – my life. Everything I put any value on.'

He cut off his plea when a steward stopped at his elbow with a tray, removed empty glasses, replaced them with full ones. Jim held himself silent. After an interminable time, the steward left.

'Harry – '

'Jim,' Morrow said carefully, 'you are my best officer, and if I *had* a best friend, you'd be that, too. But I am Commander, Starfleet, so I don't break rules.'

'Don't quote rules, Harry! We're talking about loyalty! And sacrifice! One man who died for us, another at risk of deep – permanent – emotional damage – '

'Now, wait a minute!' Morrow said. 'This business about Spock and McCoy and mind-melds and – honestly, I have never understood Vulcan mysticism. Nor do I understand what you hope to accomplish – I'm sorry! I don't want you to make a fool of yourself. Understand?'

'Harry, you don't have to *believe*. I'm not even sure *I* believe. But if there's even a chance that Spock has an . . . an eternal soul – then that is *my* responsibility.'

'Yours!'

'As surely as if it were my own.' He leaned forward. 'Harry, give me back the *Enterprise!* With Scotty's help – '

'No, Jim! The *Enterprise* would never stand the pounding.'

Kirk realized that Morrow had not understood a word he had said all evening. Harry did not believe him and did not trust him. Worse, he would not permit him to draw on a thirty years' friendship to help him complete a task that bound him as strongly as any Starfleet mission he had ever undertaken.

'You've changed, Harry,' he said with anger and contempt. 'You used to be willing to take some risks.'

'I used to have different responsibilities than I have now,' Harry said sadly. 'Jim, I'm not completely unsympathetic to your request, believe me. I'll contact Esteban. If anything comes of . . . what *Grissom* has found on Genesis, I will of course order them to bring it back.'

'How long – ?'

'At least six weeks.'

'Impossible. Harry, Leonard McCoy is being driven mad! He wasn't properly prepared for what happened to him, he wasn't trained – in six weeks the damage could be fatal!'

'You're not dictating any terms here! *Grissom's* mission is vital – we have to have the data on Genesis before we can make a decision about it! And you want me to order them to turn around and come straight back so you can – save a dead man's soul? Can't you see how that would sound? No. I'm sorry.'

'I repeat: give me back my ship.'

'I'm sorry, Jim. I can't let you have the *Enterprise*.'

'Then I'll find a ship – I'll hire a ship!'

'Out of the question!' Morrow said again. 'You can hire one – but you won't get it anywhere near Genesis. The whole Mutara sector is under quarantine. No one goes there until the science team gets back, and probably not even then. Council's orders.'

'Then let me speak to the Council!' Jim's voice rose, so absorbed was he in the urgency of his quest. 'Harry, *please!* I can *make* them understand!'

He realized that every person in the lounge was either staring at him or making a noticeable effort to avoid doing so. He drew back, forcing his temper back under control.

'No, *you* understand,' Morrow said. 'You simply have no conception of the political realities of this situation. Tensions are strung so tight you could play them like a piano! The Council has its hands full trying to deal with delegations from both the Romulan and the Klingon Empires. My gods, Jim, can you imagine the repercussions if you go in there and announce your personal views on friendship and metaphysics?' He shook his head slowly, stroked the condensation in stripes down the side of his glass with his forefinger, and clenched his fist. 'Jim – ! Your life and your career stand for rationality, not intellectual chaos. Keep up this emotional behavior, and you'll lose everything. You'll destroy yourself!'

As one friend accused him of abandoning lifelong rationality because of a duty to another friend who had continually perceived him as totally illogical, Jim Kirk felt an almost hysterical urge to laugh.

'Do you hear me, Jim?'

Jim stared at him for a long time, searching for some way to respond to having been so irrevocably refused. He sagged back in his chair.

'Yes, I hear you,' he said. He truly was not sure if he had heard everything Harry Morrow had said to him, but it did not matter. He sighed. 'I . . . just had to try.'

'Of course,' Morrow said. 'I understand.'

Jim said nothing, certainly not, No, you don't, you don't at all.

'Now take my suggestion, Jim,' Morrow said kindly. 'Enjoy your leave – and let all this tension blow away.'

'You're right,' Kirk said with reluctance. He picked up his glass and raised it to Morrow. 'Thanks for the drink.'

'Any time.'

Jim set it back down without tasting it, rose, and walked from the lounge, eyes front. He was very much aware of Morrow, watching him with concern, very much aware of all the other senior Starfleet officers, deliberately avoiding him.

This was the world in which he had lived for thirty years, the world in which he always before felt comfortable and welcome. The palpable chill said: The pressure finally got to him, Jim Kirk finally cracked.

The rumors would fly across Starfleet at transwarp speed, grow, and take on a life of their own.

He left the lounge, stepping out into the terminal of the spaceport. Restrained conversation and low lights gave way to brilliant illumination and the hubbub of crowds. He felt more out of place here than he ever had on any alien world. He wondered if there was any place left for him at all.

He looked around, feeling conspicuous in his Starfleet uniform. Finally he found Sulu and Chekov. They were a hundred meters across the terminal, wearing civilian clothes and sitting together on a circular bench, people-watching. Chekov wore a jumpsuit of relatively severe tailoring, while Sulu wore jeans and sandals and an embroidered white Filipino festival shirt. Sulu saw Kirk

160

first and nudged Chekov. They waited for him with elaborate casualness. Kirk glanced around carefully, looking for other Starfleet personnel. He wished he had asked the two younger officers to wait for him somewhere more private. The way things stood, the less they were seen with him the better. He needed their help, but with any luck he might be able to get them out of all this relatively unscathed.

He saw no one else he recognized, so he joined Sulu and Chekov.

'The word, sir?' Sulu said.

'His word is no,' Kirk said, gesturing with a jerk of his head back toward the senior officers' lounge. 'But my word˝. . . is given.'

'Count on our help, sir.'

'I'll need it, Hikaru.' He had nearly slipped, nearly said, 'Thank you, Captain.' But he had heard about Sulu's removal as captain of *Excelsior*. The young officer still retained the rank, of course, but without a ship it meant nothing. Kirk felt responsible for the change in Sulu's orders. He did not want to hurt him any more.

'Shall I alert Dr McCoy, sir?' Chekov asked.

'Yes. He has . . . a long journey ahead.'

Leonard McCoy strode down the crowded street. His body felt like someone else's. He could smell the pungent scent of eight different volatile recreational drugs. He was familiar with them all, of course: he was, after all, a doctor. But he should not be able to sort them out so efficiently from the surrounding smells of the dirty street, the fog, the rain, incense and warm oil from one establishment, raw meat from another. He could hear more clearly than usual. He listened to five simultaneous conversations, one in Standard, two in more traditional Earth languages, and two – no, that was a single conversation being carried out in two different dialects of the same offworld tongue.

He arrived at the meeting place. He paused before its brightly lit come-hither sign. He could feel the colors of the neon script illuminating his face with another dozen different languages, evenly divided between Earth and other worlds. He rubbed the scratchy stubble on his jaw. There was something else he was supposed to be doing, something Jim had told him to do. Oh. Right. Jim had told him to shave and put on more beard repressor. Was this as important? He remembered what it was he was doing. It definitely was more important than shaving.

But is it the right thing? he wondered. There's still time to turn back, go to the nearest hospital, confess to being stark raving mad, and make them lock me up before I get violent.

He reached into his pocket, but it was empty. He had forgotten his tranquilizers. He shrugged. They had not been doing him much good anyway.

He plunged into the tavern.

The noise, the smoke, the appalling scent of sizzling meat assaulted him. He staggered and only managed to keep from falling by grabbing onto the nearest person. She turned, ready to fight, then looked at him more closely and laughed.

'Honey, you look like you're having a tough time of it,' she said. She supported him easily. She was half a head taller than he. Her heavy, curly black hair spread around her head and down her back. She wore the black leather pants and jacket favored by independent couriers, with the jacket fastened only at the bottom and nothing beneath it. The skin of her throat and the inner curves of her breasts looked like warm sable. She was black on black on black, except her eyes, which were a piercing pale blue. He stared up at her and fell in love with her

162

instantly. Only that saved him from abandoning his appointment and asking her for the help he needed. He did not want to drag anyone he loved into the trouble he was heading for.

'I'm . . . I'm all right,' he said. He drew himself up straighter. He still had some dignity.

She kept a steadying hand on his elbow. 'Sure?'

'Yes,' he said. 'Yes, thank you.'

'Okay.' She let him go.

Somehow he kept his feet and continued farther into the bar. A tiny plane whizzed past his face. Startled, he stepped back and nearly fell. A second plane whined past, its propellors blurred, minuscule guns blazing with a sharp snapping sound like a fire of pitch-pine.

The planes were holograms. Nearby, two youths lay in game couches, their eyes closed and their hands on antiqued controls. Behind their eyelids they were experiencing the dogfight of the two early twentieth century biplanes. McCoy watched the three-dimensional images zoom high over the heads of the bar patrons. Each aircraft was the size of his hand, and exquisitely detailed. Suddenly they dove straight toward him. The Spad 7 vanished into his shirt front, the Albatros D-III close behind. He hardly had time to flinch. He looked over his shoulder to watch them soar into the heights again, unscathed by their passage through his strange and alien body. The fleeing Spad suddenly executed an elegant loop-the-loop, came up behind the Albatros, and quite abruptly shot it out of the sky. The Albatros screamed into a dive, emitted holographic flame and clouds of holographic smoke – and disappeared a handsbreadth from the floor. The Spad zoomed victoriously toward the ceiling and faded away.

'Gotcha!' cried one of the youths.

'Okay, okay – want to make it three out of five?'

'That is a wager.'

They were dressed alike – McCoy wondered if that was some new style he had been too out of touch to notice – and they looked so alike that it was impossible to tell if they were two of one gender, two of the other, or one of each. He supposed they knew. That was, after all, the thing that mattered.

McCoy pushed on ahead. The illumination was very dim, but he could see quite clearly, in an odd and glowing way that he had never experienced before. Nevertheless he could not find the person he was looking for. Instead he found a small unoccupied booth in the corner of the room and settled down to wait.

Beneath the din of the tavern he heard footsteps quickly approaching. He glanced up.

'Long time, Doc,' Kendra said.

'Yeah,' he said. 'Yeah . . .' He would have liked to talk over old times with her. 'Anyone . . . been looking for me?'

'I have,' she said. 'But what's the use?' She smiled. 'Well. What'll it be?'

'Altair water.' He drew himself up grandly. '"Specially carbonated from underground fissures".'

Kendra snorted at his recitation of the advertisement.

'Not your usual poison.'

'To expect one to order poison in a bar is not logical,' he said, and then he realized – though it surprised him to hear a tavern employee admitting it – that of course she meant alcohol, which was indeed a poison despite its wide use as a recreational drug.

Then he wondered what in heaven's name he was talking about. He simply did not want a drink, that was all. He had not had a drink since – since before Spock died, as it happened. This is it, he thought. Sheer lunacy. I'm talking to myself. I always talk to myself, though, he thought, it helps me think. Have since I was only a lad.

Doesn't mean a thing. As Freud said, Sometimes a cigar is only a cigar. He noticed Kendra watching him curiously. 'Excuse me,' he said. 'I'm on medication.'

'Got it.' She went away to get his water. As her footsteps receded among the hubbub, another set approached.

The alien slid into the booth beside him. 'Hello! Welcome to your planet.'

'I think that's my line, stranger,' McCoy said.

'Oh, forgive. I here am new. But you are known, being McCoy from *Enterprise*.'

'You have me at a disadvantage, sir. You are – ?'

'I name not important. You seek I. Message received. Available ship stands by.'

'Good. How soon and how much?'

'How soon is now. How much . . . is where.'

'Where . . . ?'

'Is yes. Where?'

'Somewhere in the Mutara Sector.'

'Oh. Mutara restricted. Take permits many . . . money – more.'

'There aren't going to be any damn permits!' McCoy shouted. 'How can you get a permit to do a damn illegal thing?' He glanced around hurriedly to see if anyone had noticed his outburst, then continued in a softer, more conspiratorial tone. 'Look, price you name, money I got.'

'You name place, I name money. Otherwise, bargain no.'

'All right, dammit! It's Genesis. The name of the place we're going to is Genesis.'

'Genesis!' The being recoiled.

'Genesis, yes! How can you be deaf,' he muttered, 'with ears like that?' I used to say the same thing to Spock, McCoy thought.

'Genesis allowed is not. Is planet forbidden.'

'Now listen to me, my backwards friend!' He lurched forward and grabbed the alien's collar. 'Genesis may be "planet forbidden," but I'm damn well – '

A hand closed around his arm. McCoy tried to pull away, but the grip tightened painfully. He looked up. The civilian, an ordinary man, so ordinary he should have looked out of place here, but did not, smiled at him pleasantly. When he leaned forward he loomed, and McCoy realized how big he was.

'Sir, I'm sorry, but your voice is carrying,' he said. 'I don't think you want to be discussing this subject in public.'

'I'll discuss what I like, and who the hell are you?'

The alien tried to pluck McCoy's hands from his collar. McCoy considered going for his throat, but instead clenched his hands harder around the fabric. The civilian tightened his grip again.

'Could I offer you a ride home, Dr McCoy?'

What shreds of control McCoy had regained disintegrated.

'Where's the logic in offering me a ride home, you idiot! If I wanted a ride home, would I be trying to charter a space flight?' He scowled, beginning to perceive the civilian as an obstacle to his quest. 'How the hell do you know who I am?'

The plain young man lowered his voice. 'Federation security, sir.'

McCoy realized just how serious an obstacle the young man was. He lurched away, loosing his grasp on the alien and trying to break the security man's grip. He crashed into Kendra, bringing his Altair water, which tumbled off her tray and splashed over the alien's face and shoulders. The alien leaped to his feet, brushing at the drops and stains. Kendra, surprised by the fray, fell backwards against the next table, sending icy drinks into customers' laps.

'You – you horrible doctor!' the alien cried, still brushing at the water.

166

'Come in here and punch people, will you?' yelled a customer as bits of crushed ice slid down the front of his sheer trousers. 'Whyn't you go across the street where you belong?' He punched the alien, who rolled with the blow, let himself fall over a chair that tripped up the ice-drenched patron, chose the better part of valor, and left his commission behind him.

McCoy bowed to the wisdom of his former and all too brief colleague and headed for the door. Unfortunately the Federation man still had hold of his arm. He brought McCoy up short. McCoy swung around, panicked, and grabbed the man at the vulnerable point between neck and shoulder. He squeezed with all his strength and turned to flee without even waiting to see what happened.

Nothing had happened at all.

The Federation man, his grip unbroken, dragged McCoy to a halt. He looked into the doctor's eyes. 'You're going to get a nice, long rest, doctor,' he said gently. 'Please come along.'

McCoy had a choice: walk or be carried.

He walked.

8

Saavik followed the blurry, half-obscured tracks across the snow. The wind blew ice crystals against her face, whipping them across her cheeks and freezing them to her eyelashes. She squinted to try to see into the blizzard. Movement caught her eye, and she headed toward it. The snow made ghosts all around her. She would have believed she were seeing phantoms if David's tricorder had not continued to bleat rhythmically.

She trudged through the snow, cold and unhappy, trying to ignore both sensations. But she discovered that once she had released her self-discipline, even for only a few days, she could not easily regain the complete Vulcan control she had worked so hard to learn.

With the discovery of the creatures around Spock's coffin, her hopes had crashed; a few moments later, when she saw that the coffin was intact, unsealed, and empty, her hopes had risen just as abruptly. This emotionalism was dangerous; in addition, it was illogical, for even when she dropped her mental shields completely, she could find no sense of Spock anywhere.

She knew she had erred. Whatever happened, whatever she and David found, she must re-establish dominance over her feelings and aspire to eradicating them.

Now she understood why Vulcans denied themselves any indulgence in passion. It was to protect themselves from pain.

Saavik shivered and pressed forward against the howling wind and the snow.

The ground rose beneath her. She was climbing the

flank of a glacier. In only a few kilometers' distance it had changed from a thin blanket of snow to a sheet of ice many meters thick.

The frequency of the tricorder's output increased until it was nearly a continuous shriek, even louder than the wind. Saavik stopped and motioned for David to turn the thing off.

Beneath the ragged whine of the wind, the skittering of snow across the ground, the creaking of the ice beneath her feet, Saavik heard a weak and frightened whimper. She walked toward it. Her boots crunched through the frozen crust. The snow reached halfway to her knees. The uneven footprints before her trailed atop the surface. She wondered if she were following some small and vicious predator that a member of the Genesis team had made up as 'a little joke,' a little joke that now perhaps was injured and desperate. Saavik was growing impatient with the collective humor of the group. Her phaser made a comforting weight in her hand.

A great mass of stone, one moment concealed by the snow, the next a wall of tumbled gray blocks before her, thrust abruptly from the surface of the glacier. The ice had crumpled and cracked all around it, piling up in great heaps to either side.

Saavik saw the child.

He crouched in the meager shelter of a rock overhang, naked, shuddering uncontrollably with the cold. He saw her and tried to scrabble deeper into the cleft, clumsy on his injured leg.

David saw the boy and gasped.

'Your comrades appear to have added a humanoid species to the Genesis matrix,' Saavik said. She crushed out the spark of fury that rose in her against such presumption. She could not afford to lose her temper, not here, not now.

'We didn't,' David said. 'I'm sure nobody did. We discussed it, because we realized it was possible. But nobody did it. Nobody even argued for it – it was obvious to all of us that it would be completely unethical to include an artificial intelligence in the first experiment. Besides, nobody could have put such a complex program into the matrix without everybody else noticing.'

'David, the evidence is before your eyes.' She holstered her phaser, opened the side pocket of her coat, and drew out Spock's burial robe. She stepped toward the child, carrying the heavy cloth in one hand, her other hand empty and outstretched.

'No,' David said. 'The evidence is behind us, in Spock's empty coffin.'

She looked at him sharply, unwilling to let herself begin to hope again.

The little boy huddled against cold stone, too tired to flee any farther. The wind whipped his scraggly black hair around his face and shoulders. The cold had given his skin a peculiar pallid tint. Saavik sat on her heels beside him and touched his shoulder gently. He flinched violently and stared at her, wide-eyed. She brushed her fingertips across his cheek. He continued to watch her, motionless, as she pushed back his hair, revealing his ears.

He was a Vulcan.

Saavik stared at him with wonder. She did not know what this could mean. Now was no time for analysis. The cold and the wind were too powerful. Whoever or whatever the boy was, she had to get him off the glacier.

She hoped she had shown him she meant him no harm. Moving slowly and carefully, she brought the black cloth forward, opened it slowly so he could see what she was doing, and wrapped it around his shoulders. He touched it with wonder, then hugged it tight.

'I am Saavik,' Saavik said in Vulcan. 'Can you speak?'

He cocked his head at her, but did not reply. She felt no resonances from him, no mental emanations, no hint of Spock's powerful intelligence. He was, rather, an innocent, a blank.

'It was the Genesis wave,' David said. 'It must have been. His cells could have been regenerated. Reformed . . .'

Still moving carefully so as not to alarm the child, Saavik drew out her communicator. David's theory was the most outrageous she could imagine . . . and the simplest.

'Saavik to *Grissom*. Captain Esteban, come in please.'

'Esteban here, Saavik. Go ahead.'

'We have found the source of the life signs. It is a Vulcan child, the equivalent of eight or ten Earth years of age.'

There was a very long pause before Esteban replied.

'A child! That's . . . extraordinary. How did he get there?'

'It is Dr Marcus' opinion that this is – that the Genesis effect has in some way regenerated – Captain Spock.'

Back on board the *Grissom*, J. T. Esteban clamped his jaw tight shut to keep it from dropping. He glanced over at his science officer, who stopped staring at the speaker from which Saavik's announcement had come and met Esteban's gaze with an expression of complete, bewildered, speechless perlexity.

'Ah, Saavik,' Esteban said, slowly, carefully, trying to figure out how to reply without saying that he thought she and David Marcus had gone stark staring bonkers. 'That's . . . ah . . . extraordinary. What would you, ah, like to do next?'

'Request permission to beam aboard immediately.'

He wanted to stall them for a bit. It was possible that some glitch in the Genesis programs had produced powerful hallucinogens, or even that one of its denizens could take on the form of someone the observer would most desire to see. He could not take the chance of beaming such a thing on board. Of course there was always the possibility that what Saavik was describing was exactly what was happening . . .

'Saavik . . . do Dr Marcus' instruments show any chance of, er, radioactive contamination?'

After a short pause, Saavik replied, 'None that he can detect, sir.'

'Well. All the same, I'm going to advise Starfleet and get instructions.'

'I am sure Starfleet would approve, sir,' Saavik said.

'Nevertheless . . . let's do it by the book. Stand by on this channel.' He nodded to his communications officer. 'Go.'

'Starfleet command, this is USS *Grissom* on subspace coded channel ninety-eight point eight. Come in, please.'

The comm officer flinched as a high whine came through the earpiece.

'Sir,' the comm officer said to Esteban, 'something's jamming our transmission. An energy surge.'

'What's the location?'

'Astern, sir. Aft quarter.'

'On screen.'

The viewscreen flickered from a forward view to the aft pickup. The starfield lay empty behind them, empty except for an odd interference pattern in one corner. Esteban frowned, wondering if the maintenance of the pickup had been let go.

The interference pattern suddenly coalesced and solidified.

Out of nothing, a ship appeared.

Down on the surface of Genesis, Saavik and David waited impatiently for a response from Esteban. To

172

Saavik's embarrassment, she was beginning to shiver from the cold. The child had stopped watching them. He hunched shivering in the black cloth, his eyelids drooping.

'Don't sleep,' Saavik said, shaking him gently. He did not respond.

'Just like good old J.T. to leave us here freezing our butts off while he puts in a call to Starfleet,' David said. 'Let's get off this glacier, anyway.'

Saavik nodded. Between them, they got the child to his feet. His injured leg collapsed beneath him. They would have to carry him, then call *Grissom* back when they got to a more hospitable spot.

As she was about to put her communicator away, it shrieked and squealed.

'Oh, my god!' It was Esteban's voice. 'Red alert! Raise the shields!'

'Captain,' Saavik said, 'what is it?'

'We're under attack! Stand by for evasive – stand by for – '

The cracked voice dissolved in a rattle of static.

'Captain! Captain Esteban, come in please!'

Deep space replied to her with silence.

On the bridge of the Klingon fighter, Commander Kruge watched the Federation science ship open out like a flower with a center of flame. The wreckage exploded and expanded beyond the limits of his own ship's port. Kruge's anger was only a little less explosive.

He swung around toward his gunner.

'I told you,' he said dangerously, in the lowest of the low dialects, 'engine section only!'

'A fortunate mistake,' the gunner said. His crest flared up in excitement until he realized how Kruge had spoken to him. 'Sir . . . ?'

'I wanted prisoners,' Kruge said, layering all the strata

of his words with contempt. At his side, Warrigul growled.

The gunner's crest flattened against his skull. Kruge gestured to Maltz.

'Offer him a chance to regain his honor,' Kruge said.

Maltz stopped before the gunner's station and drew his ceremonial blade.

The gunner cringed. 'Sir, please, no – it was an error!'

Maltz willed the gunner to get hold of himself and bow to the inevitable with grace. Maltz offered him his own honor blade. Every member of the crew watched, mesmerized.

Instead of accepting it and doing the proper thing, the gunner lurched backward from his station.

'Sir, no!' he cried. He stumbled toward Kruge, his hands outstretched in supplication. 'Mercy, sir – '

Kruge drew his phaser and fired. The gunner disintegrated in a flare of energy.

'Animal,' Kruge muttered. Warrigul snorted in agreement and rubbed up against his leg.

Maltz sheathed his blade, glad that its edge had not been sullied with the blood of a coward.

'Sir,' Torg said, 'may I suggest – '

Kruge whirled around to confront him. The commander still gripped the handle of his phaser, his frustration undiminished.

'Say the wrong thing, Torg, and I will kill you, too!'

'I only mean to say, my lord, that if it is prisoners you want, we interrupted a transmission from the planet's surface. I have traced it.' He gestured to the screen. 'These life signs may be the very scientists you seek.'

Kruge strode to his side, glared at the screen, and analyzed the readings. One was clearly human, the other two less distinctive. Vulcan, perhaps, or Romulan. Human was to be expected; humans were the troublemakers of the galaxy, as far as Kruge was concerned. It annoyed him thoroughly that the Romulans might be involved in this. No doubt they had abandoned their commitments to the Klingon Empire and rushed straight to conclude an alliance with the Federation, in return for a share in Genesis.

And he, Kruge, was about to catch them at the treachery.

'Very good,' he said to Torg, who stood even straighter with the pleasure of his commander's approval. 'Very good.'

The Vulcan boy huddled against Saavik's side, unable to understand the events taking place overhead, unable even to understand that events *were* taking place overhead, but upset and frightened by David and Saavik's reaction.

'*Grissom*, this is Saavik, come in please – '

The emergency channel replied with static. Suddenly Saavik snapped the communicator closed. Her transmission would clearly and easily mark their position.

'Saavik, my gods, what happened to them?'

'It would seem that *Grissom* was destroyed by an enemy attack,' she said.

Saavik thought with regret of Frederic, the Glaeziver, whose counsel she had grown to value in the short time she had known him. He had understood what Genesis might mean for him and his kind, and now he was gone.

'Destroyed . . . ?' Stunned, David looked up, as if he might see the remains of the ship drifting dead in the new sky.

Saavik put away her communicator. It was useless now. She picked up the Vulcan child and started across the ice. She was very worried about the boy. He was so cold he had ceased even to shiver.

The ground quaked gently beneath her feet. Some

distance away, ice shuddered, squealed, and ruptured. The child cried out weakly and began to tremble again. His pain did not ease until the tremblor faded.

Saavik reached the place where, half an hour earlier, the snowfield had ended. Now it stretched onward and she could not see its edge. She hitched the child higher against her shoulder and ploughed on.

David caught up to her.

'Saavik – that means we're stranded down here!'

'Logic indicates that is the case,' she said. The glacier seemed never-ending. It must be flowing at an incredible rate.

'How can you be logical at a time like this? We have to get the hell off this planet!'

'We must get out of the snow, first,' she said. 'I think it likely that we would freeze before we would starve, on this world.'

'We have to get off Genesis!' David said again.

'That will be difficult,' Saavik said. It took considerable effort to make any headway through the deep, soft snow. She trudged on.

'Why don't you just call for help!'

She looked at him. His demand was most curious, the result, no doubt, of panic. He knew her communicator was nothing but a local transceiver. *Grissom* had been the only Federation ship within its range. Whatever destroyed it was the only ship she would reach if she called again.

David's reaction disturbed her greatly. He was more frightened of remaining on the world he had created than he was of transmitting a mayday that would be picked up by enemies. He was more distressed by having to remain in a paradise he had helped design than he was by the destruction of an entire ship and its crew.

'I have already made one transmission too many,' she said.

176

David's shocked expression revealed his comprehension. He did not ask her to call for help again.

The snow ended as abruptly as it had begun. The edge of the ice moved perceptibly, creeping and grinding its way across the desert floor. Saavik stepped out of cold and into abrupt, welcome heat. She carried the child across a hundred meters of the water-worn stones, to a place where he would be safe for at least a few minutes. The snow on her hair and the ice on her eyelashes melted quickly. Cold drops slid down her face. She lowered the child to the ground, brushed away the dissolving snow with half-numbed hands, and helped him to lie in a warm and sunny spot.

David sank down nearby, drew his knees to his chest, and laid his face against his folded arms.

Saavik sat on her heels beside him.

'David,' she said gently.

He said nothing.

'David, it is time for truth between us.' She put her hands on his shoulders in what she hoped might be a comforting gesture. But what did she know of comfort? She was neither Vulcan, never needing comfort, never able to give it, nor was she Romulan, able to give full rein to her passions. 'This planet is neither what you intended nor what you hoped for, is it?'

David let his hands fall. 'Not exactly,' he said.

'Is it what you feared?'

'I didn't think this would happen – !'

'But you have not been surprised by anything we have discovered, no matter how bizarre.'

'There was one set of equations, I wasn't quite certain about them . . .'

'You were overruled by the other members of the Genesis team?'

'I . . . I didn't want to make a big thing of them . . .'

'Surely you pointed them out?'

'Why should I?' he snapped, on the defense. 'I'm a mere biochemist, as my young genius physicist colleagues kept trying not to remind me. If Madison and March didn't think their creation was going to dissolve back into protomatter – '

'Protomatter!' Saavik exclaimed. 'David, you are saying the entire system is unstable – and dangerously unpredictable! As an ethical scientist – '

'It shouldn't have happened! It hasn't, yet, maybe it won't. Maybe it wasn't a mistake at all – '

'And perhaps the ground tremors are in our minds, and the harmonic vibrations we detected from *Grissom* were instrument malfunction . . .' She shook her head. 'Oh, David.'

'I just figured, if it worked out for fusion, it would work out for us.'

'What are you talking about?'

'The first time anybody started a fusion reaction – the first time on Earth, I mean. It was a bomb, of course – '

'Naturally,' Saavik said.

'They didn't know for sure if they'd set off a chain reaction of all the hydrogen in the atmosphere. But they took the chance. They did it anyway.'

'Indeed.'

'Well, at least there's precedent.'

'I am glad to see you are able to maintain your sense of humor,' Saavik said.

'Dammit, Saavik, if those equations weren't right, the whole project collapsed – permanently! All I had was a suspicion, and it was a suspicion about a probability function at that! There was only a one in a million chance that the worst would happen even if the worst *could* happen. Besides, if we'd tested Genesis the way we intended to, instead of having it blown up by your admiral's – '

'Your father's – '

' – friend Mister Khan, there wouldn't have been anybody on the planet to be in danger!'

'You did not tell your collaborators,' Saavik said. 'Even after detonation, you did not tell Carol – '

'If I had, it wouldn't be just us stuck here! Mother would never have gone back to Earth, not if she'd known. She'd have taken the whole responsibility on herself . . . when it was mine to accept.'

'Just like your father . . .' Saavik said sadly. 'You changed the rules.' She knew now that Genesis would never benefit anyone. It would never create new resources, it would never provide a new home for Frederic's people, it would only, ever, cause grief and anguish and disaster.

'If I hadn't, it might have been years – or never!'

All Saavik could think was that if Genesis had been delayed or abandoned, none of the recent events would have happened. *Reliant* would never have visited the world on which Khan Singh and his people were marooned. Khan would never have obtained a starship. He would never have led his people on his mission of vengeance. The scientists on Spacelab would not have been murdered. The *Enterprise* and its crew of children never would have been attacked. Peter Preston would still be alive. Genesis would not have existed to be used as a weapon, and Mr Spock would not have had to sacrifice his existence to save his ship and his crewmates.

Spock would not have died.

Nor would he have been resurrected. The child possessed the substance of her teacher, but he lacked his mind, his experience, his individuality.

Saavik rose to her feet and stood looking down at David. A dangerous fury began to form.

'And how many have paid the price for your impatience?'

Saavik said. 'How many have died? How much damage have you caused – and what is yet to come?'

He raised his head. His belligerence dissolved in grief and anguish, but Saavik was still too close to the madness to forgive him. She fled from him, her fists clenched so hard that her nails cut into her palms. When she had run a hundred paces she stopped.

Saavik cried out to the dying world, a long, hoarse shriek of rage and pain.

For a jail cell, it was not half bad.

Leonard McCoy lay on the bunk with his arm flung across his eyes.

The bunk was no wider than his shoulders, the floor was badly worn, gray, spongy linoleum, and he could not turn out the lights, but, still, it was not too bad. For a jail cell.

McCoy felt quite calm and rational and single-minded, despite having been forbidden any tranquilizers. After he had prowled the cell, pacing back and forth and inspecting every crack and corner of it, after he had come to the conclusion that he could not escape (that was the one other thing wrong with it, of course: he could not pass through the open doorway; the force field threw him back into the room at every try, more forcefully and more painfully each time. But, then, it *was* a jail cell), the compulsion to return to the Mutara Sector and Genesis had vanished as suddenly and completely as it had appeared.

He wondered about that. It seemed like a terribly logical reaction to have . . .

McCoy dozed off.

'You got a visitor, Doc.'

McCoy started out of troubled sleep, wondering where he was and how he had gotten there, and then remembering. Not a dream, after all. Too bad.

'Make it quick, Admiral,' the guard said. 'They're moving him to the Federation funny farm.'

McCoy peered sideways from beneath his arm and saw the guard and Jim Kirk standing outlined by the force field. Jim shook his head sadly.

'Yes, my poor friend,' he said. 'I hear he's fruity as a nutcake.'

Oh, you do, do you? McCoy thought. A 'funny farm,' eh? Is that the kind of respect anybody with a few problems gets in here? Besides, I know my rights – they can't send me anywhere without a hearing.

However, they had put him in here without a hearing. Genesis had not only frightened the Federation and Starfleet, it had put them into a total panic. McCoy wondered what would happen when Jim called his lawyer for him, as McCoy intended to ask him to do. He wondered if the administration of this prison would even admit to an attorney that he was here.

'Two minutes,' the guard said.

McCoy watched the grid of the force field dim and fade. He had to struggle against the sudden compulsion to leap up and try to fight his way out. Since the guard was head and shoulders taller than he, and armed at that, such a course was definitely not logical. As Jim stepped inside the cell, the urge diminished in proportion to the strength of the reappearing energy barrier.

Jim knelt beside the cot.

'Jim – ' McCoy said.

'Shh.' He raised his hand, shielding it from the surveillance camera. 'How many fingers?'

His fingers parted in the Vulcan salute.

'That's not very damned funny,' McCoy said.

'Good,' said Jim. 'Your sense of humor has returned.' He reached into his pocket.

'The hell it has!' Two minutes, and Jim wanted to spend

it trading one-liners. McCoy wanted a lawyer and he wanted out of here. It was ridiculous to maintain the pretense of being asleep, so he sat up.

Jim drew out a spray injector.

McCoy frowned. 'What's that?'

'Lexorin.'

'Lexorin! What for?'

'You're suffering from a Vulcan mind-meld, Doctor.'

'*Spock* – ?'

'That's right.'

'That green-blooded, pointy-eared son of a bitch. It's his revenge for all those arguments he lost – '

'Give me your arm. This will make you well enough to travel.' He fumbled around with the automatic hypo, putting himself in considerable danger of shooting himself in the hand. 'How do you do this, anyway?'

'Give it here,' McCoy said. He took the hypo and pushed up his own sleeve. 'This once, Admiral, you're beyond your capabilities.'

Outside the prison, Hikaru Sulu ran his hands through his hair to muss it, tucked one side of his ruffled civilian shirt in and left the other free, hyperventilated for a few breaths, and, when he thought he had a properly flustered air about him, flung open the door and rushed into the reception area. The two guards looked up from their card game, startled by the appearance of another visitor so late at night.

'Where's Admiral Kirk?' Sulu said urgently.

One of the guards looked him up and down.

'He's with a prisoner. What's it to you?'

'Get him quickly! Starfleet Commander Morrow wants him – right now!'

The guard snorted with irritation, glanced at his partner and shrugged, laid his cards aside, and fumbled around for his electronic key. He vanished into the cell block. His partner glanced speculatively at the face-down cards, glanced at Sulu with unconcealed disdain, and flipped his partner's poker hand face up. Then, watching Sulu with a faint sneer, he turned the cards back over.

Sulu simply watched as if he saw men cheat their partners every day and thought nothing of it. It was to his advantage if the guard assumed he was a powerless flunky.

The guard stretched and yawned.

'Keeping you busy?' Sulu said to the big man.

'Don't get smart, Tiny.'

Sulu frowned. He had to remind himself forcibly that he was supposed to be someone's messenger boy.

'This man is sick! Look at him!' Kirk's muffled voice came from beyond the cell-block door.

The guard heard, too, and rose to his feet. Sulu took a step forward, ready to distract him. The console did the job for him.

The signal buzzed insistently. The guard frowned, glanced at the cell block door, and snatched up the receiver. Sulu relaxed, centered himself, and waited. These few minutes were crucial. A glitch now could destroy the whole plan.

'Sixth floor holding,' the guard said. He listened to his earphone. 'Yeah, come on up and get him, his visitor's just leaving . . . What? Some admiral, name of Kirk.'

Sulu could hear the squawk of protest from the receiver. He also heard a crash and thud from within the cell block, but the guard was too distracted to notice.

'How the hell am I supposed to know *that?*' the guard snarled. 'He's a damned admiral – ! All right!' He flung down the earpiece and headed for the door. He heard the commotion beyond.

The door to the cell block opened and Admiral Kirk stepped through, supporting Dr McCoy.

'What the hell is going on?'

Sulu tapped the guard on the shoulder.

'Dammit, I told you – ' The guard swung toward him, punching at Sulu's head as he turned.

Sulu stepped into and around the strike, cutting down with his hands to redirect the force of the blow. As the big man stumbled forward, off-balance, Sulu drew him in, pivoted, and spiraled him up. The guard ran out from under himself, and Sulu completed the spiral into the ground. The wall interposed itself. Sulu's opponent hit it with a thud – a hollow thud, Sulu fancied – and slid slowly and limply to the floor.

The form had not been perfect for *yokomenuchi iri-minage*, and throwing one's partner into the wall was rather bad form. But, then, this was the real world.

Besides, Sulu hated to be teased about his height.

Sulu glanced up. Kirk was watching appreciatively.

'The side elevator,' Sulu said. 'Agents on their way up.'

Kirk nodded. He and McCoy hurried out the side door. Sulu paused by the master console. He reached beneath it, sought out the central processor, and applied the confuser he had put together. A moment later it rewarded him with a small fireworks display and the acrid smell of burned semiconductors.

Sulu started after Kirk. He reached the door, paused, and glanced down at the unconscious guard.

'Don't call me "tiny",' he said.

Someone should have told the man that in Sulu's chosen martial art, being short was an advantage.

Sulu caught up to Kirk and McCoy and helped support the doctor.

'I'm all right,' the doctor muttered. But he did not try to pull away. He was steadier than the last time Sulu had seen him. Apparently Sarek's lexorin had worked.

Admiral Kirk pulled out his communicator and flipped it open.

'Unit two, this is one. The *Kobayashi Maru* has set sail for the promised land. Acknowledge.'

'Message acknowledged,' Chekov replied, his voice sounding tinny from the small speaker. 'All units will be informed.'

Kirk closed his communicator. McCoy seemed to gain strength from the interchange and, perhaps, from regaining his freedom. He cocked his eyebrow at Kirk.

'You're taking me to the promised land?'

'What are friends for?' said Kirk.

On board *Excelsior*, Montgomery Scott waited for the turbo-lift. He kept his hand thrust deep in his pocket. The sharp corners of a small and nondescript chunk of semiconductor, elegant only at the microscopic level, bit into his palm.

The lift arrived, the doors slid open, and Captain Styles stepped out. Scott started. He had not expected to see anyone, particularly not Captain Styles. He managed to greet the officer civilly; technically, after all, Styles was his superior officer.

Superior officer, indeed, Scott thought angrily. Taking this ship from our own Mr Sulu with nae a second thought nor a protest. 'Tis nae thing superior in that.

'Ah, Mr Scott,' Styles said. 'Calling it a night?'

'Aye, Captain, yes,' Scott said, trying to maintain his frozen smile.

'Turning in myself. Don't know if I'll be able to sleep, though – I'm looking forward to breaking some of the *Enterprise*'s speed records tomorrow.'

'Aye, sir,' Scott said through clenched teeth. 'Good night.' Scott got into the lift. As soon as the doors slid closed between him and Styles, he scowled.

His whole time on *Excelsior* had been like a replay of the arguments he had had with Mr Sulu about the ship. Only this time, Scott lost most of the arguments. Scott would never admit it to Sulu, but *Excelsior* was, indeed, a miracle of engineering. He had expected it to be full of complications, but its systems were elegantly integrated, clean, and nearly flawless. Scott, of course, had been looking for the flaws.

'*Level*, please,' the ship's computer said.

There were a few things on the ship that Scott did not like, such as the faintly insolent baritone voice of the computer. Had he the charge of *Excelsior*, that would change.

'Transporter room,' he said.

'*Thank* you,' said the computer.

'Up your shaft!'

The lift jerked into motion.

'Temper, temper,' Scott said.

Saavik and David struggled up the steep flank of the mountain, seeking a vantage point from which to watch for other survivors of *Grissom*. David believed it was at least possible that a few others might have had enough warning to escape. He knew Saavik thought the possibility unlikely, but she had not tried to persuade him it was impossible. In fact, she had barely spoken to him since his confession about Genesis. When he suggested they climb to higher ground, she merely shrugged, picked up the Vulcan boy, and started toward the mountain that rose abruptly from the surrounding desert.

'Are you mad at me?' David asked hesitantly.

She kept on climbing. But after another twenty meters she said, 'Were I to permit the less civilized part of my character to dictate my reactions, I would be infuriated with you.'

'I had to do it!' David said. 'It shouldn't have put anyone in danger, and if it worked – '

'Yes,' she said. 'So you have said.'

'I knew if I told you, I'd lose you as my friend,' David said, despondent.

Saavik stopped and laid the Vulcan boy down gently in the shade of a tree, out of the penetrating blue-white sunlight. Then she faced David and took his hands in hers.

'You have not lost me as a friend,' she said.

'But – you must hate me, after all this!'

'I am angry,' she said, not bothering to conceal her feelings behind a philosophical comparison of Vulcans and Romulans, no longer trying to claim that she did not possess those feelings at all. 'If I understand them properly, anger and hatred are two very different emotions. And again, if I understand correctly – it is unusual to hate a person that one loves.'

'Saavik – ' He tightened his grasp on her hands.

'Perhaps I am not capable of love, as humans know it,' Saavik said. 'But as you cannot explain it, I am free to define it for myself. I choose to define it as the feelings that I have for you.'

She looked into his eyes. She felt in his wrists his cool, strong pulse. She drew her hands up his arms, to his shoulders, to the sides of his face. He moved toward her and put his arms around her. She kissed him. David felt as if he were dissolving in a white-hot flame, or tumbling unprotected through a solar flare.

Saavik drew away.

'We must go on,' she said. 'We cannot stay here.'

As she started toward the Vulcan boy, she heard a strange sound. She glanced back the way they had come.

'David,' she said with wonder, 'look.'

Far below, the glacier lapped at the foot of the mountain, surging up in slow-motion waves. As David and

187

Saavik watched, the ice crept forward, piling and folding and crushing itself against immovable stone, squealing and cracking and shrieking. The ice had completely engulfed the desert, inundating it like a silver flood.

Scott materialized in the dark. He hated being transported into darkness.

'Chekov?' he whispered.

'Welcome home, Mr Scott,' Chekov said. '*Strasvuitche, tovarisch.*'

'None o' your heathen gibberish, Chekov,' Scott said. 'How did ye get on board?'

'We have ways,' Chekov said.

'Which ways, in particular?'

'Partner of "Unit three" was taking advantage of her good nature, was late for job. Will be more difficult for "Unit one".'

'All right,' Scott said. 'Let's get some life in tae this old tub.' He squinted across the transporter room of the *Enterprise*. He could barely make out Chekov's hands in the faint glow of the console's controls.

'How was trip?' Chekhov said.

'Short,' Scott said. 'Let's get to work.'

Uhura replied to the ten P.M. check.

'Roger. Old City Station at twenty-two hundred hours. All is well.'

She made a few adjustments to the controls of the Earth-based transporter to which she had been assigned. This was a peaceful posting; she had been here since four this evening and, officially, she had transported no one in or out. The schedule listed no travelers – officially – for the rest of the night.

She became aware that Lieutenant Heisenberg was watching her closely, with a slight frown of curiosity. He leaned back in his chair, his hands clasped behind his head and his feet up on the console.

'You amaze me, Commander,' he said.

'How is that?' she said mildly.

'You're a twenty-year space veteran – yet you ask for the worst duty station in town. I mean, look at it – this is the hind end of space.'

'Oh, peace and quiet appeal to me, Lieutenant.' Uhura smiled a private smile.

'Maybe it's okay for someone like you, whose career is winding down.'

Uhura raised an eyebrow at that remark, but let it pass.

'But me,' Heisenberg said, 'I need some challenge in my life. Some adventure. Even just a surprise or two.'

'You know what they say, Lieutenant. Be careful what you ask for: you may get it.'

'I *wish*,' he said with feeling.

Uhura glanced at the clock. She had tried to persuade Heisenberg to go home early, on the grounds that there was hardly enough work for one person, let alone two. Unfortunately, he had declined. Apparently he felt slightly guilty about arriving an hour late. She wished he would choose some other day to make it up, but that was life.

The door slid open.

Admiral Kirk, Dr McCoy, and Captain Sulu entered and headed straight for the transporter platform without a pause. Kirk appeared intent, but intent on something and somewhere else, distracted from this place and time. McCoy looked exhausted, but steady. Sulu caught Uhura's gaze and offered her his unshadowed smile.

'I talked to Sarek,' Uhura heard Kirk say softly to McCoy. 'I'm worried about him, Bones. The strain on him – '

Heisenberg dropped his feet to the floor and sat up very straight in his chair.

189

'Gentlemen,' Uhura said. 'Good evening.'

'Good evening, Commander,' Admiral Kirk said. 'Everything ready?'

'Yes, Admiral.' She swept her hand through the air in a gesture of welcome. 'Step into my parlor.'

Uhura saw Heisenberg's jaw go agape as he recognized the travelers. He was the one factor of uncertainty in this equation. She hoped he would behave sensibly. She began setting controls.

'Commander,' he whispered, 'these are some of the most famous people in Starfleet. Admiral Kirk! My gods!'

'Good for you, Lieutenant,' she said.

'But it's damned irregular – no orders, no encoded i.d. – '

'All true,' she said agreeably.

Heisenberg glanced over her shoulder and frowned at the settings she had entered.

'That's the *Enterprise*,' he said in a low and worried voice.

'And another one for you, Lieutenant. You're doing very well tonight.'

'But the *Enterprise* is sealed – we can't beam anybody directly on board!'

'Can't we?'

'No, we can't – It's directly against orders, we can't just let people waltz in here and go on board a sealed ship, no matter who they are!'

Uhura was rather glad he was making the objection, for in the long run it would serve to keep him out of trouble.

'What are we going to do about it?' he exclaimed.

'*I'm* going to do nothing about it. *You're* going to sit in the closet.'

'The *closet!*' He backed off from her. 'Have you lost all sense of reality?'

'But this isn't reality, Lieutenant,' she said sweetly.

'This is fantasy.' She drew out her concealed pocket phaser and leveled it at him. It was set on stun, of course, but stun was more than sufficient for this exercise. She hoped Heisenberg would not make her use it. Waking up from phaser stun was rather unpleasant. Uhura wished him neither harm nor physical discomfort. His psychic discomfort, though, was another thing entirely. She owed him a little psychic discomfort, after that snarky remark about her career.

'You wanted adventure?' she asked. 'How's this? Got your old adrenalin going?'

Heisenberg nodded.

'Good boy,' she said. 'Now get in the closet.'

She touched a key and the door to the storage closet, just behind him, slid open. She gestured with the phaser and he backed into it.

'Wait – '

She closed the door.

'I'm glad you're on our side,' McCoy said.

She smiled.

'Let's go,' Kirk said. 'Uhura, is it on automatic? Come on, get up here.'

'No,' she said.

It took him a second to realize what she had said. His expression changed from distraction to amazement.

'"No"?' he said. 'What do you mean, "no"?'

'I realize that the Admiral is . . . somewhat unfamiliar with the word – '

Kirk opened his mouth to speak, but she cut him off.

' – but somebody's got to stay behind and put enough glitches in communications so you don't have every ship in the sector coming after you.'

'You can do it from the *Enterprise* – '

'No, I can't. It's too easy to jam. Admiral, there's no time to argue! Prepare to energize!'

191

'What about – ?' He gestured toward the closet.

'Don't worry about Mr Adventure. I'll have him eating out of my hand.' If I have to, she thought. 'Go with all my hopes, my friends.'

Kirk nodded, acquiescing. 'Energize.'

She activated the beam.

9

After the figures of Kirk, Sulu, and McCoy turned to sparks and vanished, Heisenberg started pounding on the inside of the closet door. Uhura ignored him and set to work opening the communications channels that she would need to interfere with as soon as Spacedock realized what was going on.

Uhura was in her element at the console. She infiltrated every important communications channel between headquarters and the fleet. By the time the tangle got straightened out, the *Enterprise* would be halfway to Genesis. If the ship could evade any pursuit sent directly from Spacedock, then Admiral Kirk should be able to carry out his mission. If it could be carried out.

Sulu felt his body form around his consciousness, and then he was standing on the bridge of the *Enterprise* with Kirk and McCoy solidifying beside him. The ship's systems were running at standby level, and the bridge felt very empty with only five people. At the navigation console, Chekov raised his hand in greeting. Scott rose from the command chair to greet Kirk.

'As promised, 'tis all yours, sir,' he said. 'All systems automated and ready. A chimpanzee and two trainees could run her.'

'Thank you, Mr Scott,' Kirk said drily. 'I'll try not to take that personally.' He drew aside, with McCoy, and faced the other three. 'My friends,' he said. 'I can't ask you to go any farther. Dr McCoy and I have to do this. The rest of you do not.'

Taking the *Enterprise* to Genesis would require a good deal more than 'a chimpanzee and two trainees', and everyone on the bridge knew it. Sulu strode down the steps and took his place at the helm. Yesterday he had made a decision on where to place his loyalties. He saw no reason to change his mind now.

'Admiral,' Chekov said, 'we're losing precious time.'

'What course, please, Admiral?' Sulu said, entering a course for the Mutara sector.

Kirk glanced from Chekov, to Sulu, to Scott.

'Mr Scott – ?'

'I'd be grateful, Admiral, if ye'd give the word.'

Kirk hesitated, then nodded sharply. 'My word is given. Gentlemen, may the wind be at our backs. Stations, please!'

Kirk took his own place in the command seat.

'Clear all moorings . . .'

Sulu centered his attention on the impulse engines. They had not, of course, received the overhaul Scott had wished to give them, and they responded hesitantly, irritably, erratically, just as they had on the way in. The warp drive would be equally rocky.

The ship backed hesitantly from its slip and swung toward the entrance of Spacedock.

'Engage auto systems,' Kirk said. 'One quarter impulse power.'

The *Enterprise* reached the berth in which *Excelsior* lay. Sulu gave the new ship a single glance and pushed the longing, and the temptation for regret, out of his mind.

Sulu started hearing consternation over the communications channels, as sensors and alarms and Starfleet personnel on late-night watch began to realize what was happening. The *Enterprise* drifted like a ghost ship past *Excelsior*, toward the huge closed spacedoors. He heard the beginning of a command to secure them, a command that was abruptly and rudely cut off by a screech of static. A moment later a raucous voice spilled over the channel. Sulu recognized the voice of a popular comedian.

He grinned. Everything Uhura did, she did with flair and humor. Crossing Starfleet channels with those of a system-wide entertainment network might well produce an interesting hybrid.

Quite, as Spock would have said, fascinating.

'One minute to spacedoors,' Sulu said.

McCoy fidgeted on the upper bridge level.

'You just gonna *walk* through them?'

'Calm yourself, Bones,' Kirk said.

'Sir,' Chekov said, 'Starfleet Commander Morrow, on emergency channel. He orders you to surrender vessel.'

'No reply, Mr Chekov. Maintain your course.'

Sulu set the communications monitor to steady scan. At one channel it paused long enough for him to hear, 'What the hell do you mean, *yellow alert?* How can you have a *yellow alert* in *Spacedock?*'

The soundtrack of an old movie cut off the reply: 'Who *are* those guys?'

The one thing Uhura could not do was prevent people on Spacedock from seeing what was happening. Everyone at the space station knew the *Enterprise* was being decommissioned. By now they would have begun to notice something distinctly odd.

'Thirty seconds to spacedoors,' Sulu said.

'Sir, *Excelsior* is powering up with orders to pursue,' Chekov said.

Sulu switched the viewscreen to an aft scan. They all watched *Excelsior* come alive, preparing for the chase.

'My gods,' McCoy said. 'It's gaining on us just sitting there.'

Sulu switched back to a forward scan. The spacedoors filled the viewscreen completely.

195

'Steady, steady,' Kirk said. 'All right, Mr Scott?'

'Sir – ?' Scott answered distractedly, for his concentration was fixed on smoothing out his infiltration routine.

'The *doors*, Mr Scott.'

'Aye, sir, workin' on it.'

Sulu had his hands on the controls to apply full reverse thrust when the doors finally cracked open and revealed the bright blackness of space beyond. The doors slid aside for the bow of the *Enterprise*. With a handsbreadth to spare, they were free.

'We have cleared spacedoors,' Sulu said.

'Full impulse power!'

Sulu laid it on. The *Enterprise* shuddered and plunged ahead.

Behind them, *Excelsior* burst out into space.

Uhura had left the channels clean enough for the *Enterprise* to know what was going on, but she was also insuring that no ship could be sent after them by radio or subspace communications.

All they had to do was elude *Excelsior*.

'*Excelsior* closing to four thousand meters, sir,' Chekov said.

'Mr Scott,' Kirk said, 'we need everything you've got now.'

'Aye, sir. Warp drive standing by.'

'Kirk!' Captain Styles' voice burst through the chatter and static. 'Kirk, you do this and you'll never sit in a captain's chair again!'

Kirk ignored him; Sulu gritted his teeth. In the background of the channel he could hear *Excelsior* preparing to apply a tractor beam.

'Warp speed, Mr Sulu,' Kirk said.

'Warp speed.'

The ship collected itself and lurched into warp.

Excelsior's communications switched to subspace.

'No way, Kirk,' Styles said. 'We'll meet you coming back! Prepare for warp speed! Stand by transwarp drive!'

Damned showoff, Sulu thought. *Excelsior* could catch the *Enterprise* with warp speed alone; with transwarp it would overshoot its quarry and, indeed, have to come back to meet it.

As the *Enterprise* struggled toward the Mutara sector, Sulu aimed the visual sensors aft. On the viewscreen, the tiny point of light that was *Excelsior* shone white behind them. Scott watched with a self-satisfied smirk. Sulu glanced at Scott, and wondered.

Excelsior's aura blue-shifted as the new ship accelerated toward them.

The blue-shift died, and the ship's light reddened as the *Enterprise* accelerated away from it. Sulu's sensors revealed *Excelsior* to be intact, but without power. He felt more than a little ambivalent about what was happening.

'*Excelsior* is adrift in space,' he said.

When Captain Styles' call for a tow came through from *Excelsior*, Uhura intercepted and damped it, feeling considerable satisfaction.

Take over Hikaru's ship, will you? she thought. You can just sit there and stew for a while.

'Commander, let me out of here!'

She ignored Heisenberg's shouts and his pounding on the door, until she was afraid he was making so much noise that someone else would come along and hear him.

'Heisenberg!' she shouted. 'Shut up!'

'Let me out! What the hell is going on?'

'If you don't be quiet I'll use this phaser on you!' She continued working. Some of the safeguards had come into play against her. Each new disruption was increasingly difficult to accomplish. Tracers had already been sent out.

She had only a few minutes left before she must flee, if she were to complete one final self-appointed task before the authorities caught up with her. She did not doubt that by this time tomorrow she would be in jail.

'Commander,' Heisenberg said, not shouting this time. 'What's going on? Maybe I can help.'

She stopped replying; she had enough already to occupy her attention.

'Commander Uhura, please, if you'd just told me – '

He sounded sincere, but she did not know him well enough to know how good an act he could put on. Besides, she needed no help. If he was looking for excitement, he would surely find it if she let him out of the closet – he would find it for a few minutes, and perhaps spend the rest of his life regretting it, or trying to make up for it. The best thing she could do for him was leave him where he was. That way, it would be clear to Starfleet that he had nothing to do with helping James Kirk steal the *Enterprise*. Heisenberg might find himself embarrassed to be locked up by an officer whose career was winding down . . . but it would be less embarrassing than a court-martial.

She had done what she could here. She set the transporter controls on automatic. Starfleet would be able to trace her by the coordinates on the console, but by then she hoped it would not matter.

'Heisenberg!' she said.

'What?' he said irritably.

'Somebody will be along to let you out in a few minutes. I'm sorry I had to lock you up, Lieutenant. It was for your own good.'

'Yeah, sure.'

Uhura stepped up on the transporter and dematerialized.

* * *

Mr Scott paused behind Sulu, at the helm. On the viewscreen, *Excelsior* dwindled and vanished behind them.

'I dinna damage thy ship permanently, lad,' Scott said softly.

Sulu glanced up. What to do to *Excelsior* had been left up to Scott, and it was a relief for Sulu to know the change was temporary. He nodded, grateful for the reassurance.

'Mr Scott,' Kirk said, 'you're as good as your word.'

'Aye, sir. The more they overthink the plumbin', the easier it is to stop up the drain.'

There are always a few flaws in a new application of technology, Sulu thought.

'Here, doctor,' Scott said to McCoy. He took his hand out of his pocket and handed McCoy a dull gray wafer. 'A souvenir, as one surgeon to another.'

McCoy accepted it. His hand shook slightly. He clearly had no idea what it was.

'I took it out o' *Excelsior*'s main transwarp computer,' Scott said. 'I knew Styles surely wouldna be able to resist trying it out.'

'Nice of you to tell me in advance,' McCoy said.

Kirk hooked his arm over the back of his command chair. 'That's what you get for missing staff meetings, doctor,' he said. He surveyed the bridge, taking in everyone. 'Gentlemen, your work today was outstanding. I intend to recommend you all for promotion.' His voice turned wry as he added, 'In whatever fleet we end up serving.'

Sulu caught Chekov's glance.

'In fleet of ore-carriers of Antares Prison Mine,' Chekov said, only loud enough for Sulu to hear.

Kirk stood and laid his hand on Sulu's shoulder.

'Best speed to Genesis, Mr Sulu,' Kirk said.

* * *

Uhura had never visited the Vulcan embassy. The stately building stood in a genteel neighborhood in the city, on a hilltop overlooking the sea. The ocean was black and silver in the dark; the moon was one night past full. Uhura materialized on the sidewalk in front of the ambassador's residence, for it was protected against penetration by unauthorized transporter beams. She walked into the pool of light around the gate and pressed the buzzer.

'Yes?' The video screen tucked discreetly into a recess in the stone pillar remained featureless. The tiny camera next to it, pointing directly at her, was surely in use.

'I would like to speak with Ambassador Sarek,' she said.

'The ambassador cannot see visitors this evening. You may make an appointment and return during reception hours.'

'But it's urgent,' Uhura said.

'What is your request?'

'It's private,' she said, remembering how reticent Spock had always been about his background and his family.

'Sarek is occupied,' the faceless voice said. 'I cannot disturb him unless I know your name and your business.'

'I am Commander Uhura, from the starship *Enterprise*,' she said. 'You may tell Ambassador Sarek that my business . . . concerns Genesis.'

'Wait,' said the emotionless voice.

She waited.

She could feel the minutes ticking away, minutes during which her trail would be traced. She knew the process well enough to be able to estimate just how quickly the trace could be done, and when that amount of time had passed she began to listen for the shining satin sound of a transporter beam. Fog rolled in from the sea. She shivered.

She touched the signal button again.

'We respectfully request that you wait.' The voice had so little inflection that she wondered if it came from a machine, and a machine poorly programmed for Standard at that.

'I'll be forced to go, soon,' she said. 'If I can't see Sarek I must leave him a message – but I'd prefer to speak to him in private. It will only take a moment!'

'Please contain your emotions.'

She wanted to kick the gatepost, that was how contained her emotions were. But she knew it would do her no good, and probably break her foot as well.

She heard a transporter beam, very near. She pressed herself against the stone gatepost, trying to conceal herself in the shadows. She could not hide from the materializing security team for long. She had considered transporting to some other location and proceeding here on foot, but they would have deduced where she was heading. They probably would have arrived before she did.

She pressed the call-button again.

'We respectfully request that you wait,' the flat voice said again.

'I'm about to be taken,' she said. 'Please tell Sarek – '

The gates swung slowly open. The distance to the residence was about a hundred meters, and the hundred meters was her distance. She plunged inside just as the security team reached her. They chased her across the dark grounds of the Vulcan embassy. She outraced them to the residence, to no avail. The door remained closed. She turned.

One of the security officers strode up the stairs and took her arm.

'Please come with us, Commander. It'll be a lot easier if you don't make any fuss.'

'I'll come with you if you'll just give me ten minutes to speak with Ambassador Sarek. It's desperately important!'

The security officer shook her head. 'I'm sorry,' she said. 'That's impossible. It's directly against orders.'

She led Uhura down the stairs and halfway back to the gate.

'Do your orders include invading the sovereign territory of an allied power?'

Sarek had crossed the distance between them and the wide steps of the embassy with such long and silent strides that no one had seen him approach. His commanding presence was accentuated by his long black cape, his drawn, intense features, his dark and deepset eyes. To Uhura he looked as if he had neither eaten nor slept since word of Spock's death reached him.

The head of the security team blushed scarlet, knowing she had overstepped her authority. She put the best face on it that she could.

'That was not our intention, sir,' she said. 'Several people from the last mission of the *Enterprise* have shown . . . evidence of severe mental difficulties. We're trying to get them to treatment. If you'll give me leave to take Commander Uhura to the hospital – '

'I will do no such thing. Commander Uhura has requested political asylum, and I have granted it. I give you leave to remove yourselves from the embassy grounds.'

The security officer stood her ground and spoke to Uhura. 'Commander, is this what you want? It could mean exile. But we might all be able to get out of this pretty clean. If I give you your ten minutes – off the record – will you come with us?'

Uhura considered it, but she had burned too many bridges today.

'No,' she said. 'I'm staying here.'

The security commander took a deep breath and let it out slowly. 'Very well.' She turned to Sarek. 'My government will contact you immediately with a formal request for extradition.'

'That is up to your government. Good evening.'

The security commander led the team from the grounds of the embassy, and the gate closed behind them.

'Thank you, sir,' Uhura said. She was shivering violently. 'I came to tell you – '

'Come inside, Commander,' he said. 'There is no need to stand in the cold and the damp . . . and in public . . . for our conversation.'

Kruge materialized on the surface of the Genesis world, near enough to the high-order life signs to track them, but far enough away that they would remain ignorant of his arrival, and he could come upon them unawares. At his side, Warrigul appeared, shivering with excitement and whining, but whining almost soundlessly. The beast had been trained to recognize potential combat and to behave in a suitable manner. If Kruge ordered Warrigul to attack, the attack would be silent.

The commander inspected the glade as his serjeant and crew member materialized behind him. The place pleased him, with its dark earth smelling of mould, the tall-stalked plants that bore drooping, leathery leaves, the heat and actinic brightness of the brilliant new sun.

Kruge pulled out his tricorder and scanned with it. He located the metallic mass around which so much activity had lately centered. It lay deeper in the glade, perhaps fifty paces. Some minor life signs surrounded it, but the signs lacked the high order that would betray the presence of the prisoners he hoped to take. Still, they had been there, so there he would go too, and pick up their trail.

He set off between the gnarled stalks of the leather plants. Warrigul padded along at his side; the serjeant and the crew member brought up the rear.

The ground began to quiver. Kruge stopped. The quake intensified, till the leather plants all swayed and thumped together with a low and hollow sound. A frond broke away from its stalk, making a heavy liquid crunching noise, and the long thick leaf thudded to the ground like some dying thing at the dead-end of its evolution.

As the earthquake reached its peak, Kruge heard a long and high-pitched hissing shriek, like nothing he had ever heard before. He started toward the noise, striding steadily across the rocking surface. He made note, for future use, of the fact that his two subordinates did not follow him till the quake ceased and he was a good twenty paces ahead of them. Only Warrigul stayed with him.

He nearly stumbled over his pet when it stopped short, took a step backward, and growled.

The thick gray-green vegetation thinned slightly, letting a sharp white column of sunlight pierce the canopy to illuminate the Federation torpedo casing that had engendered so much interest.

All around its base, like the monsters in the story of Ngarakkani, a myth of Kruge's people, writhed a great mass of sleek scaled creatures. The creatures saw him, or smelled him, or felt the vibration of his footsteps, and rose up in a many-headed tangle to hiss and scream.

Kruge heard the serjeant whisper a protective curse. Kruge smiled to himself, gestured to Warrigul to sit and stay, and strode toward the casket. He ignored all but the largest of the creatures, which had squirmed to the top of the torpedo tube and coiled there. It raised its head, weaved toward him and away, hissed, and squealed a challenge. It reached as high as his shoulder.

He stepped into its sudden strike and grasped its throat, then drew it from the slithering group and raised it up to inspect it. It twisted in his hands. Several others coiled around his boots. He ignored them, as he ignored his two

204

companions, though he was aware of everything, most particularly including the impression the scene must be making. Like the hero Ngarakkani, he would wrestle with the demons and defeat them.

The creature whipped its long lashing tail around his neck and began to squeeze. Kruge thought to unwind it from him, but its strength exceeded his. The harsh scales of its belly cut into his throat, squeezing the breath out of him. Darkness slipped slowly down around him.

The creature had tricked him into going on the defensive. He let its body tighten around him; he turned to the attack. He grabbed its throat with both his hands and squeezed. He began to twist.

He heard its bones begin to crunch. As he began to lose consciousness, its strength suddenly dissipated and it sagged away from him.

He cast the limply writhing body to the ground.

His subordinates gazed upon him with awe. He intensified their reaction by ignoring it. He *tsked* to Warrigul, who leapt up and sprang to his side, snarling at the twitching body of the creature.

Kruge pulled out his communicator.

'Torg,' he said easily, 'I have found nothing of consequence. I am continuing the search.'

David sat forlornly on a stone outcropping. His world spread out around his vantage point. It was beautiful. It was strange, and growing stranger. It was destroying itself. The vines back on Regulus I had been a warning that he should have heeded, as he should have heeded the rogue equation in the primary Genesis description. Evolution was running wild. Each species was growing and changing and aiming for its own extinction, without creating any diversity, any new forms, to take over when the old died out. Not that it much mattered. If his estimates were right, the evolutionary process would be only about half done when the more violent geological processes tore the whole planet apart. Soon after that, the sub-atomic attractions would break down, and the entire mass of what had been the Mutara Nebula, what had been Genesis and its new star system, would degenerate into a homogeneous, gaseous blob, a fiery, structureless plasma: protomatter.

His shadow stretched far down the hillside as the sun set behind him. Night approached, a dark border overwhelming day. It reached the edge of Spock's glade. The group of delicate fern-trees had grown and coarsened, turning from a patch of feathery emerald green to a smudge of bulbous gray, just in the few hours since he had left it.

He and Saavik had found a vantage point, but so far David had detected no sign of other intelligent life. His tricorder showed nothing, but it was of limited range. He had heard nothing over his communicator; if anyone else had fled *Grissom* before it was shot down, they were as reluctant to broadcast their presence to their attackers as was David. Perhaps they were listening to each other's static.

More likely, no one else had survived. But until he was sure, he was keeping his communicator set to the Federation emergency channel.

Night fell quickly on Genesis. The land below the promontory had grown too dark for David to see anyone, friendly or malevolent. Darkness obscured everything, even the field of silver ice now covering the desert, nearly surrounding the glade, and grinding away at the base of the mountain itself. David rose and trudged back up the hill. Gnarled black trees with twisting exposed roots loomed over him, and great broken slabs of stone projected from the ground. Soon he reached the narrow, hidden cave they had stumbled upon.

He stepped inside, expecting the pale steady illumination of the camp light from Saavik's kit. Instead he encountered darkness.

'Saavik – ?' he whispered, but before her name had passed his lips she had uncovered the light again. She held her phaser aimed straight at him. She let her hand fall.

'Your footsteps . . . sounded different,' she said, in explanation and apology. She put the phaser away again. 'This place is most discomforting.'

The Vulcan child whimpered. He lay huddled on a bed of tree branches, his face to the stone wall. Saavik had laid her coat over him. She turned to him, touched his shoulder, and said a word or two of comfort. David did not speak the language she was using, but he recognized it when he heard it.

'Why are you talking to him in Vulcan?' he said.

Saavik shrugged. 'I know it is not logical. I know he cannot understand, but he would not understand any other language, either, and Vulcan is . . . the first language Spock taught me.'

David glanced at the child. 'It's hard to think of him as Spock,' he said.

'He is only a part of Spock. He is the physical part. The mind exists only in potential. He might perhaps become a reasoning being, with time and teaching. He is not so different from what I was when . . . when he found me – a scavenger, illiterate certainly, almost completely inarticulate . . .'

She shivered. He sat down next to her and put his arm across her shoulders. 'You're cold.'

'I choose not to perceive cold,' she said. She did not respond to his embrace.

The child suddenly cried out. David glanced up apprehensively, for they were beneath tons of stone. The gentle quake that followed the cry left the cave undisturbed, but the child moaned in pain. Saavik slid from beneath David's arm and went to the boy's side to tuck the black cloth and her maroon jacket more closely in around him.

'Sleep,' she said softly, in Vulcan.

David pulled out his tricorder and made a quick geological scan. The results gave him no comfort.

'This planet is aging in surges,' he said.

'And Spock with it,' Saavik said quietly.

David glanced at her, then at the boy, who had flung himself over.

'My gods – ' David said.

An hour before, the child had had the appearance of a boy of eight or ten. Now he looked more like a thirteen- or fourteen-year-old.

'The child and the world are joined together,' Saavik said. She looked at David steadily, as if wishing – or daring – him to interpret events in a different way.

David had nothing to say that would give her, or himself, any comfort. He nodded.

'The Genesis wave is like a clock ticking . . . or a bomb,' he said. 'For him and for the planet. And at the rate things are going . . .'

'How long?' Saavik asked. She thought that if they must die, sooner would be less painful than later. But though she accepted the logic of that conclusion, she was not yet ready to stop fighting for every instant of life left to her.

'Days . . . maybe hours,' David said. 'It's a chaotic system, Saavik. Which variable will pass the energy threshold and cause everything to disintegrate into protomatter . . .' He shook his head. 'It's completely unpredictable.' He looked away, and then, in such a low tone that Saavik almost did not hear him, he said, 'I'm sorry.'

She nodded, accepting both his verdict and his grief.

'It will be hardest on Spock,' she said. 'Soon . . . he will feel the burning of his Vulcan blood.'

'I don't understand,' David said.

I should not have spoken of *pon farr*, she thought. It is not logical to burden David with one more thing about which he can do nothing. No one has ever found a way to free Vulcan men of the loss of emotional and physical control they endure every seventh year of their adult lives.

She was saved from having to choose between an explanation and a lie by the abrupt querulous bleating of David's tricorder.

He pulled the instrument out and frowned over the life signs.

'Whoever they are,' he said, 'they're getting closer.'

Saavik estimated one chance in a thousand that other refugees from *Grissom* caused the signs, and five to ten chances in a thousand that whoever was tracking them had other than malicious intent. In all the other possibilities, the beings who had destroyed *Grissom* sought Saavik and David in order to inflict the same fate upon them. Still . . . a chance, even if it were the chance to become a prisoner, was better odds than the certain death they faced by remaining on Genesis.

Saavik stood up. 'I will go . . .'

'No!' David said sharply. 'I'll do it. Give me your phaser.'

Saavik did not want David, untrained as he was, to go out alone on a spy mission. She glanced at the Vulcan boy. She did not want to leave him alone, either, and she particularly did not want to leave David alone with him. She realized it would be marginally less dangerous, for David, if he were to go spying on the unknown entity.

And she could see that his guilt impelled him to undertake the mission. She offered him her phaser.

He touched her hand, took the weapon, and hurried out into the darkness.

A moment later the Vulcan child cried out in agony, just before the ground began to tremble.

10

The *Enterprise* sped free through space.

Excelsior lay far behind, still waiting for a tow. The communications channels were just beginning to come clear again. Kirk wondered if Uhura was all right. She was levelheaded. When Security came to the transporter station she should simply have thrown up her hands and surrendered. But accidents could happen, and Kirk could not help but worry. Nevertheless he was grateful to her, for without her help he might have the whole fleet converging on him. The one thing he knew he could not do, even to save McCoy's sanity and Spock's soul, was fire on another Starfleet ship.

'Estimating Genesis 2·9 hours, present speed,' Sulu said.

'Can we hold speed, Scotty?' Kirk asked.

'Aye, sir, the *Enterprise* has its second wind now.'

'Scan for vessels in pursuit,' Kirk said.

'Scanning . . .' The voice was an eerie facsimile of Spock's. 'Indications negative at this time.'

Kirk turned toward the science station. McCoy, at Spock's old place, looked up and blinked.

'Did I . . . get it right . . . ?' he asked.

'You did great, Bones,' Kirk said. 'Just great.'

'Sir, Starfleet is calling *Grissom* again,' Chekov said. 'Warning about us.'

'Response?'

Chekov glanced worriedly at his console. 'Nothing. As before.'

'What's *Grissom* up to?' Kirk said. 'Will they join us, or

211

fire on us?' he said, half to himself. 'Mr Chekov, break radio silence. Send my compliments to Captain Esteban.'

'Aye, sir.'

Kirk rose and went to McCoy's side.

'How we doing?' he said.

McCoy gave him a thoughtful and slightly sardonic glance, the look of a doctor who recognizes a bedside manner when it is being inflicted upon him.

'How are *we* doing?' he said. 'Funny you should put it quite that way, Jim.' He paused, as if listening to a second conversation. '*We* are doing fine. But I'd feel safer giving him one of my kidneys than getting what's scrambled up in my brain.'

'Admiral,' Chekov said, 'there is no response from *Grissom* on any channel.'

'Keep trying, Mr Chekov. At regular intervals.'

Carol Marcus hurried up the steps of the tall Victorian house and knocked on the door. She waited apprehensively, looking back over the small town of Port Orchard. Beyond it, water sparkled slate-gray and silver in the autumn sun. The chilly salt air fluttered against the rhododendrons that grew all around the porch. They were heavily laden with the buds of next year's flowers. She had hoped to see them in bloom, in the spring. But if that had still been possible, she would not have had to come here now, all alone.

The door opened. Carol turned, still dazzled by sunlight on the sea.

'I'm terribly sorry not to arrive when I said I would – I got lost,' she said. 'I have something to give to Del March's family, but I couldn't find the address, I ended up in a park – ' She stopped suddenly. She was practically babbling. 'I'm sorry,' she said more calmly. 'I'm Carol Marcus.'

'Come in.' Vance's mother took Carol's hand and led her inside. Her voice possessed the same low, quiet timbre as Vance's. Her hand in Carol's felt frail. 'I'm Aquila Madison, and this is Terrence Laurier, Vance's father.'

Both Vance's parents were tall and slender, as he had been. Carol had expected them to be about her own age, for Vance had been only a few years older than David. But they were both considerably older than she, perhaps as much as twenty years. Aquila's close-cropped curly hair was iron-gray. Terrence wore his longer, tied at the back of his neck, but it, too, had gone salt-and-pepper from its original black.

A leaded glass door opened from the foyer. Terrence and Aquila showed Carol into their living room. It was a high-ceilinged, airy place, carpeted with antique Oriental rugs. Aquila and Terrence sat side by side on a couch in front of the tall windows. Carol sat facing them and wondered what to say to them, how to start.

'Del never did outgrow that joke,' Aquila said.

'I thought I'd written the address down wrong,' Carol said. 'Do you mean he meant people to go to a park?'

'No, my dear,' Aquila said, 'he meant people to think they'd written the address down wrong.'

'I don't understand. Where does his family live?'

'He has none,' Terrence said. 'None he'll admit to, anyway.'

'Then where did he live?'

'He lived here,' Aquila said.

'What you have to understand about Del,' Terrence said, 'is that he made up nearly everything about himself – his name, his home, the relatives that only existed in a computer file, his background before he was twelve – everything.'

'But his records,' Carol said. 'In this day and age – '

'He didn't need too much,' Terrence said. 'Not here – a

213

false address, a few counterfeit relatives and school records. He had an uncanny rapport with computers, and the voice synthesizer he built stood in for an adult as long as nobody asked to meet it face to face. He was so young no one thought to be suspicious of him.'

'As it was, he and Vance had been friends for a year before Terrence and I realized just how odd some of the odd things about him were. Vance knew, but he couldn't persuade Del to trust us.'

'How did you find out?'

'I tried to go to his house once,' Terrence said. 'I went out all fired up with the intention of either jumping down somebody's throat for never getting the kid any decent clothes, or offering to get him some myself.'

'When we finally found out where he was living – it was an abandoned house – we persuaded him to move in here. We have plenty of room.' Aquila made a quick gesture with one hand, indicating the house, the surroundings.

Carol found herself already under the spell of Terrence and Aquila's home. It had the comfortable and comforting ambiance of a place lived in by people who loved each other, of a place lived in and cared for and cared about by the same people for a long time. Vance had told her that the Madisons, Aquila's family, were some of the first black landholders in the area. Her ancestors had settled here three hundred years ago, long before the Federation, even before the region had been admitted to statehood in the previous political entity.

'Did you adopt him?'

'We wanted to. But he was terrified that if we found his people and asked them to give up legal custody, they'd make him go back. Arguing didn't do any good – '

Carol nodded. She had been in a few arguments with Del March.

' – and besides, he might have been right.'

'We didn't press him about it. We were afraid he might run away from us, too, and we were already very fond of him. Though he could be quite trying.'

'He did have a reputation for being . . . a little wild,' Carol said.

'In college, yes,' Aquila said. 'Once he was of age and didn't have to fear being shipped back to – whatever he was running from – he didn't have to be careful never to attract any attention. He did get . . . "a little wild". We were awfully worried about him for a few years. So was Vance . . .'

'I didn't get to know him as well as I should have,' Carol admitted. 'We just never got off on the right foot. He and my son David were very close, though.' Carol reached into her pack and drew out a roll of parchment. 'I think you should have this. It was Del's – he kept it on the wall of his office. And Vance made it.'

Aquila unrolled the parchment. In his strong, even calligraphy, Vance had copied seven stanzas of Lewis Carroll's 'The Hunting of the Snark'. Those were the stanzas from which Madison and March had taken the terminology for the sub-elementary particles they had described and discovered. Carol remembered the end of the poem: 'For although common Snarks do no manner of harm,/Yet I feel it my duty to say/Some are Boojums – '

Aquila and Terrence read it over. Aquila smiled, brushed her fingertips across the parchment, and read it a second time. Terrence raised his head. He and Carol looked at each other. They could no longer avoid talking about Vance.

'I loved your son,' Carol said. 'I don't know if he told you, about us – '

'Of course he did,' Aquila said. 'We were looking forward to your vacation next spring, we were hoping you would come with him when he visited.'

'I would have. He told me so much about you . . . Aquila, Terrence, he was such an extraordinary man. I'm so sorry – ' She had to stop. If she said any more, she would start to cry again.

'Carol,' Terrence said, 'what *happened* out there? We never thought Vance would work on a military project – '

'It wasn't!' Carol said. 'Oh, it wasn't! It was supposed to be just the opposite.'

She told them about the project, and the least painful version of their son's and their foster son's deaths that she could without lying to them. But it still came down to the Spacelab team's being caught in the middle of someone else's quarrel.

When she finished, her voice shaking, Terrence and Aquila were desperately holding each other's hands. Carol stood up. She did not want to inflict her own grief on them anymore, and she thought they might want to be alone.

'I wish – I wish I could have met you next spring. I'm so sorry . . . I'd better go.'

Aquila rose. 'That's foolish, Carol. It's a long trip back, and it's nearly dark.'

It *was* a long trip back. Port Orchard was a historical reference site, so it was against the rules to beam in. The only way to get here was by ferry or ground car.

'We had already planned for you to stay over,' Terrence said.

When she realized they meant it, Carol agreed, not only because of the long trip. She was grateful to them simply for making the offer, grateful to them for not hating her, and glad to be able to spend more time in the company of two people who reminded her so strongly of the person she had loved.

Saavik started awake, unable to believe she had fallen asleep, and, at the same time, unsure what had awakened

216

her. She stood up and looked out over Genesis at night. Here and there across the land faint lights, like the shadows of ghosts, drifted between twisted trees.

It is merely bioluminescence, Saavik thought. What the humans call fox-fire, and Romulans call devil-dogs. And Vulcans? What do Vulcans call it? No doubt they speak of it in chemical formulae, as no doubt so should I.

She was standing on the rocky promontory that thrust out below the cave mouth. She had come out here to keep watch, and because she was afraid her exhausted restlessness might wake the Vulcan child. Genesis had permitted itself a short respite between its convulsions, and the boy had drifted off into his first painless sleep.

Saavik's tricorder beeped again, and she realized how long David had been gone. She considered, decided to take the chance of transmitting, and opened her communicator.

'Saavik to David.' She waited. 'Come in, David.'

Only static replied. She closed the communicator quickly, more worried than she cared to admit, for worry was not only an emotion, but a completely unproductive use of energy.

A low, moaning cry came from the cave. Saavik braced herself against the inevitable ground tremor that echoed the child's pain. Rocks clattered down the hillside. Saavik sprinted for the cave entrance, dodging boulders and raising her arms to ward off a rain of gravel. The huge trees rocked and groaned.

She stopped just inside the cave. The boy huddled against the wall as if he could draw in its coolness and take upon himself a stony calm. His muscles strained so taut they quivered, though the earthquake had faded. This paroxysm had nothing to do with the convulsions of the dying world.

'Spock,' she said softly.

Startled, he flung himself around to face her.

He had changed again. Before, she could see him only as a Vulcan child. Now she could see in him her teacher, her mentor – Spock. He was younger than when she first encountered him. But he was Spock.

The fever burned in his face and in his eyes. He fought what he could not understand. He struggled to gain some control over his body and his world.

Saavik knew that he would fail.

'So it has come,' she said to him in Vulcan. She moved closer to him, speaking quietly. 'It is called *pon farr*.'

He could not understand her words, but her tone calmed him.

'Will you trust me, my mentor, my friend?' I know it is no longer you, she thought, but I will help you if I can, because of who you used to be.

The sound of his labored breathing filled the cave. She knelt beside him. She was not certain that anything she could do would ease his pain. They were not formally pledged, psychically linked.

His body was so fevered she could feel the heat, so fevered it must burn him. She touched his hand and felt him flinch as a thread of connection formed between them. She guided his right hand against hers, then put her left hand to his temple. His unformed intelligence met her trained mind, and she used the techniques he had taught her – it seemed so long ago, in another life – to soothe his fear and confusion. Saavik felt the tangled tautness of his body begin to relax.

Spock reached up and gently touched her cheek. His fingers followed the upward stroke of her eyebrow, then curved down to caress her temple, as Saavik met the gaze of his gold-flecked brown eyes.

The viewscreen wavered with the *Enterprise*'s change of state from warp speed to sub-light. The new star and its single planet spun where only a few days before the Mutara Nebula filled space with dense dust-clouds. Despite everything, Jim Kirk remained taken by the world's beauty.

'We are secured from warp speed,' Sulu said. 'Now entering the Mutara sector. Genesis approaching.'

'What about *Grissom*, Mr Chekov?' Kirk asked.

'Still no response, sir.'

Sulu increased the magnification of the viewscreen and put a bit of the ship's limited extra power to the sensors, but he could find no trace of *Grissom*, either.

'Bones,' Kirk said tentatively, 'can you give me a quadrant bi-scan?'

He glanced back at McCoy. The doctor hunched unmoving over Spock's station. After a moment he spread his hands in frustration and defeat.

'I think you just exceeded my capability . . .'

'Never mind, Bones.' Kirk gestured to Chekov. 'Mr Chekov – '

'Yes, Admiral.' Chekov joined McCoy and took over.

'Sorry,' McCoy said shakily.

'Your time is coming, Doctor. Mr Sulu, proceed at full impulse power.'

'Full impulse power,' Sulu said.

'There is no sign of ship, Admiral,' Chekov said. 'Not *Grissom*, not . . . anything.'

'Very well, Mr Chekov. Continue scanning.'

Kirk rose and joined McCoy.

'You all right?' he asked softly.

'I don't know, Jim,' McCoy said. 'He's . . . gone, again. I can feel him, it's almost as if I can talk to him. But then he slips away. For longer and longer, and when he . . . comes back . . . my sense of him is weaker.'

Kirk frowned. McCoy had not added that he, too, felt weaker, but he did not have to. It was obvious to Kirk that the doctor's strength was slowly draining away.

219

'Keep hold of him, Bones,' he said. 'Keep hold of yourself. We're almost there.'

Saavik smoothed Spock's tangled hair. The fever had broken, the compulsion had left him. He slept, and he would live. She wondered if she had done him a kindness by saving his life. He was still completely vulnerable to the convulsions of Genesis, which would continue to torture him.

She sighed. She had done what she thought was right.

She was terribly worried about David. He should have returned long ago. She drew out her communicator and opened it, but on second thought put it away. Spock would sleep for some time, so she could safely leave him alone. It would be better for all of them if Saavik sought David without using her communicator and advertising their presence. She rose and started for the cave entrance.

She heard something – footsteps. This cursed world made sounds difficult to identify accurately, a task she would have found ridiculously easy anywhere else. Hoping it was David but believing it was not, she pressed herself against the cave wall.

A great dark shape filled the entrance. The tall and massive humanoid figure carried a sensor that sought out his quarry.

A Klingon – !

While he still stood blinking in the darkness, Saavik launched herself at him. If she could overcome him and escape into the woods with Spock –

Roaring with fury, he spun, knocking her back against the cave wall. His bones were so heavy and his muscles so thick that she could barely get a grasp on him, even on his wrist. He flung his arms around her and began to squeeze, shouting angrily in a dialect of Klingon that she did not understand. She struggled, pressing her hands upward.

220

Klingons had different points of vulnerability than humans, who were different again from Vulcans and Romulans. She broke his grasp for an instant and smashed her fists into the sides of his jaw. He staggered backward, dazed by the transmission of energy from the maxilla into the skull.

Saavik heard laughter.

Two of his comrades had followed him into the cave. They stood beside Spock, who sat watching, half-awake and confused. Both were armed; they held their weapons aimed at Spock. They taunted her – again in a dialect she did not know, but the meaning was clear: Get him, little one, beat him if you can, and we will laugh at him for the rest of the trip. Beat him and lose anyway, because we hold your friend hostage.

She stepped back, spreading her hands in a gesture of surrender.

Enraged by the others' mockery, her opponent rushed at her with a raging curse. He struck her a violent backhand blow that flung her against the cave wall.

The impact knocked her breath from her. She sagged against the stone, her knees collapsing. She pressed herself against the cave wall, barely managing to hold herself upright.

Her opponent snapped a harsh reply to his laughing companions, dragged Saavik's wrists behind her back, twisted her arms, and pushed her forward out of the cave. The other two pulled Spock to his feet and roughly hurried him outside.

Saavik stumbled down the rocky trail to the promontory. Dawn lay scarlet over Genesis, turning the trees a deep and oppressive maroon. Overnight the thick gnarled trunks had sprouted tens of thousands of spindly, barbed branches that flailed at the people passing beneath them. A thorn caught in Saavik's shirt and tore it. Another

221

tangled in her hair. She tried to look back, to see if Spock were all right. With only the shroud to wrap around him, he was terribly vulnerable. But her captor forced her faster down the trail. The branches thrashed and clattered, as if whipped by a violent wind.

But there was no wind.

Even the stones had changed. The sharp thrust of the promontory was rounded, smoothed, and darkened with a patina of age that implied a thousand years of erosion. A Klingon officer stood upon it in an attitude of possession, gazing out over the forest below. A creature stood at his side.

His hunting party flung Saavik and Spock roughly down behind him.

Saavik lay still, clenching her fingers in the dirt and struggling to control her anger. If she surrendered to the madness now, she could only bring death to them all.

The commander turned slowly.

'So!' he said. He spoke in Standard, but his faint accent did nothing to disguise his impatience. 'I have come a long way for the power of Genesis. And what do I find?'

He gestured sharply as Saavik pushed herself to her knees.

The rest of his landing party dragged David forward and shoved him down. He sprawled on the stone beside Saavik. She gasped at the dark bruises on his face, the blood on his mouth, the scratches and welts on his arms and hands. He looked ashamed. She wanted to touch him, she wanted to protect him from any more pain, but she knew if she betrayed any concern for him their captors would use it against them.

'What do I find?' the commander said again. 'Three children! Ill-bred children, at that. It's only what one might expect of humans, but you, and you – ' He glared at Saavik, then at Spock, and then he laughed. 'So much for Vulcan restraint,' he said.

His creature echoed his laugh with a growling whine.

Saavik rose to her feet, very slowly, her rage so great she trembled.

'My lord,' she said. Her voice was so calm, so cold, that it astonished her. 'We are survivors of a doomed expedition. This planet will destroy itself in hours. The Genesis experiment is a failure.'

'A failure!' The commander laughed with every evidence of sincere good humor. 'The most powerful destructive force ever created, and you call it a *failure* – ?' He took one step forward. Saavik had to raise her head to look at him. He was head and shoulders taller than she. 'What would you consider a success, child?' He chuckled. 'You will tell me the secrets of Genesis.'

'I have no knowledge of them,' Saavik said.

'Then I hope pain is something you enjoy,' he said.

Saavik was accustomed to being taken at her word, but she knew she could not hope for that courtesy from the enemy commander. Genesis had taken six primary investigators plus a laboratory full of support personnel eighteen months of solid work and all their lifetimes of experience to create. Even if Saavik had belonged to the team, she would not be able to say, in a few simple words, how to recreate their project.

The Klingon serjeant hurried forward with an open communicator. The commander cut off his words.

'I ordered no interruptions!'

'Sir!' said a voice from the communicator. 'Federation starship approaching!'

Saavik and David caught each other's glance, hardly daring to hope.

The commander glared at them, as if they had called the

starship to them at this particular moment, simply to frustrate him.

'Bring me up!' he said. And to his landing party, 'Guard them well.'

He and his creature vanished in a dazzle of light.

Kruge reformed on board his ship and strode to the bridge. Torg saluted him and gestured to the viewport.

'Battle alert!' Kruge said. As the bridge erupted into activity around him, he folded his arms across his chest and observed the Constellation-class Federation starship that sailed slowly toward him. He smiled.

It was his, as firmly in his possession as the three child-hostages on the surface of Genesis.

Warrigul pressed up against his leg. Kruge reached down and scratched his creature's head. Warrigul hissed with pleasure.

The *Enterprise*'s search for *Grissom* continued fruitlessly. Kirk wondered if, somehow, it had finished its work and headed back to Earth. Travelling at warp speed, they might easily have missed it. No doubt David was back home already, having coffee with Saavik. Or laughing with his mother about that lunatic James Kirk, rushing off in a stolen ship on a self-imposed mission that no one else could understand. Kirk pressed the heels of his hands against his eyes.

'Sir – ' Chekov said.

'What is it, commander?'

'I'd swear something was there, sir . . .' Chekov peered at his instruments, which had flickered with the sensor-signature of a small vessel, but now stubbornly continued to show absolutely nothing. 'But . . . I might have imagined it . . .'

'What did you see, Chekov?'

'For one instant . . . Scout class vessel.'

'Could be *Grissom*,' Kirk said thoughtfully. 'Patch in the hailing frequency.'

Chekov did so, and nodded to Kirk.

'*Enterprise* to *Grissom*,' Kirk said. 'Come in, *Grissom*. Come in, please.'

'Nothing on scanner, sir,' Chekov said.

'Short range scan, Mr Chekov. Give it all the focus you've got. On screen, Mr Sulu.'

Chekov focused the beam, and Sulu switched the viewscreen, which showed nothing but empty space.

On the bridge of his fighter, Commander Kruge listened to the Federation ship's unguarded transmission:

'I say again, *Enterprise* to *Grissom*. Admiral Kirk calling Captain Esteban, Lieutenant Saavik, Dr Marcus. Come in, *Grissom!*'

'Report status,' Kruge said, keeping his voice offhand, but secretly rejoicing. Kirk! Admiral James T. Kirk, and the *Enterprise*! If he returned home having vanquished the legendary Federation hero, and bearing Genesis as well – !

'We are cloaked,' said Torg. 'Enemy closing on impulse power, range five thousand.'

'Good.' Kruge stroked the smooth scales of Warrigul's crest and murmured to his creature, 'This is the turn of luck I have been waiting for . . .'

'Range three thousand,' Maltz said.

'Steady. Continue on impulse power.'

'Yes, sir!'

Kruge noted Torg's intensity, Maltz's uneasiness.

'Range two thousand.'

'Stand by, energy transfer to weapons. At my command!'

'Within range, sir.'

Kruge turned slightly. After a moment, his new gunner raised his head and froze, noting Kruge's attention.

225

'Sight on target, gunner,' Kruge said. 'Disabling only. Understood?'

'Understood *clearly*, sir!'

'Range one thousand, closing.'

'Wait,' Kruge said, as the *Enterprise* loomed larger in his viewport. 'Wait . . .'

At the same time, Kirk studied the enhanced image on the viewscreen of the *Enterprise*.

'There,' he said. 'That distortion. The shimmering area.'

'Yes, sir,' Sulu said. 'It's getting larger as we close in – '

' – And *it's* closing on *us*. Your opinion, Mr Sulu?'

'I think it's an energy form, sir.'

'Yes. Enough energy to hide a ship, wouldn't you say?'

'A cloaking device!'

'Red alert, Mr Scott!' Kirk said.

'Aye, sir.'

The Klingon vessel must have beamed someone on board. Chekov would have had only a second or two to catch a glimpse of the ship. If his attention had wandered for a moment . . .

'Mr Chekov,' Kirk said, 'good work.'

'Thank you, Admiral.'

The lights dimmed. The Klaxon alarms sounded: a bit redundant, Kirk thought, since every living being on the ship was right here on the bridge.

'Mr Scott, all power to the weapons system.'

'Aye, sir.'

McCoy stood up uneasily. 'No shields?'

'If my guess is right, they'll have to de-cloak before they can fire.'

'May all your guesses be right,' McCoy said.

Kirk tried not to think what the appearance of this disguised ship, in place of *Grissom*, must mean.

226

'Mr Scott: two photon torpedoes at the ready. Sight on the center of the mass.'

'Aye, sir.'

The *Enterprise* sailed closer and closer to an indefinable spot in space, more perceptible as *different* if one looked at it from the corner of the eye. The ship was very nearly upon it when –

Sulu saw it first. 'Klingon fighter, sir – '

The Klingon craft appeared before them as a spidery sketch, transparent against the stars, quickly solidifying.

' – Arming torpedoes!'

'Fire, Mr Scott!'

The torpedoes streaked toward the Klingon ship. It was as if their impact solidified the ship while simultaneously blasting a section of it away. The fighter tilted up and back with the momentum of the attack. It began to tumble.

'Good shooting, Scotty,' Kirk said.

'Aye. Those two hits should stop a horse, let alone a bird.'

'Shields up, Mr Chekov,' Kirk said.

'Aye, sir.' He accessed the automation center and tried to call up the shields.

Nothing happened.

'Sir,' he said in concern, 'shields are unresponsive.'

Scott immediately turned to his controls, and Kirk turned to Scott.

'Scotty – ?'

With a subvocal curse, Scott bent closer over his console. 'The automation system's overloaded. I dinna expect ye to take us into combat, ye know!'

On the smoke-clouded bridge of his wounded ship, Kruge stumbled over a dim shape and fell to his knees. He touched the shape in the darkness –

Warrigul.

His beast, which he had owned since he was a youth and

227

Warrigul only a larva, lay dying. Ignoring the chaos of the damaged bridge, Kruge stroked the spines of Warrigul's crest. His pet responded with a weak, whimpering growl, convulsed once, and relaxed into death.

Kruge rose slowly, his hands clenched at his sides.

Torg's voice barely penetrated the white waves of rage that pounded in his ears.

'Sir – the cloaking device is destroyed!'

'Never mind!' Kruge shouted. There would be no more hiding from this Federation butcher. 'Emergency power to the thrusters!'

'Yes, my lord.'

The lights on the bridge further dimmed as the thrusters drained the small ship's power, but the tumbling slowed and ceased. The ship stabilized.

'Lateral thrust!'

Torg obeyed, bringing the ship around to face the *Enterprise* again.

'Stand by, weapons!'

Jim Kirk watched the Klingon craft come round to bear on his ship.

'The shields, Scotty!'

'I canna do it!'

'Ready torpedoes – ' The order came too late. The enemy ship fired at nearly point-blank range. The *Enterprise* had neither time nor room to manoeuver. 'Torpedoes coming in!' Kirk cried, bracing himself.

The flare of the explosion sizzled through the sensors. The viewscreen flashed, then darkened. The ship bucked violently. Kirk lost his hold and fell. The illumination failed.

'Emergency power!'

The *Enterprise* responded valiantly, but the bridge lights returned at less than half intensity. McCoy helped Kirk struggle up.

'I'm all right, Bones.' He lunged back to his place. 'Prepare to return fire! Mr Scott – transfer power to the phaser banks!'

'Oh, god, sir, I dinna think I can – '

'What's *wrong*?'

'They've knocked out the damned automation center!' He smashed his fist against the console. 'I ha' no control over anythin'!'

'Mr Sulu!'

Sulu's gesture of complete helplessness, and Chekov's agitated shake of the head, sent Kirk sagging back into his chair.

'So . . .' he said softly. 'We're a sitting duck.'

He watched the enemy fighter probe slowly closer.

Kruge, in his turn, watched the silent, powerful Federation ship drift before him.

'Emergency power recharge,' Torg said, 'forty percent . . . fifty percent. My lord, we are able to fire – '

Kruge raised his hand, halting Torg's preparations for another salvo.

'Why hasn't he finished us?' Kruge said. He suspected Kirk wanted to humiliate him first. 'He outguns me ten to one, he has four hundred in crew, to my handful. Yet he sits there!'

'Perhaps he wishes to take you prisoner.'

Kruge scowled at Torg. 'He knows I would die first.'

'My lord,' Maltz said, from the communications board, 'the enemy commander wishes a truce to confer.'

'A truce!' Kruge's training and better judgment restrained his wish to fire, provoke a response, end the battle quickly and cleanly. 'Put him on screen,' he said more calmly, then, to Torg. 'Study him well.'

The transmission from the *Enterprise*, enhanced and interpreted, formed Kirk's three-dimensional image in the area in front of and slightly below Kruge's command post.

'This is Admiral James T. Kirk, of the USS *Enterprise*.'

'Yes,' Kruge said, 'the Genesis commander himself.'

'By violation of the treaty between the Federation and the Klingon Empire, your presence here is an act of war. You have two minutes to surrender your crew and your vessel, or we will destroy you.'

Kruge delayed any reply to the arrogant demand. Kirk was neither ignorant nor a fool. He must know that officers of the Klingon Empire did not surrender. And no one with a reputation like his could be a fool. Was he trying to provoke another attack, so he could justify destroying his enemy or increase his valor in the defeat? Or was there something more?

'He's hiding something,' Kruge said. 'We may have dealt him a more serious blow than I thought.'

Torg looked at him intently, trying to trace his superior's thoughts. 'How can you tell that, my lord?'

'I trust my instincts,' Kruge said easily. He toggled on the transmitter. 'Admiral Kirk, this is your opponent speaking. Do not lecture me about treaty violations, Admiral. The Federation, in creating an ultimate weapon, has turned itself into a gang of interstellar criminals. It is not I who will surrender. It is you.' He paused to let that sink in, then gambled all or nothing. 'On the planet below, I have taken prisoner three members of the team that developed your doomsday weapon. If you do not surrender immediately, I will execute them. One at a time. They are enemies of galactic peace.'

Listening to the transmission with disbelief, Kirk pushed himself angrily from his chair. '*Who is this?* How dare you – !'

'Who *I* am is not important, Admiral. That I have *them*, is.' He smiled, baring his teeth. 'I will let you speak to them.'

On the surface of Genesis, far below, the landing party

230

listened via communicator to the battle and to the interchange between Kirk and Kruge. Saavik listened, too, buoyed by the appearance of the *Enterprise*, disturbed by its failure instantly to disable and capture the Klingon ship. A Klingon fighter was no match for a vessel of the Constellation class. Saavik could only conclude that Kirk had come back to Genesis before his ship was fully repaired. She glanced at Spock, who sat wrapped in his black cloak and in exhaustion that was nearly as palpable. The reports *Grissom* had sent back must have brought James Kirk here. She then glanced at James Kirk's son, and saw the hope in David's bruised face. She hoped, in her turn and for all three of them, that he would not be disappointed.

The Klingon commander snapped an order. The serjeant in charge of the landing party replied with a quick assent and motioned to his underlings. They dragged Saavik, David, and Spock to their feet. Spock staggered. His face showed hopeless pain. The planet's agony, which came to him without warning and frequently – more and more frequently as the hours passed – tortured him brutally.

The serjeant thrust his communicator into Saavik's face. His meaning was clear: she must speak. She tried to decide if it would be better to reassure Admiral Kirk that his son and his friend were alive, or if she should maintain her silence and by doing so withhold the Klingons' proof that they had prisoners.

The serjeant said a single word and Saavik felt her arms being wrenched upward behind her back. She called on all her training. Though the leverage forced her on tiptoe, she neither winced nor cried out. She stared coldly at the serjeant.

He clenched the fingers of his free hand into a fist. Saavik did not flinch from him. He gazed at her steadily, then smiled very slightly and made a silent motion toward David. The crew member restraining him twisted his arms pitilessly. David gasped. The serjeant prodded Saavik in the ribs. He did not need to be able to speak Standard to indicate that he would hurt either or both of her friends until she did his bidding. She closed her eyes and took a deep breath. She could not bear to bring them any more pain.

'Admiral,' she said, 'this is Saavik.'

'Saavik – ' Kirk hesitated. 'Is . . . David with you?'

'Yes. He is. As is . . . someone else. A Vulcan scientist of your acquaintance.'

'This Vulcan – is he alive?'

'He is not himself,' Saavik said. 'But he lives. He is subject to rapid aging, like this unstable planet.'

Before Kirk could answer, the serjeant turned to David and thrust the communicator at him.

'Hello, sir. It's David.'

'David – ' Kirk said. His relief caught in his voice, then he recovered himself. 'Sorry I'm late,' he said.

'It's okay. I should have known you'd come. But Saavik's right – this planet is unstable. It's going to destroy itself in a matter of hours.'

'David . . .' Kirk sounded shocked, and genuinely sorrowful for his son's disappointment. 'What went wrong?'

'I went wrong,' David said.

The silence stretched so long that Saavik wondered if the communication had been severed.

'David,' Kirk said, 'I don't understand.'

'I'm sorry, sir, it's too complicated to explain right now. Just don't surrender. Genesis doesn't work! I can't believe they'll kill us for it – '

The serjeant snatched the communicator from David.

'David – !' Kirk shouted. But when David tried to reply,

232

his captor wrenched him back so hard he nearly fainted. Saavik took one instinctive step toward him, but she, too, was restrained, and for the moment she had no way to resist.

The serjeant permitted them to listen to the remainder of Kruge's conversation with Admiral Kirk.

'Your young friend is mistaken, Admiral,' Kruge said. His voice tightened with the emotions of anger and desire for revenge. 'I meant what I said. And now, to show my intentions are sincere . . . I am going to kill one of my prisoners.'

'Wait!' Kirk cried. 'Give me a chance – '

Saavik did not understand the order Kruge next gave to his serjeant – that is, she did not understand the words themselves, which were of a dialect she did not know. But the intent was terribly clear. The serjeant looked at Spock, at David, at Saavik.

His gaze and Saavik's locked.

The serjeant had been vastly impressed by his captain's offer of final honor to his gunner, and vastly horrified by the gunner's inability to accept the offer and carry out the deed. He recognized in Saavik a prideful being. As Kruge had shown magnanimity to the gunner, the serjeant would show it to this young halfbreed Vulcan. He would give her the chance to maintain her honor at her death.

He drew his dagger. The toothed and recurved edges flashed in the piercing light of the sun. He raised it up; he offered it to her.

Saavik knew what he expected of her. She understood why he was doing it, and she even understood that it was meant as a courtesy.

But she had never taken any oath to follow his rules.

She raised her hands, preparing to grasp the ritual dagger. She could feel the attention of every member of the landing party. They were so fascinated, so impressed

233

by their serjeant's tact and taste, that they had nearly forgotten their other captives. Saavik would take the knife – then lay about her with it, distract them, cry 'Run!' to her friends, and hope they had the wit to take the chance she offered them. With any luck at all she might escape, too, in the confusion, but that matter was quite secondary to her responsibility to David and to Spock.

She reached into herself to find the anger that had been building up for so long, the berserk rage that would give her a moment's invincibility. The fantastically recurved blade of the knife twisted in her vision. Her attention focused to a point as coherent and powerful as a laser. She touched the haft of the knife.

'No!' David cried. He flung himself forward, breaking out of the inattentive hold, and plunged between Saavik and the serjeant.

It took Saavik a fatal instant to understand what had happened.

With a snarl of rage, the serjeant plunged the dagger into David's chest.

'David, no – !'

David cried out and collapsed. Saavik went down with him, breaking his fall. She held him, trying to stanch the blood that pulsed between her fingers. She could not withdraw the knife, for it was designed to do far more damage coming out than going in. David grasped weakly at the hilt and Saavik pushed his hands away.

'David, lie still – '

If she could just have a moment to help him, a moment to try to meld her consciousness with his, she could give him some of her strength, some of her ability at controlling the body. She knew she could keep him alive.

'David, stop fighting me – '

He was very weak. He stared upward. She did not think he could see her. Her own vision blurred. He tried to

234

speak. He failed. She struggled to make contact with him, to touch his mind, to save him.

'Help me!' she cried to the landing party. 'Don't you understand, you can never replicate Genesis without him!'

If any of them understood her, they did not believe her. The Klingon commander did not rescind the death sentence he had ordered. Saavik felt David slipping away from her.

'David – '

He reached up. His hand was covered with blood. He touched her cheek.

'I love you,' he said. 'And I wish . . .'

Saavik had to bend down to hear him, his voice was so weak.

'I wish we could have seen Vance's dragons . . .'

'Oh, David,' Saavik whispered, 'David, love, there are no dragons.'

Three of the landing party dragged her from him.

Saavik's fury erupted without focus or plan. The madness took her. She flung herself backwards, turning. She clamped her hands around the throat of the nearest of her captors. He gagged and choked and clawed at her hands. She perceived the blows and shouts but they had no effect on her. She perceived the limpid hum of a phaser and felt the beam rake over her body. Her fingers tightened. The phaser whined at a higher pitch. Hands clawed at her, trying to break her grip, failing.

The phaser howled yet a third time. The sound penetrated Saavik's blue-white rage, searing her mind from cerebrum to spinal cord.

She collapsed to the rocky ground and lost consciousness.

11

Pale and tense, Jim Kirk pushed himself from the command seat. His fingernails dug into the armrests and he sought desperately for time. The channel from the surface of Genesis spun confused voices around him, but the Klingon commander smiled coolly from the viewscreen, impervious and confident.

'Commander!' Kirk shouted.

'My name,' his opponent said, 'is Kruge. I think it *is* important, Admiral, that you know who will defeat you.'

'At least one of those prisoners is an unarmed civilian! The others are members of a scientific expedition. Scientific, Kruge!'

'"Unarmed"?' Kruge chuckled. 'Your unarmed civilian and your scientific expedition stand upon the surface of the most powerful weapon in the universe, which they have created!'

'Kruge, don't do something you'll regret!'

'You do not understand, Admiral Kirk. Since you doubt my sincerity, I must prove it to you. My order will not be rescinded.' He glanced aside and snapped a question to someone out of Kirk's view.

Kirk heard the beginning of a reply.

A cry of agony and despair cut off the words.

'David!' Jim shouted. 'Saavik!'

He could make out nothing but the sounds of struggle, anger, and confusion. The transmission jumped and buzzed – Kirk recognized the interference of a phaser beam, reacting with the communicator. He was shaking with helplessness. The uncertainty stretched on so long that he thought for an instant of rushing to the transporter room and beaming into . . . into whatever was happening on the surface of Genesis. But even in his desperation he knew that he would be too late.

Commander Kruge watched, harsh satisfaction on his face.

Finally the voice transmission from Genesis cleared to silence.

'I believe I have a message for you, Admiral,' Kruge said, and spoke a command to his landing party.

Again there was a delay. Jim could feel the sweat trickling down his sides. A voice came from Genesis, but it was one of impatient command in a dialect of Kruge's people that Kirk had never even heard before.

'Saavik . . . David . . .' Kirk said.

'Admiral . . .'

Even when Saavik was angry – and Kirk had seen her angry, though she might have denied it – her voice was level and cool. But now it trembled, and it was full of grief.

'Admiral, David – ' Her voice caught. 'David is dead.'

Kirk plunged forward as if he could strangle Kruge over the distance and the vacuum that separated them by using the sheer force fury gave his will.

'Kruge, you spineless coward! You've killed – my – son!'

At first Kruge did not react, and then he closed his eyes slowly and opened them again, in an expression of triumph and satisfaction.

'I have two more prisoners, Admiral,' he said. 'Do you wish to be the cause of their deaths, too? I will arrange that their fate come to them . . . somewhat more slowly.' He let that sink in. 'Surrender your vessel!'

'All right.' He became aware of McCoy, at his side. 'Give me a minute, to inform my crew.'

237

Kruge shrugged, magnanimity in his gesture. But his tone reeked of contempt. 'I offer you two minutes, Admiral Kirk,' he said, enjoying the irony of turning James Kirk's commands back upon him. 'For you, and your gallant crew.'

His communication faded. Kirk sat staring at the viewscreen as the image scattered and reformed into space, stars, the great blue curve of Genesis below, and the marauding Klingon fighter.

'Jim,' McCoy said. He took Kirk by the shoulder and gripped it, shaking him gently, trying to pull him back out of despair. 'Jim!'

Kirk recoiled from his help. He stared at him for a moment, hardly seeing him, hardly aware anymore of the reason he had come to this godforsaken spot in space. He knew that if he did surrender, he would sacrifice the lives of all his friends. And he realized, suddenly, that if he gave Kruge the opportunity to tap into the *Enterprise*'s Genesis records, the information would lead inevitably to Carol Marcus. Kruge might be bold, but he was not a fool; he could not threaten Carol directly. But Kirk would be a fool to discount the Empire's network of spies, assassins . . . and kidnappers.

'Mr Sulu . . .' he said. 'What is the crew complement of Commander Kruge's ship?'

'It's about – ' Sulu had been thinking of a smart and angry kid, a young man on the brink of realizing an enormous potential, his life drained out into the world he had tried to make. Sulu forced his voice to be steady; he forced his attention to the question he had been asked. 'A dozen, officers and crew.'

'And some are on the planet . . .' Kirk said. He faced his friends, who had risked so much to accompany him. 'I swear to you,' he said, 'we're not finished yet.'

'We never have been, Jim,' McCoy said.

238

'Sulu, you and Bones to the transporter room. Scott, Chekov, with me. We have a job to do.' He slapped the comm control. '*Enterprise* to Commander, Klingon fighter. Stand by to board this ship on my signal.'

'No tricks, Kirk,' Kruge replied. 'You have one minute.'

'No tricks,' Kirk said. 'I'm . . . looking forward to meeting you. Kirk out.'

Kirk gathered with Chekov and Scott at the science officer's station and opened a voice and optical channel direct to the computer.

'Computer, this is Admiral James T. Kirk. Request security access.'

He experienced a moment of apprehension that Starfleet might have blocked the deepest levels of the computer. A bright light flashed in his eyes, taking a pattern for a retina scan. No: no one in Starfleet had expected him to commit an act as outrageous and absurd as stealing his own ship. The order to him to sit still and do nothing, though it would cost the life of Leonard McCoy, was deemed to be sufficient protection for the *Enterprise*. They had not bothered to protect the ship in any more subtle way. If they had, no doubt the ship's computer would have begun shouting 'Thief, thief!' the moment he stepped on board.

'Identity confirmed,' the computer said.

'Computer . . .' Kirk said. He took a deep breath, and continued without pause. 'Destruct sequence one. Code one, one-A . . .'

As Kirk recited the complex code, he ignored Scott's stunned glance. The only way he was going to get through this was by keeping it at a distance, by making the decision and carrying it out with no second-guessing.

Kirk finished his part of the process and stood aside.

Chekov stepped forward, his expressive face somber.

'Computer,' he said slowly, 'this is Commander Pavel Andreievich Chekov, acting science officer.'

The computer scanned Chekov's dark eyes and recognized him.

Was it Kirk's imagination, or did the identification take longer for Chekov than it had for Kirk? It must be his apprehension and his nerves and his sense of the clock ticking away that last minute. The computer was merely a machine, a machine with a human voice and some decision-making capabilities, but it was not designed to be self-aware. It could not possess intimations of mortality. It would not delay identifying Chekov to give itself a few more moments of existence, nor would the injuries begun by Kirk's code slow it in any fashion perceptible to a human being. The end would be quick and clean, a matter of microseconds.

'Destruct sequence two, code one, one-A, one-B . . .'

The computer was merely a machine; the ship was merely a machine.

'Mr Scott,' Kirk said, his voice absolutely level.

'Admiral – ' Scott said in protest.

'Mister Scott – !'

Scott could stop the sequence. Kirk experienced a mad moment when he hoped the engineer would do just that.

Scott looked away, faced the computer's optical scan, and identified himself. 'Computer, this is Commander Montgomery Scott, chief engineering officer.' The light flashed white, bringing the lines of strain on his face into sharp relief.

'Identification verified.'

'Destruct sequence three, code one-B, two-B, three . . .'

'Destruct sequence completed and engaged. Awaiting final code for one-minute countdown.'

If the computer were merely a machine, if the ship were

merely a machine, how could Jim Kirk perceive grief in its voice? It was just that, he knew: his perception, not objective reality. He and Spock had had many arguments about the difference between the two. They had come to no agreement, no conclusions.

The last word remained James Kirk's.

'Code zero,' he said. 'Zero, zero destruct zero . . .'

This time there was no delay.

'One minute,' the computer said. 'Fifty-nine seconds. Fifty-eight seconds. Fifty-seven seconds . . .'

'Let's get the hell out of here,' Jim Kirk said angrily.

On the bridge of the fighter, Torg felt his commander's gaze raking him and the heavily armed boarding party. Torg understood the compliment his commander offered him by permitting him to lead the force. Maltz alone would remain behind with Kruge. Admiring his commander's restraint, Torg wondered if he himself, in Kruge's position, would have the strength to let another lead the assault. By forgoing that perquisite, Kruge would gain the more important prize of seeing Kirk brought to him, thoroughly beaten, a prisoner.

Torg felt some slight apprehension about the size of his force relative to the crew of a ship such as the *Enterprise*. He wondered if the two remaining hostages would truly secure the submissive behavior of the enemy. He knew that if the positions were reversed, Kruge would sacrifice two hostages without hesitation.

'They do outnumber us, my lord – ' Torg thought to point out that even a few rebels among the crew could make significant trouble.

His crest flaring, Kruge turned on him. 'We are Klingons! When you have taken the ship, when you control it, I will transfer my flag to it and we will take Genesis from their own memory banks!'

'Yes, my lord,' Torg said. Kruge delivered into his

hands the disposition of any rebels. Torg would deliver
the ship into the hands of his commander.

'To the transport room,' Kruge said. He saluted Torg.
'Success!'

The intense thrill of excitement nearly overwhelmed the
younger officer. No one had ever spoken to him in such a
high phase of the language before.

'Success!' he replied. As he ordered his team into
formation and away he heard Kruge contact the Federation admiral again. The conversation followed him via the
ship's speakers.

'Kirk, your time runs out. Report!'

'Kirk to Commander Kruge. We are energizing transporter beam . . .'

Torg arranged his party in a wedge, with himself at the
apex.

'Transporter, stand by,' Kruge said.

'Ready, my lord.' Torg grasped the stock of an assault
gun, a blaster, the weapon he particularly favored over a
phaser.

'. . . Now.'

The beam spun Torg into a whirlwind that swept him
away.

As his body reformed aboard the *Enterprise*, he held his
weapon at the ready. But no rebels waited to resist him.

No one waited at all. Over the speakers, a soft and
rhythmic voice kept the ship's time. An alien custom, no
doubt, as inexplicable and distracting as most alien customs.

'Forty-one seconds. Forty seconds . . .'

Torg descended from the transporter platform. He was
prepared for an attack, even more than a surrender. He
was not prepared for . . . nothing.

He led his force from the transporter room and toward
the bridge. By the time he reached it, the eerie silence

beneath the computer voice had drawn his nerves as taut as his grip on his blaster.

The bridge, too, lay empty and quiet.

'Twenty-two seconds. Twenty-one seconds . . .'

Torg drew out his communicator.

'It's a trap,' one of the team members said. The fear in his voice infected every one of them.

Torg silenced him with a poisonous glance that promised severe discipline when the time was right. He opened a channel to his commander.

'My lord, the ship appears to be . . . deserted.'

'How can this be?' Kruge said. 'They are hiding!'

'Perhaps, sir. But the bridge appears to be run by computer. It is the only thing speaking.'

'What? Transmit!'

Torg aimed the directional microphone at the computer speaker, which continued its rhythmic chant. 'Six seconds. Five seconds . . .'

'Transport! Maltz, quickly, lock onto them – !'

The alarm in Kruge's voice terrified Torg, but he had no time to react.

'Two seconds. One second.'

The transport beam trembled at the edge of his perceptions –

'Zero,' the computer said, very softly.

– but it reached him too late.

Saavik lay on the cold, rocky hillside. The effects of the stun beams were fading, yet she was barely able to move. The madness had possessed her, and now she must pay its price. Her rage had drained her of strength. David's death had drained her of will. His blood stained her hands.

She forced herself to rise. The young Vulcan watched her, curious and impassive. His form was that of Spock, but the Spock she had known had never been indifferent to exhaustion or to grief. She stood up. David's body was only a few paces away.

The serjeant snapped an order at her. She understood its sense, but chose to ignore it. The crew member she had tried to throttle leaped forward and struck her, knocking her down. Even the sound of his laughter was not enough to anger her now.

She staggered back up. The guard flung her to the ground again. Saavik lay still for a moment, digging her fingers into the cold earth, feeling the faint vibrations of the disintegrating world.

She pushed herself to her feet for a third time. The guard clenched his fist. But before he could attack, the serjeant grabbed his arm. The two glared at each other. The serjeant won the contest. Neither moved as Saavik took the few steps to David's body and knelt beside him. She put her hand to his pallid cheek.

When David was near, she had always been aware of the easy and excitable glow of his mind. Now it had completely dissolved. He was gone. All she could ever do for him was watch his body through the night, as she had watched Peter and as she had watched Spock. On the *Enterprise* the ritual had been only that. But on this world his body was vulnerable to predators, indigenous or alien.

Saavik gazed into the twilight. If the *Enterprise* were in standard orbit, she should be able to locate it as a point of light in the sky. Working out the equations in her head forced her to collect her mind and concentrate her attention. When she was done she felt unreasonably pleased with herself.

Am I becoming irrational? she wondered. Under these conditions, feeling pleased at anything, much less at the solution of such a simple process, must surely be irrational.

She looked for the *Enterprise* in the spot she had calculated it should be.

She found the moving point of light.

And then –

The transporter beam ripped James Kirk from his ship and reformed him on the surface of Genesis. One after the other, McCoy, Sulu, Chekov, and Scott appeared around him, safe. They all waited, phasers drawn, prepared for pursuit. They had timed their escape closely. The enemy boarding party could have perceived the last glint of their transporter beam, could have tracked them by the console settings, and could have followed them. But they remained alone.

The air was cold and damp and heavy with twilight. All around, a hundred paces in all directions, iron-gray trees reached into the air, then twisted down, twining around each other like gigantic vines. They formed a wide circle around an area clear of trees but choked with tangled, spiny bushes. He took a step toward the forest, where he and his friends could find concealment, and where he would not be able to see the sky. But the thorns ripped into his clothing and hooked into his hands. The scratches burned as if they had been touched with acid. Jim stopped.

Unwillingly, he looked up.

Stars pricked the limpid royal blue with points of light. This system contained only a single planet and no moon. All its sky's stars should be fixed, never changing their relationship to one another. But one, shining the dull silver of reflected light, moved gracefully across the starfield on its own unique path.

Slowly and delicately it began to glow. Its color changed from silver to gold. Then, with shocking abruptness, it exploded to intense blue-white. The point of motion expanded to a blazing, flaming disk, a sphere, a new sun that blotted out the stars.

245

Jim felt, or imagined, the radiation on his face, a brief burst of heat and illumination as matter and antimatter met and joined in mutual annihilation.

The *Enterprise* arced brilliantly from its orbit. For an instant it was a comet, but the gravity of the new world caught it and held it and drew it in. It would never again curve boldly close to the incandescent surface of a sun, never again depart the gentle harbor of Earth to sail into the unknown. The gravity of Genesis turned the dying ship from a comet to a falling star. It spun downward, trailing sparks and cinders and glowing debris. It touched the atmosphere, and it flared more brightly.

Just as suddenly as it appeared, it vanished. One moment the *Enterprise* was a glorious blaze, and the next the sky rose black and empty.

It seemed impossible that the stars should remain in their same pattern, for even fixed stars changed after an eternity.

'My gods, Bones . . .' he whispered. 'What have I done?'

'What you had to do,' McCoy said harshly, his voice only partly his own. 'What you've always done: turned death into a fighting chance to live.' He faced Jim squarely and grasped his upper arms. 'Do you hear me, Jim?'

Jim stared at him, still seeing a flash of the afterimage of the new falling star, still feeling the death of his ship like sunlight searing his face. He took a deep breath. He nodded.

The tricorder Sulu carried had been reacting to the new world since the moment they appeared, but Sulu had barely heard it. Now it forced itself on his attention.

'Sir, the planet's core readings are extremely unstable, and they're changing rapidly – '

Kirk wrenched his attention to the immediate threat. 'Any life signs?'

246

'Close.' He scanned with the tricorder. 'There.'

'Come on!'

Kirk strode through the clearing toward the distorted trees. This time the thorns seemed to part for his passing.

The holographic viewer, which had blazed with light, hung dark and flat; the port looked out on empty space.

Kruge slowly realized how many blank seconds had passed during which he had failed to act, or even to react. The great ship which he had held in thrall had dissolved in his grasp.

Confused and uncertain, Maltz waited by the transporter controls. He had directed the beam to the landing party, touched them, held them – then nothing remained on which to lock.

Kruge was unable to believe what the alien admiral must have done.

'My lord,' Maltz said hesitantly, 'what are your orders?'

My orders? Kruge thought. Do I retain the right to give orders? I underestimated him – a human being! He did the one thing I did not anticipate, the one thing I discounted. The one thing I would have done in his position.

'He destroyed himself,' Kruge said aloud.

'Sir, may I – ?'

If I had known one of the prisoners was his son – if I had interrogated them before sacrificing one – ! Kruge flailed himself with his own humiliation. Killing Kirk's son was stupid! It made Kirk willing to die!

'We still have two prisoners, sir,' Maltz said with transparent concern, for he had received no real response from his commander, no acknowledgement of his presence or of their predicament, since the enemy ship exploded and died. 'Perhaps their information – '

Kruge turned on him angrily. 'They are useless! It was Kirk I needed, and I let him slip away.'

'But surely our mission has not failed!' Maltz exclaimed. They had come seeking Genesis; they retained two hostages who had some knowledge of it, perhaps enough to reproduce it. By his cowardly suicide, Kirk had abandoned them to their captors. Surely Kruge would not let one setback destroy him because of pride . . .

'Our mission is over,' Kruge said. '*I* have failed. A human has been bolder and more ruthless than I . . .' His eyes were empty. '*That* . . . is the real dishonor.'

– and then, the point of light that was the *Enterprise* flared into a nova and scattered itself across the sky.

Saavik gasped.

The ship vanished.

She felt the loss of other lives and dreams much more sharply than she felt the certainty of her own impending death. That did not seem to matter much anymore. It would have very little effect on the universe.

Spock cried out violently, foretelling an inevitable quaking of the planet. The night rumbled; the ground shook. In the distance, Genesis echoed Spock's agony. Beyond the forest, a fault sundered the plain, splitting it into halves, then ramming the halves one against the other. One edge rose like an ocean wave, overwhelming and crushing the other, which subsided beneath it. The sheer faces of stone ground against each other with the power to form mountains.

A wash of illumination flooded ground and sky. A brilliant aurora echoed the earthquake lights, and ozone sharpened the air.

The planet was dying, as the *Enterprise* had died, as every person Saavik had ever cared about had died, as she expected, soon, to die.

Her guards turned away to gaze into the looming, sparkling curtains of the aurora. Even above the rumblings of the quake, Saavik could hear the electric sizzle of the auroral discharge. The guards watched and marveled. The undertones of their voices revealed fear.

Instead of fading, the quake intensified. The massive trees rocked. The loud *snap!* of breaking branches reverberated across the hillside. The guards looked around, seeking some place where they might be safe and realizing no such place existed on this world.

The ground heaved. It flung a massive tree completely free, ripping it up by its roots and propelling it onto the bare promontory. The guards plunged out of its reach and stood huddled together, terrified, stranded between the clutching, grasping trees and the abyss.

The resonances of Genesis tortured Spock. Saavik touched David's soft, curly hair one last time. She could do nothing for him, not even guard him till the dawn. This world would never see another sunrise.

She rose and picked her way across the ragged, trembling surface. Behind her the serjeant spoke into his communicator, a note of panic in his voice. Though Saavik could not understand the words, she could well imagine what he was saying.

Only static replied. Perhaps, when the *Enterprise* destroyed itself, it had destroyed the marauder as well. If that were true, then they were marooned down here after all.

Spock lay prone, shuddering, clenching his long fingers in the dirt. Saavik began to speak to him in Vulcan. If she could calm him enough to approach him, she might join with his mind and alleviate some of his pain.

So intent was she that she did not even hear the guard stride up behind her. He shoved her roughly aside. She stumbled on the broken ground.

'No!' she cried as the guard reached down to jerk Spock to his feet. 'No, don't touch him!'

She was too late.

He reached down and grabbed Spock's arm. Spock reacted to the touch as if it burned. He leaped to his feet with a cry of pain and anger, lifted the guard bodily, and flung him through the air.

The guard smashed into a contorted tree with a wrenching crunch of broken bone. His body slid limply to the ground and did not move again.

As the serjeant drew his phaser, Saavik struggled to her feet.

'Be easy,' she said to Spock in Vulcan, 'be easy, I can help you.'

Spock covered his face with his hands and cried out to the darkness in a long, wavering ululation. He had aged again, aged years, during the short time the guards had kept them apart. Saavik touched him gently, then enfolded him and held him. He was so intent on his own inner contortions that he did not even react.

The serjeant approached, his phaser held ready. He was frightened to the brink of ridding himself of his murderous prisoner, his commander's wishes and ambitions be damned. Saavik glared at him over her shoulder. He would not reach Spock without going through her first.

A tetanic convulsion wracked Spock's body, arching his spine and forcing from him a shuddering, anguished scream.

In the dark forest on the side of the mountain, Jim Kirk heard a shriek of agony. He redoubled his pace. He plunged up the steep slope. The faint trail wound between trees that would have done credit to Hieronymus Bosch. The scarlet aurora threw moving shadows across his path. Kirk struggled upward between whipping branches that moved far more violently than the plunging of the earth could account for.

Sulu paced him, with Chekov close behind. McCoy

followed at a slightly greater distance. Kirk gasped for breath. The heavily ionized air burned in his throat.

He burst out into a clearing. Saavik stood in its center, supporting – someone – and a Klingon serjeant threatened her with a phaser.

'Don't move!' Kirk cried.

The serjeant spun in astonishment, leading with his phaser.

Kirk fired his own weapon. The beam flung the serjeant backwards. He hit the ground and did not move again.

Kirk ran past the serjeant without a second glance. He slowed as he approached Saavik, who turned toward him, cradling an unconscious young man in her arms.

'Bones – ' Kirk said softly.

McCoy panted up beside him and gently took her burden from her. When his hand brushed Saavik's arm, she gasped and jerked away as if he had given her an electrical shock. She took a step back, staring at him. Kirk touched her elbow, startling her.

'Sir – ' she said. Her voice broke, and she staggered. He caught her and drew her close.

'Easy, Saavik,' he said. 'Take it easy. It's all right.'

'I tried,' she whispered. 'I tried to take care of your son . . .'

The auroras burned in the sky and lit the clearing with a ghastly glow. Jim saw, beneath a twisting tree, the body of his son.

He hugged Saavik one last time. She took a long shuddering breath and straightened up, allowing him to break the embrace.

He left her with McCoy and the others and slowly crossed the clearing. His boots crunched on fallen leaves.

Jim knelt beside David's body.

'My son . . .' A poem whispered to him from a long-ago

time. '"To thee no star be dark . . . Both heaven and earth . . . friend thee forever . . ."'

Fallen leaves drifted across David's body, shrouding the young man in a tattered cloth that shone scarlet and gold when the auroras flared, a cloth of autumn leaves, from a world that had barely experienced its spring.

12

Jim closed his eyes tight, fighting back the tears. He heard footsteps nearby. He opened his eyes and raised his head. His vision blurred then cleared. Saavik stood before him.

'What happened?' he said.

'He . . . he gave his life to save us,' she said. She stopped, then shook her head and turned away. She said, very softly, 'That is all I know.'

'Jim!'

Kirk stood quickly, responding to McCoy's concerned shout. He forced himself away from his grief, away from the dead and toward the living.

McCoy hunched over the body of the young person whom Saavik had so fiercely protected. Kirk knelt down beside them, and in the changing light he saw –

He gasped. 'Bones – !'

'*Bojemoi!*' Chekov exclaimed.

In all the years from the time James Kirk met Spock until the time of Spock's death, the Vulcan had not much changed. He aged more slowly than a human being. No one knew if he would age as slowly as a Vulcan. Kirk had always been aware that he would not live to see Spock old, and he had not known him as a youth. The Vulcan lying unconscious before him *was* a youth . . . but he was also, unmistakably, Spock.

Spock. Alive.

Kirk wanted to laugh, he wanted to cry, he wanted instant certain answers to all the questions tumbling over each other in his mind. My gods, he thought, Spock – alive!

And then he had to wonder, What does this mean for McCoy?

'Bones – ?' he said again.

'All his metabolic functions are highly accelerated,' McCoy said. He made his diagnoses calmly, despite its implications. 'In lay terms – his body is aging. Fast.'

'And – his mind?'

McCoy glanced at his tricorder again and shook his head. 'The readings of a newborn, or at best an infant of a few months – his mind's a void, almost a *tabula rasa*.' He glanced up. 'It would seem, Admiral,' he said drily, 'that I have all his marbles.'

'Is there *anything* we can do?'

McCoy shrugged. Kirk glanced at Saavik.

'Only one thing, sir,' she said. 'We must get him off this planet. He is . . . bound to it in some way. He is aging, as is this world.'

The young man moaned. The ground shuddered as violently as he did. Saavik knelt beside him.

'And if he stays here?'

Saavik looked up.

'He will die.'

Kirk withdrew as a blaze of lightning flooded the clearing. He had to do something . . . and only one possibility remained.

He opened his communicator.

'Commander Kruge,' he said. 'This is Admiral James T. Kirk. I am . . . alive and well on the surface of Genesis.' He paused. He received no reply except crackling electrical interference. 'I know this will come as a pleasant surprise for you,' he said, 'but, you see, my ship was the victim of . . . an unfortunate accident. I'm sorry about your crew, old boy. But *c'est la vie*, as we say back on Earth.'

His answer was another convulsion of the ground,

another crash of static, another blinding burst of light from the cloudless sky.

'Well?' Kirk said angrily. 'I'm waiting for you – what's your answer?' He forced himself to relax his grip on his communicator, to be patient, to wait and think. 'I have what you want,' he said desperately. 'I have the secret of Genesis! But you'll have to bring us up there to get it. Do you hear me?'

Static drowned out any possibility of an answer. The sky and the earth rumbled, the young Vulcan moaned, the trees groaned and cracked, and in the background the aurora rustled, soft and eerie. A tremendous crash of lightning and thunder obliterated sight and sound. His shoulders slumping, Jim Kirk folded his communicator and stowed it carefully away. He blinked a few times, trying to drive away the afterimages that made his eyes water. He turned back to the remnants of his crew, whom he had led to their doom.

He joined them, but he did not know what to say to them. Spock lay sprawled on the ground, his arm flung across his face. The others were gathered around him, astonished to find him alive. Kirk sat on his heels beside them, not knowing what to say. 'Thank you' and 'I'm sorry' seemed terribly inadequate.

'Drop all weapons!'

Startled, Kirk spun toward the voice.

The sky was a luminous backdrop, a curtain of wavering auroral light pierced intermittently by stars. Against it stood a huge shadow. It loomed above them on the pinnacle of stone.

Kirk rose carefully, drawing his phaser and dropping it, then spreading his empty hands. Sulu, Chekov, and McCoy followed suit, but Saavik remained kneeling beside Spock.

The looming figure came a few steps toward them. The phaser glinted in his hand. The hair of his crest rose.

255

'Over there,' said Commander Kruge. 'All but Kirk.' He gestured to a trampled spot on the hillside.

Kirk made a slight gesture of his head. McCoy, Sulu, and Chekov reluctantly obeyed. Saavik remained where she was, next to Spock. Kirk heard the Klingon commander draw in a long, angry breath.

'Go *on*, Lieutenant,' Kirk said softly. He feared that she would argue, but finally she stood and joined the others.

Commander Kruge spun open his communicator. 'Maltz,' he said, 'the prisoners are at our first beam coordinates. Stand by.'

Kirk took one step toward Kruge, who reacted by raising the phaser.

At least I have his full attention, Kirk thought.

'You should take the Vulcan, too,' he said easily.

'No.'

'But, why?'

'Because,' Kruge said, 'you wish it.' Keeping his gaze on Kirk, he picked up the phasers and flung them, one by one, over the promontory and down the side of the mountain. Then he spoke into the communicator in his own language. Kirk did not understand the words, but it must have been the order to transport. The energy flux pulsed around Kirk's friends.

'No – !' Saavik cried, but the beam attenuated her voice. She vanished with the others.

Only a few hundred meters away, the whole hillside suddenly split open with a great roar of tortured rock. Scarlet light and intense heat fanned out of the fissure. The glowing magma thrust upward through the breach in the planet's crust. The waterfall that tumbled down the hillside flowed into the crack and over the molten rock, exploding into superheated steam.

Kruge strode closer to Kirk.

256

'Genesis!' He shouted over the cacophony of the dying planet. 'I want it!'

'Beam the Vulcan up,' Kirk said. 'Then we talk.'

'Give me what I want – and I'll consider it.'

'You fool!' Kirk cried. 'Look around you! This planet is destroying itself!'

Kruge smiled.

'Yes,' he said. 'Exhilarating, isn't it?'

Kirk stared at him, speechless, then recovered himself. 'If we don't help each other, we'll all die here!'

'Perfect!' Kruge said triumphantly. 'That's the way it shall be!' He loomed over Kirk, smiling his wolfish smile. '*Give me Genesis!*' he said. Each word struck like a blow.

As if in reply, Genesis heaved and pitched beneath him. The outcropping on which he stood shattered and flung him forward. He lost his balance and fell. His phaser skittered across the stone, sliding down the hillside to the edge of the earth fault.

As Kruge struggled up, Kirk plunged forward and tackled him. Kirk's breath rushed out as if he had run into a solid wall. Kruge roared with anger and caught him in the side with his fist. He fell hard but managed to roll to his feet. Kruge ran toward his phaser. Kirk sprinted toward him and tackled him at the knees. They both went down. Half-stunned, staggering, Kruge rose. But Kirk managed to get up first. He pressed his advantage, hitting with short, sharp jabs that did little real damage but kept his opponent off-balance and flailing. He ducked beneath Kruge's long, powerful arms and hit him again. Kirk's knuckles were raw. Each blow shot pain up his hands.

The livid glow of magma haloed the Klingon commander. He swung and missed. His momentum pitched him around. Kirk sprang at him and hit him one more time with his battered hands.

Kruge fell.

He tumbled over the edge of a bit of broken ground.

Kirk looked over the precipice. Kruge stood on the second cliff, just above the rumbling magma. Steam and smoke roiled around him.

Looking up at Kirk, he laughed.

Infuriated, Kirk sprang down on him. The heat slapped him. He struggled with Kruge. The size and relative youth of the Klingon commander began to overwhelm him. Kruge broke Kirk's hold and slammed him in the chest with both hands. The impact flung Kirk violently back against the cliff's rock wall. Dazed, Kirk slid toward the ground. He barely managed to prevent himself from falling. He was soaked with sweat. He struggled up. Kruge regarded him from the edge of the pit. The scarlet darkness silhouetted the Klingon commander, who waited, hands on hips, for Kirk to regain enough of his strength to be a fitting opponent.

The magma surged from below, scraping against the side of the cliff. Rocks fell, clattering hollowly. Great hexagonal columns of basalt split away from the cliff and collapsed like the trunks of ancient trees. The column on which Kruge stood fractured and began to sink. The magma swallowed its base.

The whole column began to topple. Kruge balanced upon it, the heat rising around him in waves. To Kirk it looked as if the commander were enjoying his peril, testing his nerve.

'Jump, damn you!' Kirk cried.

And still Kruge delayed. The column of stone continued to tilt, to sink.

Kruge leaped. But he had waited an instant beyond the last moment. He fell short. He slammed up against the fragmenting columns, gripping the edge, his feet dangling into the glowing pit.

Kirk sprinted to the edge of the cliff and knelt, peering

down at Kruge, who looked up at him with his teeth slightly bared in an expression that was more a mocking smile than a threat.

'Now,' Kirk said, 'you'll give me what I want – '

Kruge lurched upward, trying to get his arm over the edge of the cliff, trying to gain leverage. Kirk let him flail at the heated stone.

'You're going to get us off this planet!' Kirk said.

Kruge snarled something. Whatever it was, it was not agreement. He slipped precariously down.

'Don't be a fool!' Kirk cried. 'Give me your hand – and live!'

The commander lunged toward Kirk. Kirk jerked back. Kruge's fingers grazed his throat, then slipped away. He started to fall, but with a supernatural effort he vaulted upward again and grabbed Kirk's leg.

Kruge abandoned his hold on the cliff and clenched both hands like claws around Kirk's ankle.

Jim Kirk felt himself sliding along the rough surface of the cliff, off-balance, only a handsbreadth from the edge. He struggled back, digging his fingers between the hexagonal patterns where the basalt continued to fragment. His fingernails ripped, and he left streaks of blood on the dark stone as he slipped farther and farther over the edge. The fierce heat of the magma gusted up around him.

He heard Kruge laughing again, laughing with contempt and victory, laughing at the death of Kirk's son, at Kirk's determination to save his friends, at Kirk's defeat, and at Kirk himself.

'Damn you!' Kirk cried in a rage. 'I have had – enough – of *you!*' He kicked out angrily, and again, desperately.

Kruge's grip loosened, faltered, and broke.

Kirk scrambled back onto the cliff.

Kruge tumbled down, with nothing to break his fall but the glowing magma.

The basalt columns shuddered and split away from each other, tumbling one after the other into the pit. The cliff was disintegrating beneath Jim's feet. He raced for the higher cliff, leaped, caught its edge, and dragged himself up its face. He lay panting on solid ground, exhausted. He had no choice but to get up and keep going, for the solid ground was no longer solid. Other cracks opened, engulfing twisted, warty trees that exploded into flame and smoke, swallowing the hillside's streams, gushing superheated steam. Jim struggled to his feet. Spock sprawled, unconscious, near a blood-red glowing fissure.

The hot white spark of the Genesis sun burst above the horizon, piercing the darkness and the steam and the smoke. Long shadows sprang into existence. They moved and wavered like wraiths with the convulsions of the ground.

Kirk knelt beside Spock and gently turned him over.

He cursed softly.

This was Spock, Spock as he had known him. In only a few minutes he had traveled from youth to maturity. In a few more minutes he would progress to age, thence to . . . death. He moaned, as the pain of the world to which he was chained penetrated even his exhaustion and deep unconsciousness. The sound lanced through Jim Kirk.

The sun was rising so fast he could feel its progress. The rays grew hotter as their angle changed, and the shadows shortened. The planet's rotation was increasing as the world tore itself apart.

Jim looked up at the sky. Even the stars had faded in the dawn. It was too bright even to search for the reflected light of the single ship that remained in orbit around Genesis – if it had not already fled the unstable star system.

He glanced around, found Kruge's phaser, and scooped it up. Then he slid one arm beneath Spock's limp body,

260

heaved him onto his shoulder, and pushed himself to his feet. He opened his communicator, muffled the pickup by rubbing his thumbnail back and forth across it, did his best to copy Kruge's low, harsh voice, and repeated the last words Kruge had transmitted.

Then he waited. His legs were trembling with fatigue. He raised the communicator to try once more –

And felt the gentle tingle of a transporter beam forming around him. It dematerialized his body, and Spock's, and carried them away.

Saavik materialized aboard a Klingon fighter. The others appeared around her. A single officer of the ship observed their arrival.

Saavik measured the distance to his weapon with her gaze. She glanced sidelong at Captain Sulu. He stood in a completely relaxed attitude of appraisal. He was ready. If two at once –

The officer gestured with his phaser. It was set to fire in a wide fan. It was clear that if anyone moved suspiciously, the officer would stun them all simultaneously and dispose of them at his leisure.

Dr McCoy suddenly cried out in pain and fell to his knees. Chekov and Scott quickly moved to help him. Saavik and Sulu remained where they were, but they both realized they were at too great a disadvantage. As Sulu turned away to help the others with McCoy, he muttered, 'I wonder what O-sensei would have said about phasers?'

Saavik held back from touching McCoy again. When he brushed against her, back on Genesis, it was not the doctor she sensed, but Mr Spock. McCoy carried in him the unique pattern of her teacher, trapped and blind and weakening. The experience left Saavik thoroughly shaken.

Nevertheless, it explained a great deal. And it opened

so many possibilities . . . possibilities which would be closed again if they all remained prisoners, and above all if Genesis destroyed itself before those remaining on its surface could be rescued.

Composed once more, Saavik mentally ran through the forms of address in the high tongue of the Klingon Empire. She was unfamiliar with the lower dialects she had heard the other crew members speak, but no matter. It would surely be better to speak to the Klingon officer in a form too high than in one too low. If she could speak to him without offending him, she might have some chance of persuading him to rescue those left behind. She might even be able to persuade him to surrender, for the high tongue was a very persuasive language.

Whatever she did, she had only a little time. The ship lay oriented so its forward port faced Genesis directly. The tectonic activity had become so violent that even from this distance she could see the great rifts in the planet's crust and the glowing fires of its interior. Its orbit around its sun was decaying rapidly; the star's blue-white disk grew larger as Saavik watched. Before the planet destroyed itself, its surface conditions would be lethal.

'Worthy opponent,' she said, hoping that her accent was not too atrocious, 'we find ourselves in a delicately balanced position.'

He glanced at her sharply and frowned. His hand tightened on the grip of his phaser.

'You are one,' Saavik said, 'and we are five.' She neglected to point out that Dr McCoy was in no state to join in any opposition. 'Furthermore, this entire star system will soon degenerate into a plasma of sub-elementary particles. If we do not rescue our respective shipmates and flee, we will all perish.'

'Stop!'

She stopped. The tone of his voice gave her little choice.

'Why do you speak to me in this manner?' he said. He spoke quite acceptable Standard.

'I did not know you spoke our language,' she said.

'Of course I speak your barbarian pidgin – do you think me so ignorant of my enemies? But you speak to me in Kumburan, and I am Rumaiy. Could it be that you have not been taught the difference?'

'It could be,' Saavik admitted. 'I did not intend offense.'

'Could it be that you believe the slanderous cant put about, that Kumburanya are in the ascendancy over Rumaiym?'

'I confess to an unforgivable ignorance of the subject,' Saavik said, not altogether truthfully. She had been told at the Academy that the language she was studying was the only significant one in the Klingon Empire. That did not seem quite the appropriate response just now. 'In the Federation we employ a single language in public, so we may all communicate.'

'Reductionists!' he said with contempt. 'Obliterators of diversity!' He muttered something unpleasant in a language Saavik did not know, and then he started to say something which she feared would be a lengthy tirade against the social or political group that opposed his own.

'But I am not ignorant about the world below us,' Saavik said quickly, taking the risk of incurring his anger by interrupting him. 'And it is close to destroying itself. Look at it! You cannot pretend the signs do not exist! We must cooperate to survive!'

'I have my orders.'

'Orders from a commander unaware of the dangers on the surface, or beneath it – a commander who may even now be dead? If you value diversity . . . my worthy opponent, this system will soon lose its diversity completely. In a matter of hours it will consist of nothing but a homogeneous mass of highly entropic protomatter.'

263

The officer said nothing, but gazed at Saavik thoughtfully.

The communicator erupted in a muffled burst of static. Saavik cursed silently, for it broke his consideration. She would have to start persuading him all over again – if she got the chance. No doubt this was his commander with new orders, orders that could not be of any benefit to Saavik and her companions.

When she heard the voice she started. She glanced at Captain Sulu and knew her suspicion was correct, because he was forcing himself not to react, not to burst out in surprised and relieved laughter. They both looked surreptitiously up at the command seat.

The officer hesitated before replying to the order. Saavik dug her nails into her palms.

The officer touched controls.

Then they all waited.

The last thing Jim Kirk saw on the surface of Genesis was the body of his son, drifted over with scarlet leaves and outlined by the fires of the world that had meant so much to him.

That world faded like a dream.

A transporter chamber solidified into reality around Jim Kirk. He blew his breath out in a sharp reaction of relief, for if he had been under suspicion he might have found his and Spock's atoms spread all over space by the transporter beam.

Dredging from the depths of his mind the layout of a Klingon fighter, he settled Spock's body more firmly on his shoulder and headed for the control room. He saw no one as he strode through the corridors, and he could not help but think, with some trepidation, that this was precisely the sort of emptiness the boarding party had confronted on the *Enterprise*. He drew the phaser. It fit his hand strangely, having been designed for different joints and different proportions.

Doors opened for him. He stepped into the control room.

Kruge's second in command revealed no surprise when Kirk entered. Like Kirk, he held a phaser. Unlike Kirk, he was alone. Even if he fired now, he would fall to Kirk's phaser, and the prisoners behind him would become his captors.

'Where is Commander Kruge?' he asked. He spoke as if the question were his final duty. Kirk knew, then, that his masquerade had not fooled the officer for a moment.

'Gone,' Kirk said. 'Dead. Engulfed by Genesis.'

Defeated and resigned, the officer spread his hands. Kirk nodded once, sharply.

Saavik vaulted from the work-pit and relieved Maltz of his phaser. Chekov helped McCoy to his feet. The strain in the doctor's face, the strain of having been removed again from proximity to Spock, began to ease.

'How many more?' Kirk said.

'Just him, sir!' Scott said.

Kirk lowered Spock to the deck. 'Bones, help Spock! Everyone else find a station.'

Saavik put Maltz's phaser in her belt, and waited. Slowly, reluctantly, he drew his dagger and surrendered it to her.

'You!' Kirk said to him. 'Help us, or die!'

'I do not deserve to live!'

'Fine – I'll kill you later! Let's get out of here!'

He sprinted to a place on the bridge, leaving Kruge's second confused and defeated. Everyone else had already taken a spot. Kirk trusted that they had all spent their time here trying to figure out which instrument performed which function.

Beyond the viewport, the Genesis sun contracted and

brightened. It was a few minutes, no more, from nova. The instability of the planet affected its orbit in an accelerating manner. As the path decayed, the world spiraled toward the sun, drawing the ship along with it.

Kirk glanced at the beautiful and unfamiliar alien script, of which he could not read a word.

'Anybody here read Klingon?' he said.

No one answered, though Saavik glanced at him sharply, then looked away as if she were embarrassed.

Just like Spock, Kirk thought. She considers it a personal failing if she can't do absolutely everything.

'Well, take your best shot,' Kirk said to his friends.

'If you can bypass into this module – ' Chekov said to Scott.

Scott made a sound of disgust. 'Fine, but where's the damn antimatter inducer?'

'This?' Chekov replied. 'No, this!'

'This,' Scott said, 'or nothing.' He touched alien controls, took a deep breath, and moved another control to its farthest extent.

The ship whined. Everyone flinched as the sound wavered, then relaxed as it steadied and strengthened.

Sulu occupied a station as if it were built for him.

'If I read this right, sir, we have full power.'

Kirk did not doubt that the young captain read it right. 'Go, Sulu!'

The ship arced around, accelerated out of orbit, and hurtled at warp speed from the deteriorating system.

There was no conversation, there were no orders, there was simply a consensus between people who had known each other long and well. At what he judged to be a safe distance, Sulu pulled the fighter back from warp speed. If navigating the *Enterprise* was like driving a team of proud and immensely powerful draft horses, handling the Klingon ship was like being perched on the back of a skittish two-year-old colt during its first race. Sulu oriented it so the viewport faced the system they had just fled.

The planet fell toward its sun, which burned with an intense blue-white light. Stellar flares burst from the incandescent surface, reaching out to capture anything within their grasp.

The only thing within their grasp was the Genesis world. With shocking suddenness, the sun engulfed it.

The Genesis world was gone.

'Good-bye, David,' Jim Kirk whispered.

The disk of the star expanded, exploding to millions of times its previous volume until it was nothing but a tenuous, vaguely luminescent, spiral cloud of plasma.

'It will form another world,' Saavik said.

Kirk glanced at her sharply.

'The protomatter will condense to a plasma of normal matter,' she said. 'The plasma will cool. It will condense to dust, thence to a star and a family of planets. This time, lacking the Genesis wave, it will be stable. A surface will harden, oceans will form, the sun's radiation will induce chemical reactions. Life will begin. In time . . . it may evolve as David and his friends intended.'

'In millions of years,' Kirk said.

'No, Admiral,' she said. 'In billions of years.'

'I'm glad you find some comfort in the long view, Lieutenant,' Kirk said.

Sulu spoke, breaking the uneasy tension between Kirk and Saavik. 'We're clear and free to navigate,' he said.

'Best speed to Vulcan, Captain,' Kirk fell gratefully back into the role he knew best. 'Mr Chekov, take the prisoner below.'

'Aye, sir.'

'Wait!' Kruge's second in command drew back from him and turned angrily on Kirk. 'You said you would kill me.'

'I lied,' Kirk said, and gestured for Chekov to get him off the bridge.

After a quick and dirty self-taught course on the finer details of navigating a Klingon fighter craft, Sulu laid in a course for Vulcan. Saavik puzzled out the communications system.

'Lieutenant Saavik of Federation science ship *Grissom*, calling Starfleet Communications. Come in, please.'

'Communications to *Grissom*. We've been trying to reach you folks for days! A freighter just picked up a lifeboat with a couple of survivors from a merchant vessel – they claim Klingons raided their ship!'

'It is likely their claim is true,' Saavik said. 'We . . . experienced a similar encounter.'

'Are you all right?'

'I regret that we are not. We have a serious and continuing emergency. We have incurred many fatalities. We need your cooperation.'

'You have it, Lieutenant. What do you require?'

'A patch into your library's data-base, and a general message to all ships between Mutara sector and Vulcan.'

'The patch is made.' The Starfleet communications officer paused a moment, then said in a startled voice, 'Lieutenant, what communications protocol are you using? What the devil are you flying?'

'Please stand by,' Saavik said. She instructed the Starfleet data-base and waited for the information she needed before she replied to the question. She assumed her answer would cause consternation at the very least. At worst, it would result in so much suspicion that the data link would immediately be broken, and hunters would be sent out for their heads.

A new voice broke into the channel. 'Cut that damned data link! Lieutenant Saavik! This is Starfleet Commander

Morrow. What the hell is going on out there? Let me speak with Esteban!'

'I am sorry, sir,' she said. 'That is impossible.'

He cursed softly. 'I want some explanations! Have you seen the *Enterprise*?'

'The *Enterprise* is not within our range, sir,' she said. She did not know how to react to her newfound ability to dissemble nearly as well as a human being.

'What is the message you want us to relay?' Morrow said.

'"Klingon fighter on course to Vulcan – "' Saavik heard exclamations of astonishment. She continued. '"This ship is not an adversary. It is held by a contingent of Federation personnel. It is running with shields down and weapons disabled. Essential that we reach Vulcan. Delay will result in further casualties. *This ship is not an adversary*".'

'A Klingon fighter! Lieutenant, I ask again, Where is *Grissom*? What in blazes is going on out there?'

'Saavik out.' She shut down the channel.

'Good work, Lieutenant,' Kirk said. He had known perfectly well that if he or anyone else from the *Enterprise* contacted Starfleet they would have been ordered to return immediately to Earth, to surrender. They were without doubt already under arrest, albeit in absentia.

Saavik could think of no suitable way to respond to a compliment for dishonesty. Instead, she transferred the Starfleet data to Captain Sulu's station. He gave her a smile of thanks.

She brought up the second information module on her own screen and began to read the dense Vulcan prose.

'Estimating Vulcan at point one niner,' Sulu said.

Federation ships dogged their path, but none offered a direct challenge. Saavik left her ship's systems open to surveillance, but continued to let Starfleet believe that she was the only Federation member on board.

'Lieutenant,' Kirk said, 'transmit a message to

Ambassador Sarek. Tell him we bring McCoy, and Spock. Tell him . . . Spock is alive. Ask him to prepare for the *katra* ritual.'

'Aye, sir. But . . .' She was still trying to sort out the basic facts of what she had just finishing reading. She could hardly presume to comprehend the philosophy. For centuries, the most intellectual citizens of Vulcan had dedicated their lives to its study without claiming to have reached the limits of its meaning.

'But what, Lieutenant?'

'I do not know if that is possible.' Her lack of knowledge brought home to her, with redoubled force, her profound isolation from Vulcan society.

'What? What are you saying?'

'The *katra* ritual is meant to deposit Spock's consciousness in the Hall of Ancient Thought. Not back into his body.'

'But we have Spock – alive! Why can't they return his *katra*?'

'The circumstances are most unusual. The procedure you suggest is called *fal tor pan*, the refusion. The conditions required to perform it have not occurred for millennia. There is considerable disagreement about whether it succeeded then, whether it could succeed at all, and indeed whether it should succeed. The elders may not choose even to attempt it.'

'And if they don't? What will happen to Spock?'

Saavik wished she could avoid answering James Kirk as easily as she had avoided the questions of Starfleet Command.

'He will remain,' she said finally, unwillingly, 'always as he is . . .'

Kirk looked blankly at her, then turned and strode from the bridge.

* * *

Spock lay on one of the pallets in the small sick bay. McCoy stood beside him, his hand on the pulse-point at Spock's throat. The weak, thready beat pulsed far too slowly for a Vulcan. McCoy passed his scanner over Spock's body. The fragile, feeble signal gave him no confidence. Spock had stopped aging since they freed him from Genesis, but he had fallen into a deep unconsciousness. As the strength of his body ebbed, so did the strength of his spirit.

'Spock,' McCoy said softly, desperately, 'I've done everything I know to do. Help me! You stuck me with this, for gods' sake, teach me what to do with it!' He paused, without much hope, and received no answer from within or without. 'I never thought I'd ever say this to you,' he said, and thought, You green-blooded . . . but the old, familiar gibe rang hollow, and he could not bring himself to speak it aloud. 'I've missed you. I couldn't . . . I couldn't bear to lose you again.' He could feel his own strength failing him. In despair, he hid his face in his hands.

He felt the touch of another hand. Jim Kirk stood beside him, one hand on McCoy's shoulder, the other on Spock's. Their lives had been intertwined for so long . . .

Jim's face was full of grief, and yet of determination. He gripped McCoy's shoulder hard, as if, like a Vulcan, he could transfer to him some of his strength.

13

Vulcan.

A desert world, limited in material resources, yet limitless in the intellectual and philosophical achievements of its inhabitants.

Saavik gazed upon it and wished what she had wished since the first time she learned about this planet. She wished she belonged here. She wished she had some right to this world, some claim to a place upon it and within its society. She had none of those things. She suspected she could never earn them, no matter her achievements.

'Home, eh, Lieutenant?'

'I beg your pardon, Admiral?' Saavik said.

Kirk nodded toward the viewport. 'Vulcan.'

'Vulcan is not my home, sir. I have never been here before.'

'Oh,' he said, taken aback. 'I would have thought you would at least have visited it.'

'I have never been invited to Vulcan, sir.' She tried to speak as she had been taught, without emotion. She almost succeeded, but Kirk sensed something of her isolation.

'I think we'll find that we're welcome,' he said gently.

'The planet Vulcan is in hailing distance, Admiral,' Captain Sulu said.

'Thank you, Sulu. Saavik – send a message to Ambassador Sarek. Tell him we're coming in.'

She obeyed. A ground station accepted her message. She waited for an answer.

'Rescue party – '

In reaction to the voice, everyone on the bridge swung toward the speaker. Sulu gave a cheer of surprise and delight that mirrored all their feelings. Hearing Uhura's voice, knowing she was well and free, was the first purely joyful thing that had happened to any of them in far too long.

' – this is Commander Uhura. Permission is granted to land on the plain at the foot of Mount Seleya. Ambassador Sarek is ready.' She paused. Her voice close to breaking, she said, 'Welcome. Oh, welcome back.'

The fighter shivered as its wings spread into flying configuration. Sulu felt the energy of the ship glide into his hands and arms and suffuse his body with a powerful glow. He had never flown anything like this ship before. He had developed a considerable and more than grudging respect for the engineering abilities of the opponents of the Federation.

He wondered what would happen to the ship. No doubt Starfleet would seize it and send it back to Earth to be dismembered and analyzed. The idea pained him greatly.

He realized that this was quite probably the last time he would ever fly any ship, of any sort.

'Captain Sulu,' Kirk said, 'you're on manual.'

He nodded. 'It's been a while, sir.' He had not landed a ship of this size without gravity propulsion since his student days. And, of course, he had never landed a craft of this design. 'Here we go. Retrothrusters!'

The ship replied, responding like a dream. The dust of the plain at the foot of Mount Seleya billowed up around it as it settled to the ground.

The ramp hissed out and lowered itself to the ground. Spock's friends carried his litter out into the scarlet dusk of Vulcan.

At the foot of the ramp, Kirk stopped short and looked out amazed. The plain led to the temple. To either side of the long steep path, Vulcans stood watching and waiting, curious and silent. Here and there a torch flared against the dim light.

'My gods . . .' Kirk whispered.

'Much is at stake,' Saavik said.

Kirk knew little of the Vulcan philosophy of what he was about to ask, and he cared less. All he wanted to hear was an acquiescence to his demand.

The light faded to the state of dimness where everything took on an eerie cast. More torches flared. Kirk heard running footsteps before he could tell where they came from.

Uhura appeared before him. Jim embraced her with his free arm. Uhura's eyes were bright with tears.

'Sarek is waiting,' she said. 'Above – '

She slipped in between Kirk and Sulu and helped carry the stretcher up the long path to the crest of the hill, where the temple loomed dark and mysterious.

Strange music teased the limits of Kirk's hearing. As he trudged up the slope the music grew only a little louder. It and the flaring of the torches were the only sounds. The enormous crowd of people watched somberly and in utter silence.

Kirk's legs began to ache. He had fought off his exhaustion for so long that he could not even remember when last he had slept. He kept going.

A young child let go her father's hand. She walked with great dignity to Spock's side, and followed for a few paces. She looked down into his face, saluted him, and whispered, 'Live long and prosper, Spock.' Then she slipped away and vanished into the crowd again.

Sarek waited on the steps of the temple, accompanied by several dignitaries and by six members of the priesthood. The tall, stately women watched with utter impassivity.

Finally Sarek strode forward to meet them. Kirk stopped, no longer sure what he should do.

The music faded so gradually that he was uncertain of the transition between sound and silence.

Sarek gazed at Spock. He reached down and placed his long, graceful hands against the sides of Spock's face. Kirk wanted nothing more than to grab him and shake him and make him explain what would happen now. He glanced sidelong at McCoy, who had reached the raw edge of his strength.

Sarek said nothing. He took one pace backward and nodded to the members of the priesthood. They moved between Kirk and his friends so easily, so gently, and with such assurance that they hardly seemed to be displacing them. The women took Spock in their hands and carried him away. Sarek followed.

Kirk watched, astonished. The Vulcans carried Spock easily, but their hands were not underneath his body.

They were on top of it.

Kirk hurried after them.

He passed between massive stone pillars and stopped at the edge of a circular, slightly dished platform. An altar rose at its far side. T'Lar, the leader of the Vulcan priesthood, waited in stately silence as her subordinates brought Spock to her. They began a low chant that penetrated to the bones.

Sarek paused and faced Kirk.

'This is where you must wait.'

Unwillingly, Kirk obeyed. The music began again. Sarek faced the altar as his son's body sank gently to the age-smoothed granite and lay motionless as stone. The music and the chant ceased simultaneously.

'Sarek,' T'Lar said. Her voice, barely a whisper, carried

to them sharp and clear. 'Sarek, child of Skon, child of Solkar. The body of your child breathes still. What is your wish?'

'I ask for *fal tor pan*,' Sarek said. 'The refusion.'

'What you seek has not been done since ages past. It has succeeded only in legend. Your request is not logical.'

'Forgive me, T'Lar,' Sarek said. He sounded very tired, and Kirk realized this must be the most difficult thing he had said in a hundred twenty years. 'My logic falters . . . where my son is concerned.'

T'Lar looked beyond Sarek to Kirk and his friends. She looked Kirk straight in the eye. Her gaze, as sharp as a weapon, touched him, then granted him mercy. She turned her attention to McCoy.

'Who is the keeper of the *katra*?' The question, clearly, lay in ritual; she knew the answer to what she asked.

Sarek nodded at McCoy. McCoy stared straight ahead, fixed by the power of T'Lar's eyes.

'Bones – ' Kirk said urgently under his breath.

McCoy finally replied. 'I am,' he said hesitantly. 'McCoy . . . Leonard H.' He took a long breath of the rarefied air of Vulcan. 'Son of David and Eleanora . . .'

'McCoy, son of David, son of Eleanora . . .'

McCoy shivered.

'Since thou art human, and without knowledge of our philosophy, we cannot expect thee to understand fully what Sarek has requested. The circumstances are extraordinary. Spock's body lives. With thine approval, we will use all our powers to return to his body that which thou dost possess: his essence. But, McCoy . . .'

T'Lar let the silence surround them and press down against them. Kirk could see the faint sheen of sweat on McCoy's forehead.

'You must now be warned,' T'Lar said, speaking with complete formality. 'The danger to you is as grave as the danger to Spock.'

Now Kirk shivered, and tried to tell himself it was only the rapid cooling of a desert at night.

'You must make the choice.' T'Lar waited for McCoy's reply. Her dispassionate expression offered neither encouragement nor warning.

McCoy, in his turn, let the silence stretch out.

'I choose the danger,' he said. Under his breath, to Kirk, he muttered, 'Helluva time to ask.'

Kirk repressed a smile and fought down a laugh, knowing it to be a laugh of apprehension. He and McCoy both knew the choice to be between madness and the risk of death.

'Bring him forward!' T'Lar said.

Sarek led McCoy across the long empty platform and stopped before the altar. Kirk knew he could do nothing, yet he hated letting McCoy go alone, to face . . .

A bolt of heat lightning shattered the silence.

McCoy let Sarek draw him forward to the altar. Abruptly he stood all alone.

Spock lay before him, and T'Lar stood above them both. McCoy was aware of music, a rhythmic chant, and the thin sharp sighing of the wind. The powerful voice of the Vulcan leader echoed around him. 'All that can be done, shall be done, though it take full turn of the Vulcan sun.'

T'Lar stroked her fingers along his temple. Her touch was like fire, and he gasped. An alien consciousness stirred deep within his mind. Terror-stricken, he struggled against it.

The voice he heard was wordless and silent, yet so loud he feared it would strike him deaf. He could not see, and he feared he had been blinded as well.

'Yes! Strive, fight! Employ the power of thine alien emotions! Wrest back thy life!'

Thunder pounded at him, and he screamed.

Built high on the slopes of Mount Seleya, the retreat of the adepts of the discipline of ancient thought had grown and changed over many generations. Its hallways and galleries cut deep into bedrock. It was said that they looped back upon themselves and never reached an end; it was said that one could wander through them for a lifetime and never walk the same path twice.

Amanda Grayson, student and adept of the discipline, citizen of Earth, knew of no one who claimed complete familiarity with the maze. Most of the deepest caverns had long fallen into disuse. Even the most ascetic of Vulcans preferred open spaces, open air, and the heat of the huge red sun.

The retreat overlooked the plain at the foot of Seleya. Amanda stepped out onto her balcony, into darkness. The face of the retreat stretched away to either side, a long stream of carven rock. Its organic curves and graceful arcs flowed easily and imperceptibly into balconies, pathways, entrances, windows.

Amanda put her hands on the smooth surface of the parapet. The stone held the heat of the day, though the air had already grown chilly.

Long stretches of time often passed during which the plain far below remained deserted. In all the years Amanda had studied the discipline, she had never seen more than a few people at a time approach the temple. Citizens who had reached the death of the body were brought to Mount Seleya by close family members, perhaps by comrades with whom they had formed intellectual ties. The student-adepts then helped the citizen sever the bond between body and mind, between sub-

278

stance and soul. After that, the body could go to dust and ashes, but the presence retired to the Hall of Ancient Thought. Always before, the student-adepts carried out the procedure in private, in an atmosphere of calm.

All that was changed. An enormous, silent, curious crowd had gathered on the plain. Their torches cast an eerie glow over the land, the courtyard, the temple. The light was far too dim for Amanda to see the processional, but she knew every detail of the ceremony. She followed it, in her mind, as if she could affect it with her imagination and carry it to the conclusion she sought. And perhaps she could. She dared not try to reach out to her son with her thoughts, not now, not yet; but her heart was with him.

T'Mei knocked softly on the door, entered, and paused at the balcony's doorway. The young Vulcan was still many years away from adding 'adept' to her title of student, which Amanda had done not too long before. Adepts of the discipline never abandoned the appellation, 'student.' They preferred always to be reminded that the universe still held things they did not know. T'Lar, the most learned of them all, had recently and without comment ceased to use the title 'adept.' She now called herself merely student.

'Amanda?'

'Yes, child.'

'Do you need anything?'

'No, my dear,' Amanda said. 'I don't need anything, except to have my wishes answered.'

'I cannot do that,' T'Mei said.

Amanda smiled. 'I know it. Come stand by me.'

T'Mei joined Amanda on the balcony. She moved so gracefully, with such self-possession, that she made hardly a sound. Her dark gold hair fell free past her waist.

'One of your wishes is to be in the temple,' T'Mei said.

'Yes. I never thought I'd live to see the time when my own son was a subject of the discipline. Certainly I never would have wished it! I *do* wish I could be there. Spock is balanced between refusion and oblivion – and I can't even help him!' She slapped the parapet with anger and frustration. From the time of her marriage to Sarek she had known that to adopt Vulcan manners completely would be her destruction. Exhibiting her emotions beyond all courtesy would have run counter to her own upbringing, but neither did she try to smother or deny her feelings. At the beginning of her training, this all-too-human characteristic counted against her, but she proved herself worthy nonetheless.

Once in a while she appreciated, and even envied, the equanimity of Vulcans. For Amanda, the days since Spock's death had been an unending succession of powerful emotions: grief when the news first came, and hope of saving his presence, then a desperate anguish when it seemed that even Spock's *katra* had been lost. And now she was faced with the powerful, incredible possibility that her son still might live.

But it hasn't been easy for Sarek, either, Amanda thought. Equanimity or no, he's felt these past days deeply.

T'Mei rested her elbows on the parapet and gazed thoughtfully down at the temple.

'It would be most fascinating to attend the refusion,' she said. 'It is unlikely that this precise constellation of circumstances will recur in our lifetimes.'

'Or in this millennium,' Amanda said. 'But I want to be down there for personal reasons – not historical ones.'

'Your position is ironic,' T'Mei said. 'A student-adept, yet a relative of the subject, when the subject is unique.'

'Ironic's hardly the word for it,' Amanda said. No student-adept could ever participate in, or even observe, the transfer of a close relative. The *katra* was fragile and easily lost. To free it from the bearer and place it in the Hall of Ancient Thought, the student-adepts formed delicate, temporary psychic ties around it, and dissolved them again on completing the passage. If mental connections already existed between a subject and an adept, as they did when the two belonged to the same family, the resonances created an interference that invariably proved disastrous.

How the interference might affect the refusion, no one even attempted to speculate.

When James Kirk's message arrived, it had a galvanic effect on the inhabitants of the retreat. Many questions had to be answered instantly, questions that for generations had been discussed, analyzed, and debated without any final resolution. Amanda would have had no time to prepare her case, even had she wished to argue against her exclusion from the ritual – which she did not. She knew from the beginning that she could not be a member of the group that assisted her son. She understood the logic of avoiding such a completely unnecessary risk. But her intellectual acceptance of matters did absolutely nothing to diminish her emotional desire, her need, to be in the temple, to try to help.

'It is unfortunate that you must forgo participating in this unique experience,' T'Mei said.

'I don't give a hang for the uniqueness of the experience!' Amanda said angrily. She had to switch to Standard to get her point across. Vulcan was far too refined for what she had to say. 'Dammit! Right this minute I wish I'd never studied the discipline!'

'Amanda,' T'Mei said, perplexed, 'I do not understand.'

'If I weren't a student-adept, I wouldn't endanger Spock just by being near him! At least I could be down there! At least Sarek and I could be together tonight!'

She turned away from T'Mei and stared down at the

bright sparks of the torches. She was furious at her helplessness and at the injustice of the universe, too furious even to cry.

T'Mei stood beside her in silence, unable to comprehend her hope, her grief, her anger, or her love.

Jim Kirk was exhausted. He had spent the long cold Vulcan night knowing he could do nothing but wait, knowing that it would make sense . . . that it would be logical . . . to rest. But he was too tired to sleep, too keyed up. It seemed that this night he might lose all the people who meant the most to him. He had lost David already, and he had not even been permitted to contact Carol and tell her what had happened. Or, rather, he had not been prevented, but it had been made clear to him that if he left the mountain and the temple before the end of the ritual, he would not be able to return. To the Vulcans, the stricture seemed completely logical. To Kirk, it seemed a cruel choice. In the end, he had stayed. He could not help his friends, but he could not leave them, either, not when they both ran such a tremendous risk.

Jim envied Scotty, sprawled against a stone pillar, gently snoring. Chekov sat with his knees pulled to his chest, his arms folded, his head down. Uhura lay on the stone with her cheek pillowed on her hand, as lithe as a cat, and, Jim thought, as alert, even in sleep. Saavik waited for the dawn, her legs crossed beneath her, her hands palm down and relaxed, her eyes open and unblinking. Sulu knelt motionless on the stone, sitting *seiza* with his eyes half closed.

Kirk strode from one pillar to the next and back again, trying to fight off the bone-deep chill. At night, what little moisture was in the Vulcan air condensed out as frost. Kirk's lungs ached and his throat was dry and raspy.

He made himself sit down; he pretended to rest. The

stars in Vulcan's empty sky were marvelously bright and clear. The dawn-wind began to blow, cold and harsh, whipping up dust-devils from the desiccated land.

Within the space of a few breaths the stars faded and vanished, and the sky changed from black to a brilliant royal purple. The dawn-wind died abruptly. The scarlet disk of Epsilon Eridani burst above the horizon, casting impenetrable shadows through the temple and searing the desert as it had at every dawn for countless millennia.

A gong rang.

Kirk leaped to his feet.

T'Lar appeared first. She lay supine in a sedan chair carried by the dignitaries who had waited silently all night long. Kirk took a step toward her, but she neither stirred nor opened her eyes. The power she wielded had drained and exhausted her, leaving her wan and frail. The Vulcans bearing her toward the dawn passed Kirk without acknowledging his presence.

McCoy stepped wearily into the sunlight that pierced the shadows behind the altar. Though Sarek supported him, the doctor was moving under his own power. The members of the priesthood, tall and serene in their long hooded cloaks, followed behind. The Vulcans remained completely impassive, showing neither exultation nor despair.

For gods' sakes, Jim cried in his mind, what happened? *What happened?*

At the end of the procession, a single figure, robed in stark white, moved past the altar. The hood was so deep, the robe so brilliantly white, that the thick scarlet light of dawn obscured the being's features rather than illuminating them.

Nearby, Saavik drew a quick breath – of recognition? Of distress? Jim Kirk could not tell.

He became aware of his shipmates, if that term had any

meaning for them anymore. They clustered close around him, Sulu and Uhura on his right, Chekov and Scott on his left, the engineer stiff and sore and sleepy. Saavik stood a little apart from the rest.

As the procession crossed the platform, Sarek broke off from the group and brought McCoy to join his friends. Sulu moved forward to help support him.

'Leonard – ' Jim said.

'It's all right . . .' McCoy said. Weariness faded his voice to a whisper. 'I'm all right, Jim.'

Sulu drew McCoy's arm across his shoulders and supported most of his weight. McCoy managed a smile, a grip of his hand on Sulu's upper arm, as he accepted the aid gratefully.

The white-robed figure at the end of the procession walked past without a glance or hesitation. Jim still could not see beneath the hood, but he knew the stride, the carriage. Saavik started toward the figure, but Jim grabbed her arm. He could not stop her if she chose to break free, but she halted at his touch.

'What about . . . Spock?' Jim said to Sarek.

'I am not sure,' Sarek said. 'Only time will answer.' He turned his head toward the robed figure, then back to Jim.

'Kirk. I thank you.' Sarek's voice, if not his words, admitted that the night's work might have failed. 'What you have done is – '

'What I have done, I had to do,' Kirk said harshly. He thought he saw a flicker of sympathy, even of pity, in Sarek's eyes. He did not want pity.

'But at what cost? Your ship.' The lines around his eyes deepened. 'Your son . . .'

Jim felt that if he acknowledged what Sarek was trying to say to him, his whole being would shatter with grief.

'If I hadn't tried, the cost would have been my soul.'

Sarek nodded, accepting Jim's unwillingness to speak

284

any further or any deeper. He turned and walked silently away. Vulcan's star hung just above the horizon, an enormous scarlet disk, silhouetting first the procession, then a tall and solitary figure. The wind whined mournfully and fluttered the edge of the white robe.

Jim shaded his eyes with his hands, squinting into the dawn for one last glimpse of his old friend.

Live long, he thought. Live long and prosper.

And the figure slowly turned.

One of the members of the procession heard or sensed his motion and reached back, but Sarek stayed her hand. The sun shone incandescently through the fabric of the white hood, from behind, casting the face into deep shadow.

He hesitated, then walked slowly toward Jim Kirk and his friends.

He stopped, reached up, drew the hood back from his face, and let it fall to his shoulders.

The pain had left Spock's face, the pain, and the horrible emptiness. His deep gaze questioned Jim gently and wordlessly. An intent intelligence, impatient with uncertainty, lit his eyes.

He glanced from Jim to each of his other shipmates in turn: Sulu, Uhura, McCoy, Chekov, Scott; and finally Saavik. It seemed to Jim that he reached the brink of recognition with each of them, but could not quite cross the boundary.

Spock returned his gaze to Jim Kirk. The hot wind of Vulcan wailed over the desert with a keening cry.

'I know you . . .' His voice rasped across the words. 'Do I not?'

'Yes,' Kirk said. 'And I, you.'

'My father says you have been my friend. You came back for me.'

'You would have done the same for me,' Kirk said,

willing Spock to remember something from *before*, something that had happened before they brought him home.

'Why would you do this?' Spock asked.

'Because – ' Kirk fumbled for words that would form even a tenuous connection between past and present. 'Because the needs of the one outweighed the needs of the many.'

Spock stared down at him, still without real recognition. He turned away again and took a few uncertain steps toward his father, toward the other Vulcans. Kirk reached out, but he knew he had been right when earlier he prevented Saavik from stopping him. They might provide a key, but none could force Spock to remember.

What could I have said? he wondered. What was the right thing?

He let his hands fall.

A few paces away, Spock paused. He looked up into the deep sky.

'I have been . . .' he said.

At his strained and tortured voice, Jim moved instinctively toward him.

'. . . and always shall be . . . your friend . . .'

'Yes,' Jim whispered. 'Yes, Spock.'

Spock half turned. 'The ship,' he said. 'Out of danger . . . ?'

'You saved the ship, Spock. You saved us all! Don't you remember?'

Spock said nothing for a moment. He cocked his head, as if listening to some far-away inner voice. He arched his eyebrow and slowly faced Jim Kirk.

'Jim,' he said softly. 'Your name is Jim.'

'Yes!' Jim's voice broke, and he caught his breath.

Spock nodded once, briefly, as if acknowledging to himself that he had found the proper path. He glanced at McCoy, and then at the others.

Suddenly all his old shipmates clustered around him, laughing and crying at the same time. None of them knew for certain an instant of what the future would bring, but each knew that for now, for this moment, everything was all right.